THE
ROOSTER
PALACE

_5/29/98_

To North Country Books— warm regards,

THE
ROOSTER
PALACE

Jeffrey g. kelly

JEFFREY G. KELLY

ILLUSTRATED
by
LINDA A. SMYTH

Published by
Adirondack Empire
Saratoga Springs, NY

This is a work of fiction.
Except for a few details relating
to the author's own life, all the
incidents, names and characters are imaginary.

Published in the United States of America by Adirondack Empire
Saratoga Springs, New York.

Printed in Troy, New York, by Integrated Book Technologies

The author wishes to acknowledge the book, *Calcutta, Insight Guides*,
of APA publications as a valuable reference book he consulted
for various particulars of contemporary city life in Calcutta.

The artist, Linda A. Smyth, who designed the cover,
used black paper, a knife and scissors
to create all the chapter illustrations.

Library of Congress Catalog Card Number: 98-70877

ISBN 0-9663423-0-5

First Edition

Acknowledgments

Ann Booth was the first person to read this book, and I thank her for editorial tolerance and encouragement, and at a crucial stage of this project, for her technical wisdom. Norman Mendenhall helped me format the book on the computer for presentation to the printer. My readers, each of whom gave me valuable tidbits of constructive criticism, were Stephen and Susan Kelly, Theo and Talby Page, Schelling McKinley, Ed Amyot, and Susan Shanley. Finally a thank you to Terry Hamilton who weighed in at the end and advised me on what to leave in and what to leave out.

Dedication

To my wife, Linda
and my sons, Spencer and Faber.

THE
ROOSTER
PALACE

I

The Broken Plate Cafe

My senses were overloading, and I was feeling dizzy. Though I was excited to be exploring Calcutta, it was past noon, and I wasn't used to the suffocating heat. We were moving in zigzag fashion, arms held out from our sides to ward off being knocked down and trampled by the crowds.

I glanced up at the white, reflective sky, and the sun dotted my vision with light prisms, tiny geometric figures dashing about under my flickering eyelids. In the blinding, relentless sun, I felt like I was twirling on a merry-go-round. I grabbed Chaleea's shoulder for support.

"Are you all right, Mr. Jack, Sahib?" asked Chaleea, looking up at me.

"Do you have any water? Anything to drink?" I asked. Remembering my churning stomach from the two glasses of water at the Howrah Station, I added, "Any tea?"

"There are cafe's, but they are impossibly crowded," said Chaleea. He looked at me again and then thought for a moment. "We'll try."

Chaleea saw an opening. We veered to the left, towards a narrow alley, pushing others aside. "He's sick, he's sick," he said in response to some grumbles.

After trotting through passageways no wider than the two of us, we emerged onto a side street. We stopped in the shade of an overhanging metal roof of a brick building, then ducked our heads, and stepped down three steps. Chaleea knocked on a solid wooden door. Through a removable slat, a man with a black mustache peered out at us. Chaleea jabbered to him in Hindi, while I smiled weakly.

Chaleea turned to me and said, "He wants some rupees. We can't stay long." Chaleea paused and lowered his voice to a whisper, "And please, this is a political cafe."

I was desperate to get out of the sun and dust, and sit down. The doorkeeper pulled back the door, and we descended into a cellar-like tea room where murmuring Indian men sat facing each other on straw mats sipping Ceylon teas and Coca-Colas. They glanced at me with only mild interest.

As a foreigner wearing bluejeans and a denim jacket, usually I was stared at. Ever since I had disembarked, I had been wandering the streets wide-eyed during the day and resting at night at the Red Shield Guest House. By now I was acclimated to all but the heat and was ready for a different place to stay.

With relief, I crumpled to the carpet-covered earthen floor, handed Chaleea a wad of rupees, and said "Cokes."

In time, a thin man appeared carrying a circular silver tray with two white straws besides two unopened cokes, proof they had not been contaminated. A bottle opener in the shape of a tiger's head rattled on the tray. The Coke bottles were the bottles of my youth - thick, greenish glass, chipped at the bottom, holding seven ounces.

I savored my first sip and then snapped off a banana from the bunch I carried in my shoulder bag. A banana and a Coke. This was heavenly. I immediately felt better.

Chaleea spoke. " We must leave for The Rooster Palace soon, before nightfall."

"Okay, but let's sit here a while," I said sighing.

2

Covering his mouth to muffle his words, Chaleea reinforced his warning. "You can not go to The Rooster Palace after dark. Remember the Naxalites. They roam the city at night, looking for officials to kill."

One of the Sikhs, a big man in a Sherwanis long coat, his crimson turban at his side, chuckled. "It is our little revolution known only in India. And only in the lawless streets of Calcutta can Naxalites get away with practicing their ruthless terror. They're Communists who want to do away with our fledgling democracy by assassinating our public officials and greedy Rajas. They want chaos. And when it comes, the Communists will operate in daylight and seize power. In the meantime the Naxalites strike at night. You know Calcutta," he gestured with the sweep of his arm, "very few street lights."

The regular patrons in the tea house, leaning back on bolstered cushions, appreciated his short lecture, and immediately challenged his statements, saving me the task of forming an intelligent reply. They were the merchants of some of the larger stalls in the bazaar, taking their long afternoon break from their time-honored profession of selling. These Indians prized participating in a good conversation, especially in the coolness of a cellar cafe.

Chaleea nudged me. "We must go. We will be heading into the heart of Native Town, the hidden section of Calcutta," he said quietly as he rose up off the carpet.

"A few more minutes," I knew the heat and the crowds were waiting outside. But I knew that few foreigners had ever seen The Rooster Palace, and we were close to our destination.

Looking around absorbing the atmosphere of the cave-like cafe, I got up and bowed slightly to the Sikh with the stringy, oily hair. Next to his crimson turban, atop his embroidered velvet bag, I spied his carved, ivory-handled sword. He observed me staring and asked my name.

"Jack Hamilton," I said in a monotone, taking no particular pride in my name. Maybe I was tired of being an American with money.

"And yours, Sir?" I asked.

Narrowing his eyes, he said "Jean Paul," with a threatening edge to his voice. Somehow I doubted he was telling the truth.

I nodded hello and bowed slightly, my hands in prayerful gesture. Standing up straight and firm, I steadied myself and walked up past the Nepalese guard at the door, back to the bright, white heat of the day. As Chaleea and I shielded our eyes and ventured out, I turned and asked him the name of this blessed sanctuary. He said, as casually as he could, "The Broken Plate Cafe."

Startled, I checked in my bag to make sure I still had the mysterious package from the freighter. I stammered that I had a mission to complete.

Chaleea cut me off. "Please Sahib, we will come back. Besides your man would not want that transaction made in public." He seemed to know more than I did about my package.

I hesitated, trying to decide whether or not to go back in, when the door swung open, and out stepped Jean Paul and two merchants, talking politics.

Interrupting, I blurted, "Jean Paul, Sir, do you know a man called Nandalla? I have a package for him."

An abrupt silence ensued. A flicker of uncertainty crossed Jean Paul's face, and then he regained his composure and replied. "I do not." And looking squarely at Chaleea and switching to Hindi he said, "I may know of someone who does, and she is of American descent, I believe. Why don't you take your traveler there tomorrow," enunciating carefully, "to Annapurna's, shall we call it a guest house, at the far edge of The Square." As he spoke he slid a five-rupee note in Chaleea's hand, both the words and the tip smoothly executed.

II

Pondering the Package

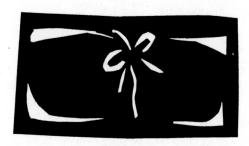

I lay still on my cot at the Red Shield, my eyes open, my legs tired from our walk back from the clandestine cafe. This time tomorrow I would be somewhere in Native Town. I stretched out, stared upward, and let my mind wander over the days since my arrival in Calcutta off the Martha Bakke. As the darkness grew, I looked around at two rows of Indian strangers breathing heavily, and struck a long wooden match on the peened metal hinge of the side table. Carefully I turned the brass knob of the kerosene lamp and exposed the wick a centimeter more. A flame leaped to life. I jerked my head up, afraid my hair would catch fire. After adjusting the wick, I set the hurricane glass over the flickering light.

I held up the package from the freighter wrapped in a frayed newspaper and read the headline, dated November 1, 1968, about a year past. "Naxalites Assassinate V.P. Candidate" with a sub-heading of "Maoist Urban Guerrilla Insurgency Feared." The newspaper wasn't yellowed, so it must have been kept out of the sunlight. The name of the paper, printed in English, was The Calcutta Daily Sentinel. The package had the weight of a clay brick and was rounded at the corners, like a loaf of bread.

I had taken possession of the package somewhere in the Bay of Bengal the evening before our Norwegian freighter docked in Calcutta. The second engineer gave me a signal to come to his cabin. We talked as we had before. Though he called himself Hans, he was a Hindu. In 21 days at sea, including three extra days in Manila being blasted by a typhoon, you got to know someone pretty well, especially when Hans and I were the only two with long hair.

That night Hans had opened his porthole, and we smoked a ceremonial chilum of hash. He asked me a favor and pulled out the package from underneath his bunk bed. He made me promise to deliver it to a hard-to-find cafe called the Broken Plate and to ask for a man called Nandalla. We shook and I promised I would. He said he had observed that once Americans gave their word, they followed through with the deed.

Now just as he had foretold, I was bound by my word. I held the package in my hands above my head and brought it down to my nose to smell. I thought maybe it was opium. I had read that for nearly one hundred years the East Indian Company shipped chests of opium to China to keep Calcutta prosperous. Carefully I put it back in my shoulder bag, next to my duffel, with still no real clue as to what was inside.

On Gurusaday Road below, eerie fires danced to the background din of cows and rickshaw wallahs. I was drifting alone with my thoughts, but I was capable of being alone. And I knew other young travelers like me lay tonight all over India connected by the web of a grand movement spun around exploring ourselves and the values our parents took for granted.

In India, my concept of time, the passing of time, had changed. Now, I just sailed along talking to other travelers, finding out where the best banana milk shakes were, sharing secret places to exchange dollars for rupees on the black market, and warning other young travelers, hippies I suppose, of the occasional bad places. Sometimes we smoked Indian cigarettes called Beedes, and sometimes we smoked marijuana or ganja as we liked to call it. Days floated by. Time lasted. A week was a long time. I did a lot of walking in dear old Cal, fed a lot of monkeys and sought out a lot of erotic temples.

I was nearly asleep nestled on top of my army-surplus, down-filled, mummy sleeping bag. This was my home away from home. Once I slipped into my sleeping bag, I felt more secure. I was in my own world, my own green camouflaged cocoon, the same sleeping bag I had slept in Vermont, Colorado, Banff, Vancouver Island, California, crossing the Pacific on my bunk, and now India. I unsnapped the outer covering, since I didn't need it here one story up off the ground, and folded it up between my duffel bag and the package.

I zipped myself into the mummy bag using the inside zipper. I was thankful for the dual zipper which eased fears of claustrophobia and allowed for a quick exit. My brother, Stephen, had given me the army-surplus bag, and I thought it symbolized the different paths we had taken, him getting drafted, me getting the high lottery number.

2

One night not too long ago back in America, in the basement lounge of our Alpha Delta Phi fraternity at Kenyon College, we all gathered about the TV and watched and waited. We laughed and hooted, slouching on the broken, red leather armchairs that reeked of spilled beer. But by evening's end some guys were pissed, one was crying, and a few were resentful of guys like me, who seemed too carefree and lucky.

My born-with-a-silver-spoon buddy Smithy and I had gotten high lottery numbers. Numbers 315 and 278 out of a possible 365. The TV analysts predicted nobody would be drafted above 200, but of course the U.S. had yet to bomb Hanoi. The bombing really turned me against the Vietnam War. I had been wavering up to then, given my football heritage. I had even wanted to enlist in the Marines, but that spirit soon left me.

Marijuana and LSD flooded our campus in the spring. I wasn't walking around campus in pajamas with a fixed smile like some of the jocks-turned-gurus who had found their peace through mescaline, but I had changed my mind about the Marines.

The campus turned topsy-turvy in one spring weekend. Someone brought these beauties down from Columbus, and the place was never the same again. Ed Carsons, our best black football player with an afro the size of the top of a palm tree, was hugging everyone, strolling arm and arm from fraternity party to fraternity party with the heretofore opposite-type, white, conservative, right-wing, campus intellectual. They weren't high on Ohio 3.2 beer. They were high on these yellow mescaline pills, these little peyote buttons, that revealed inner beauty.

No one knew what was going on, least of all the administration. All of a sudden these hard core athletes, straight guys from Youngstown, Ohio, started growing beards, looking and acting like Jesus Christ; not eating, but smiling all the time, sharing joints, going to classes in their pajamas if they went at all.

I turned on my side in my canvas cot. I was too tired to continue reminiscing, and I knew, with the help of my street urchin named Chaleea, that I was leaving the Hotel tomorrow headed to some untraveled places called The Rooster Palace and The Square. I stole a last look at my shoulder bag and touched my passport hanging from my neck. I lifted up the glass and blew out the flame.

III

Native Town

Chaleea clutched my sleeve, leading me onward without losing me in the crowded, crooked streets entangled like dried spaghetti. We wound our way back towards the undulating throngs of the market place, where people behaved like herds of animals, restless and alert for change

My young beggar turned guide kept the gangs of other beggars away. He led us through a corner of the vast Maidan area, past cricket playing fields to Curzon Park, where we stopped in front of a statue of the Russian dictator Lenin, next to a monument to Karl Marx and Friedrich Engels. The Calcutta Communist Party often held meetings of thousands of Party members at the Maidan. Unlike the activities of the Naxalites, their meetings were peaceful.

I was distracted from reading the plaque by a gang of bare-chested boys with rags tied around their waists, sticks in their hands, running around crazily on all fours, screaming and laughing, chasing what turned out to be a large rat. The boys cornered the rat against a clay wall. Then two boys placed a wire mesh trap a few feet in front of the trembling rat while the other boys tossed bits of grain to it. A few nuts were balanced on a scale in the center of the trap, the slightest move-ment on the scale triggering both wire doors to slam shut.

The boys were eager to catch the rat, Chaleea explained, and then to sell it either as a pet or for food. He felt sad for the rat, and kept a pet rat of his own at home. He had even built a maze in hopes of training her.

Looking around at the yellowish, dry fields, I spied dozens of rats popping up and down in hundreds of holes. Chaleea told me this was the Colony of Rats which had been adopted and fed by the people of the Park. The rats' underground network of tunnels had spread across Esplanda Row to the respectable Esplanade Mansions, and city offi-cials had wanted to poison them. But the puchkawallas, or street hawkers, who peddled grain and nuts to passerby's to feed the rats, protested and prevented the poisoning.

The large rat was still cornered and frightened and hadn't moved towards the bait. To end the standoff, one boy rolled a nut under its whiskered head, while another small boy leaped with cat-like agility and grabbed the rat by its large naked tail.

The rat raised its dangling head, showing its pink mouth and sharp, white teeth; curled up, hissed and bit the air close to the boy's hand. The boy wasn't phased. He whipped the rat into the trap, and the gang had its prize. When the boys sold this rat, they would make a profit of several rupees.

Chaleea, who was 14 years old, proudly told me that each day he tried to return home with at least one rupee for his family. For the past six months he and his friends and his little sister, Da, were living in the open end of a six foot diameter concrete culvert that was originally meant for diverting a creek around a construction project.

We left the rat colony behind us, crossed Dharamatala Street, and turned up a large alley. As we quickened our pace, the pungent smell of rooster dung hit us. Chaleea swished away the bangs of his black hair covering his eyes. He smiled mischievously and mentioned we were nearing the Square of The Rooster Palace, a place I had never read about.

"We haven't taken a foreigner here before," Chaleea said excitedly. "It's a different place."

Chaleea pointed to the runners passing us with their rooster cages darting through the waste of Calcutta's humanity. Toothy, skinny, brown men jostled by carrying wooden cages made of vines or branches with a rooster or hen inside.

An old man with a scrawny rooster held his cage up to my face. "For you, 20 rupees."

The cage was made of wicker and long twigs, with a large circular removable top set neatly into position. I could see the blond whittle marks at the end of the carved twigs. The oriental basket-like cage reminded me of a miniature piece of Adirondack twig furniture. Though I admired the delicate prison the rooster was kept in, I waved him away.

He left hurriedly, dodging around a woman scrounging for food, and then pushed between puchkawallas blocking his path. This bare-footed soul was intent on delivering his cage to his once powerful Maharaja who had sent him to The Rooster Palace with a handful of rupees to bargain for hens and roosters.

The hens would be used to lay eggs and bring sustenance and well-being into a Raja's princely palace. The roosters would be used to fight and bring prestige and power to the Rajas, who now in decline, once commanded for themselves.

The Roosters were colorful, entertaining pets helping to pass the idle time for these fading, frolicking monarchs who seldom worked, but preferred to scheme and play. Roosters were believed to bring good luck, so if a Raja's fortunes improved, the Raja shared some of the glory with his rooster.

The Maharajas were desperate for attention now that the government had removed their annual princely stipend and stripped them of all their titles and privileges. No more privy purses. Those Rajas who aspired to or descended from historical wealth and highness in the Indian hierarchical caste system visited The Rooster Palace often; to buy roosters of course, but also to be spotted themselves, to be singled out from the tattered masses as special, to be viewed as royalty. The average poor Hindu obliged, and on the numerous festival days kept an eye out for the tarnished self-proclaimed royalty.

Some of the messengers weaving through the crooked streets of the Hati Bagan market might be delivering a rooster to a still-wealthy Raja; a Raja who owned a chest of the cherished gold and emeralds of India - jewels with historical and mystical value, and real, present-day cash value. One such Raja was the Maharaja of Cooch Behar who showed up at festivals in his vintage Rolls-Royce Phantom and hobnobbed with the other royalty who longed for the good old days of croquet and caviar.

The runners for these Rajas could expect big tips, especially if the Raja was taken with the rooster or fancied the woven pattern of the cage. After the rooster died, sometimes from mating too often - in front of the watchful, gleaming eye of an aged Raja, the cage was kept for display purposes, almost the way Americans keep old things and call them antiques. The Raja would remember that a certain break here, to those aspen twigs, was from his rooster constantly trying to peck his way free of his tiny prison. In his idle time, the Raja might recall how he himself had repaired that spot, carefully tying it closed using hemp fibers. Eventually each cage told its own story. This peculiar penchant and appreciation for the tale of the rooster cage thrived in Calcutta.

2

Only through the underground network of cafe conversations passed along by travelers was the location of The Rooster Palace, whispered about as being somewhere in Native Town.

Over banana fritters or sharing a chilum, if you genuinely felt a deeper camaraderie with a traveler. If he or she had given you some good, reliable information on where to stay, or what to eat, or where to go, cheaply off the beaten path, where to experience something Eastern, something you might later call mystical, (Yes, visit the monkey temple, Swayambhu North, stay the day, and in the evening an old woman dressed in black will appear among the rhesus monkeys, and for three rupees she will tell your fortune.) then in return you might reveal the existence of the inner labyrinth of the fabled Native Town.

If the traveler you were confiding in was of your ilk; long-haired, not concerned with time, but conversely energetic; or if she were pretty, sun-tanned, and not from your country, or if an American and not from your home state, and therefore different, maybe more exotic, more sensual, then, yes, you might reveal your tarnished gem tucked among the dangerous back alleys of Native Town, a place reserved for the Indians who revered ritual, strong beliefs and ever-lasting festivals. You might then tell her about The Rooster Palace.

3

Along with the runners and their cages, even more people, shoulder to shoulder, moved with us in the direction of The Rooster Palace. Many with scarves over their noses and mouths, not for religious reasons, but to filter out the dust particles swirling arround the Untouchables who inhabited the fringe around The Rooster Palace. This was their turf, and like a moat surrounding a soccer field, anyone who wanted in or out of the Square of The Rooster Palace had to pass through this ring of ragged Untouchables, who earned less respect in vegetarian India than the cattle who roamed the streets.

Many of the Untouchables were curled in balls, arms sticking out at odd angles, begging or moaning beneath our feet. We stepped around them or hopped over them, careful not to lose our balance.

"Ahhhggg," I heard a cry to my left. A woman in a dazzling purple sari had stumbled on a cluster of alive but motionless bodies. She had been walking behind her golden-turbaned husband who looked to be a Sikh. He quickly reached back and caught her before she fell to the ground, and she just as quickly regained her composure. Without hesitating, however, they turned around and walked back the way they had come, their scarves pressed even firmer over their mouths and noses. Disgusted, they headed back to their brick house to wash her clothes and attempt the trip another time.

As the two passed by us, I eyed the majestic Sikh. He maintained an intelligent almost haughty look which said he knew exactly who I was - a foreigner trespassing on a sacredness peculiar to Calcutta. But I felt I represented a new breed, not here simply to see the Taj Mahal, buy a rug or a jewel, have it delivered to a palatial hotel, and then leave. I actually liked the experience of the dusty, smoky, curry and urine smell of the poverty and decay of Calcutta. I knew the journey equaled or surpassed the joy of the destination.

After I taught elementary school for the Urban Teacher Corps in Harlem for one year, I traveled West, until I was all the way East, here in my army surplus bag in fetal position smelling the smoky sweet smell of a third world city I called Cal. Thinking, well, I'll go to India, to Nepal, to find a spiritual purpose and trek in the mountains of the Himalayas. And then being here. This was magical.

When I was on the road for a long time, traveling light, I got emotionally attached to each item I carried. The close identity I felt with those familiar things, such as my denim jacket and bluejeans, helped make me feel at home. My sleeping bag and duffel bag were like that. I was proud to travel with just one piece of luggage, though I was careful to avoid a backpack which with my long straight hair would immediately label me as a hippie traveler. I thought of myself as more of an adventurer, not just a hippie, or just a traveler. Plus I figured I was too given to action to be a true, mellow-yellow hippie.

We came by train, by bus, by VW bus, by hitchhiking and occasionally by ship and by plane to India. And if by a plane stopping to refuel on its way to Hong Kong or London, other passengers would inquire incredulously, 'You're getting off here?' In fact, one fellow traveler told me out of 200 passengers, he and a man in a brown suit with a suitcase full of wrist watches were the only two to get off the plane in Calcutta.

The sharp odor of roosters broke my reverie. I started to cover my nose, but then I was forced to use both hands to cover my ears. An unearthly rumble, a reverberation of noise, pitched us backwards. The sound of the roosters grew like a diesel train screeching its brakes as it rumbled into Calcutta's grand Howrah Station.

"What is it?" I asked my guide.

"It's the roosters. They're cock-a-doodle-dooing," said little Chaleea, smartly. "We're almost there."

IV

Happy Carcasses

No one could deny the creeping misery in Calcutta increased with each new country peasant that got off at the Howrah Station, who ended up begging in the city a week later. No system had come forward to replace the civil-service bureaucracy of the Imperialistic British which enabled a colonized country like India to function, a country with 18 totally different states and languages, different Gods, different weather. When Mahatma Gandhi sat defiantly with crossed legs in front of a spinning wheel, and forced the British to retreat from India, all that was left were happy carcasses. These happy carcasses were the masses, who danced for joy with big smiles and fired their few guns into the air, in disbelief that they had finally gained their political freedom. But they were stuck in a labyrinth of paperwork and payoffs and became slaves to the lack of a new workable economic system. This is where the Naxalites saw an opportunity to feed off the failure of the current beaten and outmoded economic system left by the British.

India became know as a country of mighty squalor, a country of primeval mystery and ooze, a place of heat and wandering, a place so distinct from the order and structure of the Western world, particularly the affluence and drive of the United States, that the rebellious youth of the 1960's and 70's flocked to India and its mountainous neighbor Nepal to wander in search of spiritual resuscitation, where you could live for pennies a day, where the order was whatever order you wanted to give to the day. The destination was whatever you decided for the day. Delicious alienation bred lovingly among the hippies, among the Peace Corps workers; the contrast to the United States was the next best thing to the war in Vietnam, only without the bullets and risk of life and everyone spoke English.

The long-haired youth grew thoughts that undermined all the structure and striving and property they had been taught to revere. Instead they cherished change; they worshipped themselves in an innocent, tolerable way, sought out the bizarre, and embraced the romantic poverty of places like Nepal. For most young Westerners, Calcutta, with its parade of deformed beggars, was just too much and too immediate. The city was too big, too crowded.

But for me, the city was still wonderfully wild, still part of one big, luxurious, playful adventure. The smiling braided, blond-haired youth, carrying harmonicas, took themselves seriously, as most young adults do while their search their way to their own adulthood, carving out their own niche distinct from their parents.

I contemplated the Westerners - the Germans, the Australians, the British, the Canadians, the French, the Americans, whom I had observed wandering through Calcutta. They all dressed in bluejeans, a military garb of sorts, for a non-military army of sorts. The most garish and laid back, the ones who stayed the longest, positioned themselves as our leaders, because they had discovered the ins and outs of certain untraveled pathways of India. They became the guru's within the hodgepodge of young travelers high on pot and hash, sitting yoga style on top of moving trains smoking huge rolled joints of fresh ganja, in spite of protestations from the third class Indian travelers who felt insulted by these young, long haired, aimless kids with money. How many traveling Californians were there, anyway? And did they all like have their own language? How did they get here? Why did they come?

Maybe there was some grand and compelling, spiritually redeeming quality about India, a land of a myriad people. Once you got over the squalor, the place was warm, wet and beautiful, like a naked woman searching for her bathing suit, looking through some brush under a bench, where two boys, giggling have tossed her suit on a Goa beach and watching the unsexy but so sexy, awkward, not posed for a magazine, woman, as she reached with her long white arm through the dune grass and cactus, her head arched upwards, her breasts squished together scraping the sand, grabbing for her lime green bikini, the hair of her underarms reminding the boys of pubic hair.

Calcutta was a woman's crotch wonderfully and smelly repulsive yet drawing you forward by its odd shape and look, just so unlike anything male. The female has holes and tunnels and flaps, (and where's the doorknob) all for what purpose; the obvious, yes, but why do I like it here? I really can't stand it, especially up close, but here I am back again.

V

The Square, The Palace and The Rooster

High in the sky, shimmering in the afternoon sun above the rickety two story wood and brick buildings, I could see a mammoth array of stacked cages, forming a primitive structure shaped like an irregular pyramid. They contained thousands of prized roosters -- a Herculean feat of labor-intensive engineering. The pyramid pulsated in waves of heat and animal energy. Gesturing to Chaleea, I pointed up.

"The Rooster Palace?"

"Yes." he nodded seriously.

We moved on and nudged our way closer. The alley-ways opened to a vast stone-cobbled Square. In the middle, cages were piled ten stories high forming a living pyramid that dominated the Square. On the ground to one side men shoveled the rooster waste into a gutter-like moat of putrid, brown liquid that eventually flowed into the Hooghly, part of the celebrated Ganges River.

Torches lit the base of this castle of handmade cages. During the cooler evenings, the roosters' handlers and buyers conducted their business there, watched by the many unemployed who gathered to beg and pass the time in the Square, around the towering Rooster Palace.

Only a certain sect or caste of honey bee harvesters, called placers, was allowed to install or extract a rooster cage from The Rooster Palace. Their work in extracting honey from hexagonal cells in the hive, on a miniature scale, was much like the Gargantuan task of fitting and extracting roosters cages on the vast scale of The Rooster Palace. They were skilled in the knack of removing cages without causing the whole precarious structure to tumble down.

Part of the placer's job was to remember where to find each individual bird. Only the placers, who actually earned a small commission tied to the daily auction of the roosters, would risk the perilous climb and the pecking of the birds to place or retrieve a rooster. Because The Fat Man paid them, and because they were brave, the placers enjoyed a certain status in the lowly hierarchy of The Rooster Palace.

Another sect, called the handlers, fed the stacked roosters using old fire hoses. They sprayed a mixture of grain and water high up onto and through the pyramid. Inevitably the mixture did not quite penetrate the core of the palace-like pyramid of cages. Some of the roosters who had been stacked in the sunless interior of the ramshackle pyramid for months were near starvation, but others were still hardy and dangerous. Those tough ones that did survive, after proper care and feeding, often made great kings, fertilized many eggs and won many cockfights for those Rajas who had the gift for picking roosters with promise.

After we were more than half way across the Square, Chaleea pointed to a wooden ladder, which led to a porch above the crowds. We headed there. We climbed up, until a woman with cotton in her ears and a broom in her hands, appeared at the top blocking our way.

By now I knew what was expected. I handed her two rupees, then three, then four, and finally at five her squawking stopped and she welcomed us to her porch, where in fact, three wooden carved stools, one with inlaid red and blue beads, were placed outside for guests to witness the strange phenomena of The Rooster Palace.

In the exchange of money I couldn't help notice her long, cherry-red fingernails on hands that were warm and smooth to the touch, in contrast to her working image. Apparently she had found a way to make a few rupees a day without wearing out. Once she relaxed and smiled, I observed that she was attractive and self-assured and spoke both the casual English of travelers and the proper English of the Indians.

From my new vantage point on her balcony, I looked out at the Palace, mesmerized. Circling its base, emaciated men balancing cages on their heads trotted back to their masters. In one quarter of the Square, old women sat between mountains of dried corn and grain, pulling and weaving vines together to make new cages. Elsewhere scrawny children whacked away at rats scurrying around nibbling at the edges of the piles of grain.

Above the pinnacle of the mountain of cages, vultures circled. The mottled black birds with eight foot wing spans and red beaks had their own mournful caw and ruled the sky. They dived and landed and clawed at the cages. The roosters protected themselves by pressing against an interior side of their cage, or shrinking to a corner, while down below the older boys hurled stones up at the vultures.

One street leading to this ancient hub was wider. Through this street, rickshaws and trucks delivered more roosters who were examined, weighed, paid for and locked into cages. Then the specialized squad of workers, the placers, wearing pads on their knees and gloves on their hands, climbed the living walls of The Rooster Palace to place cages high up where they got the most air, and wouldn't be smothered by others. The Rooster Palace thrived as a living temple that generated income and diversion in the squalor of Native Town.

2

Chaleea pointed to a distant, brightly painted, delivery truck -- a flatbed, with improvised rope sides. One magnificent rooster stood on the bed of the truck, and a crowd was gathering around it. Even from our balcony across the Square, the rooster loomed large.

Annapurna was incredulous yet skeptical at the size of the bird, given the haze and the distance away. She did recognize the colorful truck as belonging to a man from the southern state of Tamil Nadu who periodically showed up with an exotic rooster.

"This is a rare one. One of the giants." Chaleea called to me. "Let's go."

I wanted a closer look too. Trusting our business-like but beguiling hostess, I left my duffel bag and my shoulder bag with the package on her balcony. We climbed down the ladder, and I steeled myself for the crossing of the Square. We wound our way through the maze of people, rubbing against the streaked rags of the Untouchables who vigorously followed the Indian custom of right hand for eating food, left hand for wiping themselves.

Our scramble across the Square came to a halt as we got closer to the truck and the giant rooster. People clogged the way trying to catch a view of this freak of nature.

I could see, but Chaleea was too short. I bent over and motioned to him to climb up on my back. He was puzzled and didn't know what I was talking about. With some effort I pulled him up, and soon he perched happily atop my shoulders. Now we were like father and son craning our necks to watch a float in the Macy's Thanksgiving Day Parade..

Chaleea liked the warm attention of someone he could trust. He realized I knew less than he did about getting around Calcutta, and though he was eight years younger, it had dawned on him that in some ways I was more innocent.

Yet I was big and strong and had money. He said my arms were bigger than his legs and he was right. He liked walking by my side hearing street kids he knew whistle and click their tongues. I was his prize for as long as he could stay with me.

"The rooster is huge!" gasped Chaleea.

"How big?" I demanded in a friendly tone.

"He's as big as me," stated Chaleea. "The handlers have put a rope around his neck. They will choke him," he protested. "No," he changed his mind. "No, they are parading him," he said knowingly.

The rooster marched deliberately, raising each foot to exaggerated heights and then stamping down. He strode around the makeshift ring like a feared, man-eating tiger, somehow aware he was king of the jungle.

We marveled at his appearance. The points on the rooster's comb, which I called his crown, were a magnificent crimson red, tall and strong. The blade at the back of his head was bright yellow. The wattle beneath his beak was colored orange, longer than Chaleea had ever seen on a rooster, like the long beard of an ancient warrior. His eyes were the size of eggs. The hackle beneath his head was a fierce dark brown. The saddle of his back where the feathers were thickest, was multicolored with a black stripe down the center all the way to his tail feathers.

A dark skinned man swung gracefully up on to the bed of the truck. He was holding the other end of the rope. The King Rooster was his. The trainer and the rooster were almost of equal size. The man was shirtless, and like a man showing off his tattoos, displayed the scars from raising this majestic monster.

"Qu'et n'a paisas?" He yelled at the crowd, "How much?"

Through the roar of the crowd, someone yelled "500 rupees!"

Facing the crowd, the trainer leaned back and laughed to show how ridiculously low he thought the offer was. As he did so, the rooster, in a malicious mood and full of stage presence, swiped his clawed foot at the shoulder of the trainer, and brought him down backwards. The crowd pulled back in awe of the power and unexpected swiftness of the rooster's blow.

The rooster stunned the Tamil man, but slowly he got up. He methodically tied the end of the training rope which held a noose around the rooster's neck to a corner post of the flatbed truck. The farther the rooster backed into the opposite corner the tighter the noose became. Someone from down on the ground pushed a long bamboo pole into the ring. With a bloodied hand from where he had touched the gash on his shoulder, he grabbed it. Chaleea could see that there was a thin wire attached to one end that ran through eyeholes the length of the pole. The Tamil man wrapped the wire of the bamboo pole around his gloved hand and tugged. A shiny reflective blade popped firmly into place at the other end, a more sinister version of the simple device my grandfather used to trim the high branches of apple trees in the Adirondacks.

The blade reflected the late afternoon setting sun. The attention of the peasant masses of the entire Square had shifted from The Rooster Palace to the ring of the flatbed truck. The crowd wondered if the bloodied trainer would now kill his giant prize, and for a moment there was silence. The Tamil trainer made a clean pass with his pole and blade, and the rooster backed farther into the corner of the ring, stretching the rope to its limit and tightening the slipknot on its neck.

I half expected the chant of "Kill, Kill, Kill" from the crowd. But roosters were their trade, their daily sustenance and entertainment, and they respected roosters. This one was too big to be killed without a proper ceremony, and for no reason but to avenge cutting his captor.

A group of the seasoned runners from the wealthier Rajas was quickly conferring, eyeing this wonderful bird. Together they yelled, "To the top. To the top."

At first I didn't know what they meant. Then others yelled, "To the Top. To the Top," like the chant of 'Ali! Ali!' between rounds in a boxing match. Now Chaleea, and I were yelling "To the Top! To the Top!

Take the vicious king bird to the top of The Rooster Palace, I thought. Have the bravest and strongest placers climb carrying this beast of a bird to the top of The Rooster Palace, where he rightfully belonged.

The Tamil man stood poised to unleash a lethal slash at his King Rooster. He touched the bamboo rod with its glistening blade to the red breast of the rooster, and demanded of the crowd, "How much? How much?" for 'To The Top,' as if he was still furious enough to kill his own King Rooster.

Chaleea caught the fervor of the moment, and innocently reached into my pocket for rupees.

"Chaleea?" I reprimanded.

"Rupees, rupees" he stammered.

From all around the truck now, rupees were passed forward to the Tamil man in small amounts, two here, three there. No individual dared pass up too much, as the notes would never reach the truck - but fine to spend a few rupees for a day like this, perhaps history, good for many future conversations. This was a moment to travel for, something different. A sea of small rupee notes washed over the truck. The crowd knew he had turned down 500 rupees. A cardboard box held the mounting pile of paper money. Soon another cardboard box appeared.

The Tamil man touched the blood on his shoulder one more time, and looked from his helpers catching the floating bills fluttering like rare butterflies, to the box of money at his feet and finally to his prehistoric rooster. He withdrew his bamboo pole with the sharpened blade at the end, and with arms outstretched, hands aloft, and a big grin that shown like a flashlight in the dark, he roared "To the Top! To the Top!"

And the people of Native Town cheered "To The Top! To The Top! To the Top!"

The Tamil man vaulted the roped sides of the truck, reached back for the two boxes stuffed with rupees, and shoved them in his truck cab at the feet of his wife, who must have been pleased.

Now the rooster took center stage, inflated his chest like a prehistoric blow fish of huge proportions, and let out a deafening, "Cock a doodle, dooo! Cock a doodle dooo!"

He marched proudly around the ring, flapping his powerful feathered wings stretching the ropes. High above vultures soared in uncertain patterns.

The frenzy of excitement gave way to the realization by those on the ground that there was work to do. The most agile and daring placers must somehow transport a gigantic cage to the top of the pyramid of roosters, which the spectacle of the King Rooster had shaken to life. The climb would be dangerous.

We covered our ears, crouched low and wound our way back towards our perch on the porch, where to my dismay the woman with the crooked-handled broom waved us away.

"You've gone. You've gone. You have to pay again."

"No way, no way," I said, and we climbed quickly up the ladder. But after seeing my package and duffel untouched, I relented and gave her a five-rupee note, which, between disdainful shrugs, she tucked into a fold in her sari. For a moment, a subconscious whisper from her of something else for sale breezed through my mind. I let that tantalizing thought pass and looked out beyond her to the vast Square in the dim, dusty sunset. I watched the shifting masses swirling like the treacherous waters where a river meets the sea.

"Over there," pointed Chaleea.

A group of men trotted through the crowd carrying a long, snake-shaped vine above their heads, like an undulating dragon riding on top of a Chinatown parade. The vine looked to be the length and thickness of the ropes in high school attached to the gym ceiling to be climbed to the top - tap the painted red, steel girder, and then back down to the mats below. I was good at that and could pull myself up just using my arms.

I asked Chaleea, "Why the big vine?"

By the time I finished the question I knew the answer. It was for the biggest cage ever to be built for a rooster. It was for King Rooster. The men dropped the thick vine on an area of large smooth stones, where dozens of white-clothed men and women sat on their hunches face to face making basket-like cages. From our distance the sight was like an impressionistic painting with spots of pure white in the foreground against brown skin and gray slate in the background. Pairs of men struggled to bend the vine. Pairs of women unloaded six feet long de-barked blond sticks. Out of what appeared to be utter randomness, I saw there was a crude efficiency and a division of labor. What the Indians lacked in mechanical and technical equipment they made up for with manpower and creativity.

The Fat Man brushed aside the smaller weavers and took over. "I need some curved sticks," he commanded. "Get me some curved sticks." He plunked himself down on a smooth round stone in the middle of his mindful minions, who in his presence referred to him by his real name, Ali Kahn. Since being fat in India was synonymous with having money, he even took a perverse, unspoken pride in the title, The Fat Man, though no one dared address him as such to his face.

Soon pairs of bent, old women with leathery skin appeared carrying crooked, blond wood in the shape of an oxen's back. They walked up to him, stooped even more while he picked over their load and removed two or three peculiarly bent pieces, and dismissed the women with a grunt and a flick of his hand.

"Those are for the corners," Chaleea whispered wisely in my ear.

Like honeybee drones buzzing around the queen, The Fat Man's servants supplied him with whatever he needed to make the grand cage for King Rooster soon to adorn the pinnacle of The Rooster Palace. A hand drill, a basket of wooden pegs, straw matting for the bottom of the cage, and smaller vines used to tie the larger ones together were placed in a circle around The Fat Man. While he muscled a section of the mighty vine with his arms the size of logs, two boys tied smaller vines through the grooves at each end, keeping the thick rope-like vine permanently bent.

Chaleea said to me, "This is a rare day. You are very lucky."

The woman whose balcony we were on quietly reappeared. "Soon you will be hungry," she said. "I have some dal and chipati."

Chaleea looked at me with big, pleading eyes.

"Qu'et n'a paisas?" I asked.

"Whatever you wish to pay," she responded kindly. Her appearance and apparently her disposition had changed. She wore a large brilliant red silk cloth wrapped over her blue sari. She had on circular gold earrings. Had she just put them on, or was I now only noticing them? Her bright red lipstick matched the color of her shoulder sari.

Perhaps catching my wandering eyes, she pulled her sari across her hidden breasts and commented, "It soon will be evening, and the chill will come."

"Are you interested in some food?" she asked again, with a touch of impatience. She looked at me, and I imagined her brown eyes gazing into my soul.

Willingly mesmerized, and with a slight gentlemanly bow, I said "Most definitely."

"You may come in then."

As she turned to go back into her second floor abode, she stared disapprovingly at my feet. Chaleea pointed to my shoes while taking off his. We set them in a row on the porch outside her wooden door. I puzzled over this chameleon-like woman whose mood and manners changed so.

VI

Annapurna's Bungalow

The hubbub of the market was subsiding. The Tamil man and his wife had moved the truck with King Rooster. The Fat Man was still twisting and weaving and notching, but the crowd around him was thinning out.

Evening was coming and the city dwellers feared the darkness. Only the desperate or downtrodden ventured out. I had been warned at the Broken Plate Cafe that in a peaceful, passive country, where Gandhi was revered, the Naxalites were violent Communists who lusted for power and ruled the night.

I suspected the man Nandalla was a Naxalite who frequented the Cafe. I eyed the package and wondered about its contents, and I wondered about the Sikh at the cafe who had sent us here and revealed the most about the Naxalites.

I pulled my socks up, shook my head free of thoughts of the past or future and stepped inside a clean room. A straw broom with a long wooden, debarked handle leaned in the corner. Silk hung on the walls, and large pillows used for cushions were spread about the carpeted floor. One of the cushions, which was tied with twine in the shape of a cylinder, doubled as our host's bed roll. One doorless closet was the home of a small propane stove with two burners. I looked for a separate bedroom or bathroom, but didn't see either.

She lit two candles and a hurricane lamp. The one window was open a few inches at the top. With the same match, she lit a small stick of incense and placed it near a carved statue of Krishna on a painted tile table. I sat cross-legged on the floor breathing slowly, purposely, peacefully.

She glided to the stove and cracked two eggs into a copper pot of rice, unrolled some tinfoil and picked out bits of chicken meat to add to the pot. She sprinkled curry from between her fingers and stirred it with an elaborate silver spoon. She lit another gas burner for a kettle of tea.

As I inhaled the aroma of incense and cooking food, she placed brightly covered red and orange place mats on the floor in front of the three of us, and I observed with inner delight, one for her next to me. She kneeled with the sizzling pan in her gloved hand and ladled the concoction into our wooden bowls. Pancake bread was on the side. The sounds of the roosters, and their pungent smell wafted through the room and mingled with our incense and food to create the sweet intoxicating smell of India.

Chaleea was busy eating, savoring each spoonful, dripping none. I waited for our hostess to begin, but she gestured for me to start. I tore the bread patty in half, stirred my rice and chicken with it, and took a luscious warmly-soaked bite of the bread.

Showing a bit of restraint, I spooned the rest of the concoction into my mouth. She watched and giggled.

"Is it good? she questioned.

"Is it good?" I repeated. "It's delicious." I reached over with my hand to reassure her, thinking how wonderful Chaleea, and now she, had been to me, a stranger from America.

Instinctively, she withdrew her hand. Chaleea, who had been watching, whispered to me. "Do not touch her with your left hand, Sahib." Of course my wooden spoon was in my right hand, and the moment was lost.

But she didn't seem too upset and serenely served tea. I got up to help but she shooed me away, as if I would disrupt the rhythm and flow of the ritual of tea. Without the slightest noise our hostess placed a rectangular, brass tray in front of me. The tray was etched with the scene of a tiger peering our of a flooded, bamboo jungle. She kneeled on one knee to pour the tea into three, pure white, ceramic cups on the tray, and I sat on my hands and watched the hot, boiled liquid arch out of the copper kettle into the thick cups. She rose gracefully and returned silently. We sipped together holding the warm, organic cups in our hands, our eyes joyfully swimming about the room like fish inspecting a coral reef.

We savored the tea while dusk departed and the darkness arrived. The only words spoken were when our hostess formally introduced herself as Annapurna, and I told her my name was Jack. The tea ritual over, Annapurna latched the shutters and clicked a bolt on a narrow door which must have led to the hallway and the stairs.

Both Chaleea and I had to go to the bathroom. Chaleea spoke to her in Hindi, and she explained where the one bathroom for this building was. With candle in hand I unbolted the door, and we walked down a tilted hallway. Over the rickety banister, down the stairs in the candlelit darkness, a heap of clothes at the bottom appeared to shift position. Then the entire floor below appeared to move. At least ten bundled persons off the street were down there finding their spot for the night, respecting the stairwell as a boundary.

One man in a turban and a white shirt which glowed bluish in the darkness, stepped over and around the bodies and climbed the stairs. We made way for each other at the top corner, and he eyed us carefully as he walked down the hall and inserted a large key into the lock of a small inlaid door. To fit through the doorway, he bent forwards and twisted sideways.

We reached the bathroom door, and Chaleea knocked. It was locked, so we stepped back and waited. A young girl emerged, only her eyes showing above her purdah. Chaleea rushed in. I nervously waited my turn, watching for the next robed figure to sidle by in the night.

Everyone knew their place, accepted their position. Why the mound of bodies at the base of the stairs didn't just walk upstairs, I didn't know. The people who lived here obviously tolerated them. I suppose as long as they remained in the hall below.

The caste system seemed to be fading on the exterior only. The lowest castes still had no chance of climbing up out of the hovel of the streets. Outwardly they harbored no resentment towards the system, and, unlike the Naxalites, no desire for change. The British and the Indian professional classes were convinced that without the structure of the caste system, India, one of the poorest countries on earth, would have erupted in violence long ago.

When it was my turn, I held my nose and breathed through my mouth. Thankfully the thing flushed. Chaleea led me back to Annapurna's flat with our one candle. We knocked gently and slid in sideways.

Annapurna had changed clothes, and again I wanted to touch her manicured hands as a way of saying thanks. She was the first Indian woman to have some genuine contact with me. I reached with my right hand, but she withdrew just enough not to embarrass me, and with the grace of a fencer handed Chaleea and me each a warm, clean wash cloth. I watched Chaleea as he first wiped his face, and then his hands, and I did the same.

On the floor her mattress was unrolled, and across the room Annapurna had lined up pillows for us. Chaleea curled up on one of the plump red pillows while I unrolled my army surplus bag.

"Good night princess," I said playfully.

"Good night stranger," she said with a sweet message of reproof.

VII

Festival Fever

In the morning, the market stirred, the roosters crowed, and The Rooster Palace, the hub of intrigue and ritual within the decaying labyrinth of Calcutta, called to Native Town to awaken to another day. A day with some promise in the air. All the players; the runners, the weavers, the messengers, the placers, and the master craftsmen, knew that an attempt would be made to cage the King Rooster and lug him to the top of The Rooster Palace. He would fetch a price that had not been heard of in years.

Word had been spreading to the Gothis in North Calcutta, to the richest Marwaris in posh bungalows in Ballygunge and to the Bengali families in South Calcutta, that a giant of a rooster would be auctioned off. The Babus, the wealthy and decadent Bengali families, descendants of Rajas, might want to buy the King Rooster to upstage a rival Babu family. Their festival of parties was to start soon, and they competed with each other in every way imaginable. On the first day of the week-long festival, the Babus adorned their palaces with costly colored electrical lights and gay decorations the way families back in the States decorated their homes at Christmas.

To pay for the King Rooster a Babu family would simply trade in one of their smaller rubies; unlatch their golden chest and reach in for a handful of jewels. The ones which fell between their fingers; those tiny jewels bought exotic Balucharis' saris, custom made silver ornaments from the Jaggu Bazaar, and hilsa fish dinners and pink gins at the Tollygunge Club. The remaining handful of rubies could go for King Rooster.

Whichever Babu family bought and owned the King Rooster would command crowing rights. That Babu family would win the most attention. They would be gossiped about. Rumors would abound at the Calcutta Cricket and Football Club as to how much they had paid. The more the better - up to a point. Even the Babus occasionally checked their wallets, or called up the few remaining working bankers in their families. The Babu dynasty was on the decline, but it was a gloriously decadent decline filled with hookahs of hashish, dancing women, gambling men and scotch.

The Rajas too would bid for the King Rooster, but more with an eye towards investment. They would want to know the age of King Rooster, his weight, where he was raised. Could he in fact grow bigger? And, smiling wickedly the princes asked, could the female hens withstand the attention of a rooster that large? Show us some of the eggs his hens produced. Were they edible, or just extra large?

The Babus, the Rajas, the nouveau rich Marwaris families, and the riffraff, myself included, all were interested in The Rooster Palace. Of course if things got out of hand, the military would appear and spoil the fun. But the handlers around The Rooster Palace were crafty. They would bribe them, find them women, somehow keep them away.

"Good morning, Annapurna," I said. Chaleea sat up and bowed slightly, pleased to have slept inside a room, instead of inside a culvert.

"The bathroom is probably free by now, since you lazy heads have slept way past the sun," said Annapurna happily.

When Annapurna opened the door to the hallway, I wedged by her, and brushed her chest with mine. "Excuse me. I'm sorry," I stole a look at her and for a moment she met my eyes and then quickly looked down to the floor,

I was still waking up and needed to splash cold water on my face. It was one of those mornings, when you're traveling a lot, and you first wake up; you're not sure where you are.

As I brushed my teeth side to side with baking soda, I wondered what was going on back in America. Football games. God it was great to watch a football game in October, sit in the wooden bleachers next to a girl in a yellow sweater who would be with you at a party that night, and park with her in your Chevy Impala before you drove her home. I swirled the brownish water around in my mouth and purposely spit it all out, hardly aware that I had been thinking back to my past.

As far as activities on the toilet, so far, so good - no diarrhea. Staring at the feeble hook and eyelet which kept the bathroom door closed got me to thinking. No matter how long the line, Indians honored this weakest of locks as a way to prevent embarrassment. The simple setup symbolized for me the fragile dignity of the destitute souls of Calcutta. The slightest push and the old eyelet would have come unscrewed. The respect of a hook and a wobbly eyelet is all that separated civility from hostility. In America that door would have been pushed open and the lock sent flying long ago.

I heard the crowing of the roosters and smelled my stench and walked out with as much dignity as I could muster. Back in Annapurna's room, I observed how tidy and comfortable and even cozy her place was. Silk on the walls covering the crisscrossing cracks in the plaster, large green and orange pillows on the floor embroidered with pictures of elephants and tigers, incense in the corners. There was Annapurna smiling, working merrily over a small two burner propane stove.

I put on my familiar denim shirt and bluejeans. I padded the slight bulge underneath my shirt in the center of my chest made by the thin embroidered leather case hanging around my neck containing my passport, American Express travelers checks and U.S. dollars. I knew the bulge looked a little strange, but it was the only worry-free way to travel.

Awake and ready for breakfast. How nice, Annapurna had prepared something. I touched the tea pot with the back of my hand. The milk was in a small silver pitcher; probably goat's milk. As long as the water was boiled I guess it was safe, but I was still worried about the milk. The preparation of the tea and patty bread with white butter seemed British except for balls of puffed rice mixed with some fresh mashed mango fruit in three ceramic bowls. Chaleea dug in and told me it was a popular Bengali dish called moori. Once I started eating, I didn't stop.

When I was done I felt I owed Annapurna some money. From my soft leather pouch hanging off my leather belt, I took out my flattened wad of 50 rupees folded in my silver and turquoise money clip from Santa Fe. I reached out and gently touched her hand with a couple of folded rupee notes, nodding to her.

"We can settle later," said Annapurna calmly. "right now I have a confession to make."

"And what's that Mademoiselle?" I asked smartly.

Annapurna turned and faced me standing straight. "I think you think I am a Bengali Indian." She paused as I looked at her closely.

I didn't know if she was waiting for an answer, but I gave her one. "Yes, I assumed you were," I said matching her somewhat formal style of speaking.

"By blood, I'm Indian, both my parents are Indian, but by birth I'm an American, just like you. I was born and grew up in Albuquerque, New Mexico."

"Well, you could have fooled me," I said casually. And she had completely fooled me. But I didn't feel deceived. Later she explained that she was passing here as a native, ever since she had joined the Peace Corps three years ago and worked out in the countryside near Dharamasala. She liked the perception that she was an Asian Indian, which gave her a disguise and a chance to be someone different. From then on she played the part so much so that she forgot sometimes she was an American. With gusto she embraced the Bengali culture and Hindu religion. Emotionally, the change wasn't difficult since she felt alienated from American culture anyway.

"So," I said with a touch of forwardness, "You're wearing bluejeans today, dressing like a western woman, are you?" I was about to say 'girl,' but switched to 'woman.' Smiling broadly, I added, "You look good."

"Do you truly think so?" she asked.

In the spirit of the exchange, I ventured on. "It was your figure in those tight bluejeans that I was commenting on."

She blushed in front of me and choose not to respond to my un-dignified comment. Instead she asked, "Do you want eggs this morning or not? They are three rupees apiece," she said.

She was back to business. Realizing I had blundered, I tried to re-cover from my flirtatious remark. Why didn't I just keep my mouth shut sometimes?

"What I meant, Annapurna, was that you look very nice this morn-ing, even in bluejeans. And I appreciate you having us here. And for me it's a pleasure to be the guest in the home of a beautiful Indian woman." I recoiled inwardly, knowing now she was not a native Indian woman. But still, I sensed she saw herself as Indian.

41

She listened and said, "Thank you," with a warm smile. I was relieved. "The eggs are only one rupee each," she mentioned while facing the closet wall and its decorative calendar of festivals. She flipped the eggs from the pan to her best blue ceramic plates.

Eager to keep the conversation rolling, I showed her the package that the second engineer wanted me to deliver to the Broken Plate Cafe.

She listened in absolute silence and then asked to see the package. With a resigned look on her face, she said simply, "I can take care of the package." She pursed her brow. "I know the Broken Plate Cafe and I know a man who frequents it. His name is Nandalla."

I was a bit surprised that here in this teeming city, she happened to know this man. I hesitated on her offer. "I promised my friend on the freighter that I would deliver the package personally."

"I will fulfill your promise, Jack. Nandalla is a man I see regularly."

Her last comment quieted me. I held the package in my hands as if I were trying to guess its weight. I was satisfied that she would make sure he got the package, but I had promised to personally deliver it. "Do you know what's in it?" I asked feeling I was the naive one. "Why don't we open it?" I asked recklessly.

"This package is not to be opened by just anyone. He who opens it will have heavy responsibilities. Enough said, Mr. Jack."

Annapurna's phrase, 'I see regularly,' kept rolling through my mind, distracting me. I exhaled a long breath and concentrated on the issue of the package, recalling again that I had given my word. "I guess we'll have to wait. If you see this Nandalla fellow regularly, I'll give it to him next time you see him."

She said nothing as Chaleea returned from the bathroom and picked up his plate of eggs, gleefully carrying them out onto the balcony while shielding his eyes from the glare of the morning sun. The Fat Man and his servants were not yet at work. The circle of smooth, round stones was clearly visible. In fact the Square was nearly empty but for the scurrying of rats and the idle hosing of the mountain of rooster cages by a couple of workers.

"Where is The Fat Man? Where is everybody?" asked Chaleea.

"Where is your religious training?" answered Annapurna. "Aren't you a good Hindu?" She paused and Chaleea dared not answer. "Today is Kali Puja and you should be at home with your sect getting ready for the parade."

Chaleea had forgotten, and I hadn't been told that today was another holiday where good Hindus did not work. Today was both a parade by the Hindus and self-flagellation by the young and restless Shiite Ashoura high on bhang who might otherwise by thinking of revolt.

Looking at me, Annapurna said, "Today the sects compete by retracing their rise and fall from saintliness to debauchery and back. And I must warn you nastiness could erupt towards Westerners and their English language. Signs will be ripped down, or the English will be crossed out and changed to Hindi."

"The Rooster Palace too," I inquired. "It closes down?"

"Yes, Mr. Jack. You'll have to stay another day at least, to see if that King Rooster actually makes it to the top."

She explained that she had seen other roosters almost as big and almost as impressive, fail. The ruling families vote no. Or a genuine chicken farmer offers the seller enough money prior to the risky ordeal of getting the rooster to the top of The Rooster Palace. Vultures can strike too. They don't like to be upstaged, and that top cage is constantly under attack by vultures working in tandem. For defense the cage has to be especially large and the vines tightly woven.

I listened intently remembering my first stroll through an open-air meat market, beseeched by beggars. I almost had my head taken off by an ugly, gray vulture sweeping in from my right, landing just to my left on a side of beef hanging from a gaff. While the vulture dug in with his yellow claws, the evil-looking bird tugged at a chunk of stinking meat with his beak. He flapped off, dropping a smaller piece which was caught in mid-air by one of two ravens who fought over it. No one else in the market paid any attention. The vultures were a part of life in Calcutta, and I was told they kept the city clean.

"This is so different from where I come from," I told Annapurna.

"Yes, I have seen pictures of New York City," she said.

"No," I said quickly, "I do not live in New York City. I live in the country, in a mountainous region called the Adirondacks. And I can't believe you've never been to the Big Apple." I knew that to anyone living in Indian, or even anywhere outside the state of New York, New York meant New York City.

I told her and Chaleea that where I lived there were no tall buildings and very few houses. Mostly there were lakes, rivers and trees; lots of pine trees. And in the winter it was terribly cold. A couple of days each winter, Saranac Lake, where I built my house with a chain saw, was the coldest place in the nation.

"How cold does it get?" asked Chaleea as he helped Annapurna wash the dishes.

"Maybe 35 degrees below zero."

Chaleea looked puzzled.

"Cold enough so that if you spit, it shatters when it hits the ground. You hear a crackle."

"I don't believe you," chimed in Annapurna.

"You don't believe me?" I repeated, standing up. And I went out on to the balcony and spit over the railing to the edge of the empty Square below. "So cold, that no matter how many saris you wrapped around yourself, or what long underwear you wore under your bluejeans, you would be freezing."

I turned and stared at Annapurna, entertaining myself. "I'm sure it gets that cold in the mountains of New Mexico or Nepal. Go to the top of your namesake in the Himalayas and you'll see."

"I am not named after that mountain. My friend Nandalla gave me that name when I told him Anna was too plain and too American. I felt like a Pilgrim with that name. He said Annapurna was the name of the Goddess of the Harvest."

I decided not to argue and asked which she preferred to be called, Anna or Annapurna? After a moment, she said hesitantly, "Annapurna." I felt that inwardly she wasn't clear about her identity, even her nationality. But I could relate to that.

"For your information," said Annapurna, " I do not go north to the mountains to get away from Calcutta. I go south to the jungle. I love the warm, wet heat. You have probably never been to the Big Jungle," she chided, mocking my reference to New York City.

With my usual directness I said, "Then take me to the jungle today, and with your permission, I will stay another night . . . with Chaleea," I added, not wanting my intentions to be misconstrued. Or maybe I did have amorous intentions.

"How long would it take for us to get there?" I asked.

"Most of a day," she answered slowly, perhaps thinking things over. "But we would have to catch a train from Howrah Station. And after the train we have to ride a bus and then some sort of dinghy. And we have to be in the Sunderbans jungle before nightfall, safe in a cottage. The Bengali tiger prowls at night, and two weeks ago . . ."

"The Bengali Tiger is a man-eater!" interrupted Chaleea.

"Yes, Chaleea, you're right, and a village surveyor was killed two weeks ago, eaten by a tiger." remarked Annapurna.

"Once the tiger tastes human flesh, he is a man-eater for life." Chaleea said with conviction.

"Annapurna, take me there. I will pay for everything," I said, though I knew money was not the issue. I simply yearned to be in a jungle.

She admonished me. "Third class on the train costs close to nothing. The bus is nothing too. Getting a dinghy and a pilot to take us to an island in the jungle is expensive, however. And if we stay at a guest house . . . ," she paused. "Out there is not Cal, and they will think the wrong thing. Even traveling with a foreign man will look bad for me."

"I'm not going to the Sunderbans," stated Chaleea. "That's where you're talking about? No, not me. The tiger is there."

Thinking out loud, Annapurna said decisively, "The Gods have willed it." Quickly she tidied her apartment, and hid her rupees under the sink in an empty can of Ajax. In a conversation in Hindi between Chaleea and Annapurna, they agreed he could stay until we returned. She handed him a note to give to her friend Nandalla if he showed up. The note explained both where she was and who Chaleea was. She instructed Chaleea not to say a word about me.

Chaleea was delighted. This one room would be the most spacious and cleanest accommodations he had ever stayed in. He would remain inside and rest and listen to the stirrings of the roosters.

Chaleea felt he had done well these two days. He felt complimented that two adults were trusting him, and felt pleased I took a genuine interest in his splendidly decayed section of Cal called Native Town. He too in turn was interested in the package and had his own idea of what was inside. Being a street person, he knew of the feared Nandalla and his connection to the Naxalites.

"If you go out, you must lock. Here is the key," Annapurna said. The two of us shuffled backwards out of the narrow door, past the bathroom which now stunk. She looked like she was wearing long underwear with a big white shirt hanging out and a scarf around her head and across the face. The bright red lipstick and the dot in the middle of her forehead told of her Hindu stature.

Hands clasped, Chaleea bent at the waist, and said, "Thank you Annapurna. And I will pray to Ma Bono Bibi, the Goddess of the Forest, for you."

VIII

Jungle Love

We were off to the infamous Howrah Railway Station and then to the jungle. Annapurna led and I followed, but not too closely. For the first time since I came ashore, a few side streets were deserted. Everyone was at the parade, frolicking, happy to be shirtless in the sun, flogging themselves, proving their Indian manhood.

We walked towards Brabourne Road where no one paid us any heed but a starving woman holding the smallest baby with the biggest eyes and a disfigured man who leaned on the sole of his upturned foot with his other foot crossed underneath him like a three–dimensional pretzel. A couple of paisas were in his bowl. I reached in my packet, but Annapurna reprimanded me.

"Do you want to go to the jungle? Well, we have a train to catch. There will be many beggars at Howrah, I assure you. Many grand deformities," she said.

I wished that we could magically just close our eyes and be in the green jungle. I was getting weary of the dust and the red and brown colors worn proudly by the bricks and mortars of the buildings which Annapurna told me reminded her of the canyons of New Mexico.

Graffiti in the form of the Maoist hammer and sickle and star was painted in orange on a building on the corner of Cotton Street. "That is a new one," remarked Annapurna. "That is probably the workings of an artist the Naxalites have paid."

We talked of taking a taxi the rest of the way but I liked to walk. The only time I took a cab was after I had witnessed a snake charmer with two hooded king cobras, Najas Hannahs, as they are called in Calcutta. I stumbled upon the scene after leaving a Congress Party rally. A California hippie acquaintance of two hours was with me. We stopped to watch a snake charmer entice a cobra up through the eye of a human skull. Using some type of ceramic flute and a rhythmic motion the charmer kept the snake upright and on guard flaring its spectacled hood. We knew something was wrong when the Indians around the charmer started to yell and gesture at us. We tried to nonchalantly saunter away, but a tight group of seven or eight ragged street people surrounded us as we turned a corner in search of a paved street and traffic. We were saved by a cabby who reached around to his back seat to open the door for the two of us. We piled in and he yelled at me to close the door. As he accelerated, the Indians had trotted along side banging their bony fists against the Plexiglas window.

Soon we were trekking across the steel Hooghly Bridge, one of the landmarks of Calcutta and the longest cantilevered bridge in the world. A parade was on the other side, and the bridge was jammed with double-decker buses, jitneys, motor scooters, rickshaws, hand-pulled carts and people. The whole suspended structure vibrated with life. We stopped in the middle to gaze at Cal, one of India's great cities, the home of the East India Company and the Imperial Capital of India, a City of Palaces. I was absorbing its decayed present state, marveling at its wonderful, serene chaos.

"There's the station," pointed Annapurna.

We quickened our pace on the downhill. A pulsating vibrancy greeted me once we pushed through the first pack of beggars milling around the rows of glass doors to the railway station. "Get out of my way," commanded Annapurna. "It's the only way," she whispered to me. "Otherwise they will be all over us. And while you're looking into a suckling baby's eyes, her older brother will have your leather pouch."

"Yes, not unlike the market. I know," I said flatly. At some point you have to turn off, and not make comparisons. Not everyone can be Mother Theresa, bless her. This was the worst I had seen. Men, barely able to stand up, urinated openly down onto the tracks. Starving families of Bangladesh refugees slept on the concrete floor, a foot or two from where an almighty diesel engine wrenched its black tonnage of iron and steel to a halt.

"Backshish, Sahib, Backshish," I heard over and over again. I wanted to hand out some coins and finally I did. Some paisas which maybe equaled a tenth of an American cent, but the black-haired boys threw them back at me. One dwarfish woman, no taller than four feet, wrinkled and sun dried, held on to my hand, and begged me to take her with me. I held tightly to my wad of rupees in one hand, breathed in the diesel-tinged air, and shook her off. Then I thought what are you doing, give her something. What is she to do? I went back and handed her two crumpled rupees, and she limped away, one leg shorter than the other, sweeping the pavement with arms which were full-sized and as long as her legs. She was quite nimble, and dodged through the crowds, gypsy-like and delighted, back to her group of beggars. And I thought the simple thought we all think in the face of ill health and tragedy - lucky me.

Sometimes beggars grouped together to form cooperatives. Begging was considered a legitimate form of employment in dear old Cal and was on the verge of gaining recognition as a trade union. I wondered if they split their earnings.

The Howrah station was immense and open, airy and light, with windows high above, and a noisy and decadent world down below, but with no weapons, no clenched fists, only a search for money to buy food, and a tolerance for misery. This was the hard edge of Eastern spirituality.

The trains came and went roughly on schedule. Third class cost less to the edge of the jungle than the rupees I had given away here at the station. As I worked my way through the masses living on the concrete platforms, I was easy to spot.

One platform away two European travelers waiting for a train gave me a holler. They wore red bandannas tied like turbans, long braided blond hair, glittering earrings running from their nose to their ears, and gold bracelets and rings like the Indian women in today's parade.

"Hey, how ya doin?" I said smiling happy to see two American-looking travelers like me.

"We're good. This is Wendy. I'm Charlotte." Charlotte kind of waved to me, twinkling, even though she was just a few feet away. God they looked great. They were standing with their feet spread apart forming a teepee over their back packs on the floor, trying to keep the beggars at bay. They were probably a couple of years older than me.

"Going to Kathmandu?" I asked.

"For sure, how 'bout you?" asked Charlotte.

"Yeah I am, but not just yet. I gotta hit the jungle first. My friend Annapurna is taking me."

"Far out."

Anna, as I sometimes silently referred to her, was standing erect behind me. So I introduced her and she bowed slightly.

The girls, Charlotte and Wendy, who I could tell by now were not Americans, but probably Aussies or Kiwis, were really curious to talk to someone whom I think they assumed was a young Indian women. They asked her questions about piercing her nose, and if they wore a sari would that offend an Indian.

Charlotte was wearing a cut-off, sky-blue T-shirt with the picture of a breaking wave and the words 'California Dreamin' zapped across it.

No bra of course. They didn't seem particularly interested in me personally, though I think they were happy to see a young white guy.

"How do you keep these poor beggars away?" Wendy asked me.

I shrugged. I really didn't know. "I guess you develop one big callous."

A tall blond sauntered over. A guy with blond hair longer than the girls'. "Hey, you from the States?" he asked me, clasping my hand, thumbs held high, the hand shake of the young and the restless. "Isn't this place too much?"

Why did I instinctively like these three, the way I liked almost all the foreign travelers I met. They were honest, open and friendly, just being their goofy, obnoxious selves.

"I'm riding on top, once we get out of Calcutta," he said with a wondrously large smile.

"On top of the train?" I said angling my head with a look of curiosity.

"Yep, and I'm lighting up the papa of all ganja joints as soon as I climb up there."

I just smiled. What was it about these Californians? They were just as free and as big as the ocean breeze.

He put his arms around both of the girls and yelled, "Honcho, boncho."

I smirked. this guy's in heaven, I figured. Two blondes from Down Under, and a pouch full of pot from Afghanistan.

Annapurna shot me a look of reproach, and I moved backwards.

"Hey, New York, come with us. Come on, come to Kathmandu. You know it flows up there. You don't want to stay here too long, man. Kind of nasty. And the food's better in Kathmandu. More Chinese."

He was right on all counts, but I was committed. "I'm going to the jungle and I have an escort," I said proudly, nodding to the retreating Annapurna.

"See you up there," he said. The crowd closed in around us, and I caught his peace sign high over the heads of the Indians - a signal of good-bye to Annapurna.

51

Suddenly I was lonely, seeing those Westerners, looking like they were having fun. Why was I so intense, so serious about really getting to know Calcutta? I guess I thought it was the most bizarre place I had ever been to. There seemed to be little order, except for the tedious bureaucracy leftover from the British, which was why the train system worked so well. The network of trains was the single common thread running throughout the patchwork quilt of states called India.

Their train to Benares and Patna onto Kathmandu was leaving, packed with penniless people. When they arrived at the border town of Raxaul the three blondes would cross into Nepal on rickshaw to catch a ride on top of a truck load of grain winding its way towards Kathmandu, the land of hippiedom, where the head honchos issued their own hippie passports to christen the newly arrived. I had researched the route well, and planned to be taking it soon.

2

Our train to the jungle was pulling out too, circling south, away from Mother Everest and the mountains and towards the open sea. We were traveling third class, which cost only six rupees apiece. I pushed in behind Annapurna. She sat on a slice of an empty seat near a corner.

Annapurna patted a sliver of a board next to her and motioned for me to sit. But all around, old, malnourished persons stood, and I thought I should defer to them. Thankfully, she insisted and somehow I wedged myself between her and a small, neatly, dressed boy. Groups of three and four passengers hung out the windows, cackling, passing Beede's back and forth, and at the last moment buying some pistachios as the train started to pull out. The vendor ran alongside the chugging train handing them their goodies through the window. Inside the car, agile Indians maneuvered towards the ceiling, and curled up on the luggage racks. I waited for the air of the open countryside and the breeze from the moving train.

"Those blonde girls were nothing but children," Annapurna said.

I was hot and sweaty and shrugged my shoulders in response. I felt her next to me, more like a mother protectorate than a woman I fancied. I wondered what her figure was like but couldn't tell through her layers of clothes.

Two gaunt men across the way who had been eyeing me warily decided to risk a smile, and I smiled back, and addressed them with my hands together, temple fashion and uttered my standard greeting. "Namesti." The boy next to me dropped his head on my shoulder, eyes closed. We slept, my head on Annapurna's shoulder, and the three hours passed.

At Lakshmikantapur, which was the end of the line, we dragged ourselves off the train and rode across the village in a rickshaw, an experience I could never get used to - being pulled by an old man. Next to a flat building we lined up for a bus to Raidighi where the waterways of the jungle began. I was thankful Annapurna had been here before and knew what she was doing, and I admired her more and more.

On the bus, she talked to me for the first time about Nandalla and how she empathized with his Naxalite cause, but not his means. More so than in the States, here she needed a man to progress socially and to find a job at Calcutta University, which had been her goal. Otherwise she would be viewed as a quirky American who stupidly had fallen in love with India, a country most educated Indians tried to leave. Now she was having doubts about everything. For once I simply listened.

In a disheveled state from our impetuous journey, we rumbled and rattled across a moist savanna, the tall grass blowing in the sea breeze. The afternoon rains were past. Annapurna and I were still sleepy from the hypnotic train ride, but I wanted to make a foray into the fabled jungle before the darkness descended.

Our driver indicated that our dirt road ended, that up ahead the rice fields and shrubs which followed ended, and the swampy waterways of the Sunderbans jungle began continuing all way to the Bay of Bengal. The framed jungle of the Bengali Tiger. The driver backed up without us, and we walked onward with a group of village children over the last cultivated field to a beach and a few rickety wooden docks with pinnaces for rent.

Four hundred yards away across a salt water inlet a green island of mangrove trees entangled with lower leafy plants stood like an inviting puzzle. While Annapurna haggled over the price for the boat, someone to pole us across, and a thatched hut on the other side, I took my boots off and walked barefoot in the black sand.

I noticed the natives treated Annapurna with respect and deference. The man polling our boat reached out and helped her aboard, while I barely had time to jump aboard as he pushed away from the dock. On the other side of the khol, packed leafy trees and bamboo stalks hid a path which led into the jungle thickness, prickly with the unknown. Before our poler had beached our boat, he warned Annapurna away with stories of the Bengali tigers turning into man-eaters because of all the salt water they drank.

Evening was upon us. We were told this was the only dry path leading through the mangrove jungle to our hut. My senses came to life, the path narrowed, and I felt a hot damp coolness that contrasted with the feel of the air in Cal. With my forearm I brushed aside leaves the size of frying pans and the thickness of pancakes, large droplets of moisture running in rivulets along the indented veins.

"Annapurna!" I gasped. On one of these leaves at eye level, a dazzling red creature the size of a silver dollar slid off the leaf and floated horizontally to the ground.

"A miniature flying frog," remarked Annapurna calmly, "though I have not seen one that vivid red before."

We walked silently onward on our jungle path. Beneath the high canopy, a black-capped kingfisher flew across, in undulating patterns, noisily announcing the presence of intruders.

Thick vines crisscrossed the view skywards. We stopped and listened. I reached out to the dripping trunk of a mangrove tree and touched a striped snail almost as big as my hand. Near my foot a fiddler crab disappeared under the brackish water.

I thought I heard human laughter in the distance. Annapurna smiled knowingly. She pointed ahead, and we walked farther. Then the laughter exploded in the trees around us. A family of rhesus monkeys clamored high up in the trees. During a mid-air leap a monkey tossed a small orange at us.

"Pick it up," said Annapurna. "Throw it back. They are playing with you."

I tossed it high up into the green leafy sky above, and a monkey showed itself as it leaped off a vine, catching the orange in mid-air and landing with a rustle of leaves on a swaying branch. What sounded like clapping broke out from the rest of the group.

A real gang. We were just like them, I thought. Now either they were gone or silence had arrived. I felt invigorated to be away from all the dirty, dusty, throngs of people. I touched Annapurna's hand and thanked her for bringing me here. She didn't resist and took delight in my enthusiasm for the jungle.

We pushed onward. I led. The leafy forest got darker, and Annapurna's mood changed. The path became spongy and full of waist-deep ferns. Out of the wet moss grew trees two feet high - perfectly shaped miniature banyan and bo trees. Tiny webbed frogs leaped away. Then I saw a part of the path move and Annapurna froze.

I didn't see the head, but the spotted body of a snake was still crossing a dirt mound ahead of us. I had never seen a snake so thick or so long. It was the size of a fire hose full of water, and the snake gave off a repugnant odor. Finally the body passed, gliding from side to side as it propelled itself forward with surprising speed.

Annapurna was feeling apprehensive and spoke carefully. "The Anaconda python swallows the farmer's small calves. There is always a reward for these snakes. But they are not poisonous. They squeeze their prey to death."

We stayed still. We heard a different rustling sound; bushes getting pushed aside. The birds had stopped their songs. Annapurna raised her hand, motioning for silence. We remained absolutely frozen. This bush smasher didn't care who heard him.

Maybe the animals used the remnants of this path much like a Grand Trunk Road of the jungle. Instead of remaining standing with leaves and branches rubbing against us, blocking our vision, we crouched down, feeling suddenly vulnerable. Light no longer streaked in between the leafy canopy. On the ground something was approaching. The bushes parted at a turn in the path, and the bristly, pink nose of a squat, wild boar with yellow tusks appeared grunting.

Annapurna whispered, "Do not move. He is dangerous, but he can not see well."

I had started to slowly rise, looking around for some sort of weapon, a stick perhaps. Then two smaller boars, with no tusks, probably babies and kind of cute, stumbled on short legs out onto the path. The big tusked boar prodded them back into the protecting thicket of the bottom layer of the jungle. The babies squealed and all three disappeared.

Annapurna grabbed me by my shirt, passed me and said, "We better leave." Neither of his spoke. The invisible aura of the tiger had our souls by the throat.

Soon we were out, into the glow of the sunset, onto a field, away from the dense, entangling greenery, walking with relief to a distant shack. Another world, the jungle, I thought, feeling exalted.

"I have seen the wild boar before, but never with its young," said Annapurna. "Both the Anaconda and the Bengali Tiger will challenge the boar. That is a rugged fighter we saw," Annapurna said with some respect. "Was it worth it, coming all this way to the Sunderbans?"

"Are you serious? I haven't been as excited since kayaking the Moose River."

"Kayaking? I am not familiar with this sport."

"It's like paddling a canoe, only there's a blade at each end and the canoe is covered. If you know how to roll over in it without getting out, you can paddle the wildest rivers you can imagine." I was pleased to find a subject I knew more about than Annapurna.

She pointed to the shack in the field, and said we can go there. Gracefully she twirled, executing her own Eskimo roll, unwrapping my arm from around her waist. We walked, hardly talking. I paused once and stared back, wondering about a real expedition into the jungle, with maps and tents and guides. Now that I had penetrated the jungle I jogged forward to Annapurna, happy with today's ending, looking forward to a night with her.

The broad skies were darkening, reddening in the West. Growing from the sides of the shack was the same grass we were walking on. The roof was made of thatching and mud, low down to avoid cyclone winds and pitched to shed monsoon rains. I opened the door made of uneven wide, wooden planks, once painted. Two cots were inside separated by a solid rectangular oak table with a white table cloth and food - grapes and bread and two cokes, and some bananas to the side.

I looked at Annapurna for her reaction.

"I asked the poler to make arrangements to leave a simple dinner. Two hours have passed and for a few extra rupees Indians can be very resourceful," she explained.

"Then I owe you some money," I stammered.

"Yes, you do," she said, as if to say all right, if it makes you feel better. "We will settle later."

The mattresses on the cots were large burlap bags stuffed with hay on a few rusted springs which creaked when I sat. Annapurna lit the hurricane lamp. I got up and walked outside to go to the bathroom. I always carried some crumpled toilet paper in a pocket. But I discovered, since I was eating less, and hardly any meat, I was going to the bathroom less. As Woody Guthrie said, 'The more you eat, the more you shit.' All I had to do was take a piss.

Annapurna opened the door for me, and the shack glowed regal with her knowing presence.

"What are you thinking about?" she asked with a warmth I had not sensed before.

"I'm thinking about you." I blushed, leaving it at that.

She took me by the hand, softly, and we sat on the edge of her cot. "You know, of course, I shouldn't be here with a Westerner, whom I do not know."

"Yeah, I know, this is a delicate situation for you, and I appreciate you bringing me here," I said in rather "ah shucks" fashion.

She patted my hand, rose and said, "Let us enjoy this meal, here at the edge of the great Bengali Jungle. And let us pray," she paused, "that all the needs of great Bengali tiger are fulfilled in the jungle and that he prowls far away from us and our field shack."

She put her hand around one of the chipped, greenish bottles of coke and handed it to me. Not yet ready to ponder what lay ahead of me, I thought, thank God for Coke Cola. It wasn't cold, but it refreshed me.

I reached out and touched Annapurna's leg. Sometimes when I'm embarrassed or at a loss for words, I let my physical nature take over.

"Sit," she said. "You know that I'm less certain about things than I appear to be. Please, tell me about New York City."

I drew a long breath, not particularly eager to speak. "It's got energy, but you have to have money to enjoy it. Not like here. Not like Calcutta. I could live for a year in Calcutta on what I would spend to live for a week in New York - $250." I fingered my Indian embroidered leather case hanging around down from my neck under my dhoti.

I explained that New York City is cold in the winter, with smoke and steam rising from portals in the street, as if there were a thousand underground fires, and sometimes a manhole cover over one of these openings will get blasted up by an explosion.

"Let's see. I always eat a hot dog and a slice of pizza when I come to New York. Just like in your markets, there are vendors with carts on wheels selling hot dogs all over the city. And pizza stands, or kiosks, are on almost every corner.

"You're either rich or poor in New York; there's no real middle class. Anyone with kids usually moves out. I lived with a concrete sculptor on Delancy Street when I was teaching way uptown at P.S.154, behind the Apollo theater in Harlem.

"Most everyone lives in high rises, tall concrete and glass, or brick and stone buildings, called tenements in the poorer sections. In the richer sections they live in brownstones.

"Do you have brownstones in Albuquerque?" I asked.

I do not know. I grew up in a ranch house in one of the Mexican sections of the city. Keep talking about New York."

"Sometimes at schools, kids at recess play on the tops of these buildings enclosed by high steel mesh fences.

"Fast, everything is fast in New York City. The people talk fast. And time goes by fast. People work and walk fast. The cabbies all drive fast. It's noisy. Cabbies honk their horns all night. If they're legal they have a photograph of the driver in each cab. I suppose so a passenger can see and compare if it's him or his brother that's driving. Gypsy cabs are unlicensed, and they come and go at night, like wisps of wind. A cab driver gets robbed each night somewhere in the City, and a cabby is probably murdered in a hold-up each week. The cabbies are almost all foreigners. I've talked to cabbies from Pakistan, Albania, and of course from here, India

"There's a large Indian population. In fact I've seen women dressed like you in your saris, not as pretty, walking seriously a few feet behind their husbands.

"Some parts of the City you can go out at night and feel safe and other parts you go out at night only if you dress like a Bowery bum.

"How would a Bowery bum dress?" asked Annapurna.

"Like any of the characters around The Rooster Palace," I said quietly.

The shack was dark except for the dancing light from the wick of the lamp. A dry wind blew outside, and the green wall of the jungle beyond the grasses awed us with a threat of peril. The predators came out at night. The Bengali Tiger ruled at night.

"The roaring screech of the tiger could be a scary gift indeed," said Annapurna, reading my mind.

We were seated next to each other on the cot. I had said what I could about New York, and now the shack was quiet. I was silent, not wanting to break any taboos. Annapurna stood up, and looking at me kindly, she unwrapped her red and gold sari. Like watching a sacred dance, I stayed respectful, and tried to push any lust away. Underneath she wore a sleeveless T-shirt that a trapeze artist might wear. She moved close to me, standing and brought my head to her stomach, a lone lane of soft skin touching my ear. I nuzzled her tummy. I kissed her there and searched for her belly button and kissed her there.

With her long finger nails she massaged my head, and grabbing the back of my hair, she jerked my head upwards so that I was staring up into her face, praying to a goddess.

"The screech of the tiger will make this a special night," she said.

"I don't think we need the tiger," I said moving up her body.

I pressed my cheek against her face. I felt very alone. We were born and fought against living alone, and finally died alone.

She stood tall and still like a statue. I touched her nose with mine. I rubbed her cheek with my cheek. She remained standing. I felt her chest against mine through the red silk. I stepped back and started to unbutton my cotton shirt. She slowly took my hands and put them on her hips, while she looked me in the eyes and skillfully unbuttoned my shirt letting it fall to the floor.

"Shhh," she said her finger to her lips. "I feel the tiger."

Chills of anticipation and excitement swept across my chest. She drew me forward, and gently kissed me, playing with my lips, tugging at them. I felt like I was floating away, like a slippery red jungle frog flying in a new direction.

I was mouthing her, her face, smelling her earthen hair, my hands on her back, cupping her ribs, saving her breasts for as long as I dared, waiting for the heavenly zone to envelope us.

She pushed me down on the cot and undid my rope belt. "Silly thing," she muttered.

I reached down to grab a pant leg. This is not the first time for either of us, I thought. But it was the first time in India next to the jungle.

I worked her silk shirt upward with my head and kissed her wide brown nipples which were large and tough like the callused hands of a farmer. They hardened and softened in my mouth.

Her bottom was soft and pliable cushioning. She took my hands and placed them where she wanted them. Not yet. I'm not ready yet, she told me without speaking. She guided my hand in the thick of her black pubic hair. I rubbed her there with my fingers, kissed her all over with my lips. I wanted to please her. If only for a few eternal moments, I had forgotten about the jungle and even myself. I was lost in the heavenly zone.

Annapurna, not yet all feeling, thought of herself as the seasoned one here in India, and it was for her to lead. She felt her wetness spreading. No urge to push forward, no desire now to be knocked about; just kiss me, touch me. She guiding me while she held my head, kissed my ears. I felt wonderfully free and new to her and to me. She liked my intuitive ways. She wanted my imagination. That's why tonight she loved me.

"Now," she murmured, getting lost herself, feeling foreign and apart from herself, feeling her arms like the flapping leaves of the jungle pulling me forward, on top of her, reaching down for me, guiding my erection into her. She put her arms up over her head and thrust her pelvis up, embracing a quiver of pain, then grabbing my bottom, clutching the flexing muscles and holding tight, giving me direction. Then she was mine and she let me go; let me on my short wild ride. She pulled my head to hers, and mouths wide like fish feeding, we kissed with tongues and teeth and sweat, and she wrestled my head aside. An uncontrollable burping noise swelled up from within her. My moans vibrated nose and mouth, and then I shot straight, felt like a heavy board, soon to bend around.

She made love wonderfully, powerfully. I lay limp over her, whispering some nonsense in her ear. Was I crying? No, I was thankful and she was too. I was young and the night was young. The wick still flickered. We both came alive, came back from being lost, and now the jungle spoke. We felt naked and unmasked. She wished it were an aftershock of love. We listened and the jungle spoke. A breeze came.

The shack had one window. I stood up naked, still erect, and she curiously examined me with her eyes. Would she want me again tonight?

I went to the door and unlatched it, swung it open and peered out. Part of the sky was covered with clouds, puffy and gray, harbingers of the monsoon season. Brightness, the clouds opened, and a moon shone. Not a full moon, but close - a night or two away.

In the moonlight, I saw the towering wall of vegetation across the field, and like a man on the bow of an ancient vessel at sea, I spied danger in those cliffs, in that jungle wall.

I turned and latched the door. "It's beautiful. The moon wants to be full." She cuddled close to me.

The breeze becalmed and the noises of the jungle ceased while the silence intensified. The distant birds had stopped squawking. Annapurna, who said she always had to fight against her superstitions, opened her mouth to me to say she was afraid.

As if from her, we heard a distant screech, like the cry of pain from a human prisoner fighting fiercely. The first screech froze us halfway between lying and sitting, our muscles tight. Again and closer we heard the wail of a great cat out hunting in the moonlight. Pray she wasn't near starvation for that is when the Bengali Tiger leaves the jungle.

"Blow the flame out," commanded Annapurna. I did and checked the lock on the pine door. I felt afraid but alive, and though it was a warm Indian night, I was chilled. I lifted the thin blanket back and lay down next to my mate, my partner and pressed next to her warmth.

"Have you ever seen the tiger?" I asked.

"No, and please God, not tonight."

3

Early the next morning, while it was still dark, the raucous callings of the jungle awoke us, and we clung together, happy the deep of the night was over and happy the morning streaks of light were near.

Like a little boy bragging, I whispered, half to myself and half to Annapurna, "We made love last night."

"You are such a boy," she whispered, "but a game one." She had thrown off her background last night. Her Indian friends would be aghast if they knew. They would think of her as a prostitute, like they thought of all the traveling white women. Indians called the unmarried girls, their long hair down, their shoulders bare, who traveled around with foreigners, 'sleeping dictionaries.' What were these women doing, Indians would ask? Why aren't they taking care of children? Why aren't they working for a living? Or taking care of a home for their husbands?

63

No, no, no, Indian women would say to Annapurna when they sensed a wandering in her or a longing for a Western style of life. Western women have no tradition, no character. Yes, Annapurna agreed, but they have fun.

She took one of my hairy, sinewy legs and wrapped it around her tummy like an arm. I'm evil she thought, kneading the memory of last night in her mind, while with her hand she worked on a morning memory. I tingled for her touch, my mind open only to the physical sensation. I stopped thinking. I knew enough to enjoy these foreign minutes, in a beguiling land, where the exotic is mixed with the religious. I too felt some guilt lying naked next to Annapurna. Usually I couldn't wait to leave a women after a session in bed, even on a straw mattress near a jungle. But it felt right with her, and I liked that she liked holding me, and scratching me.

The morning light and hint of heat took over the inside of the shack, so I kicked the blanket off to inspect my dark skinned woman who ruled and risked in her adopted homeland. I looked at her thighs and her crotch and her hairy bottom, and rubbed my paws over her tits.

"I'm hungry," I said deliberately.

"Have a banana and get dressed," she cooed.

She was about to toss me my flowered boxer underwear, but then held them up in a streak of morning light. "I want these." And she yanked them and hopped into them. Full of desire, I stared at her. She blushed, and grabbed her sari from the bed and held it to her breasts - breasts she had never been satisfied with.

"Your breasts are perfect," I said smiling, and she accepted the compliment.

Unfortunately for me, she was also getting more businesslike with each piece of clothing she found and put on. Finally she kissed me hard and directly on the mouth, followed by a long silence, while she tidied the bed, and then with a matter-of-factness which gave no hint of the precious and exciting night of love we had just shared, she said simply, "We have a train to catch. Let us go."

I too remembered The Rooster Palace, and the topping of the pyramid by the caged, King Rooster. I finished my banana, left four rupees under a coke bottle, which Annapurna said was the proper amount, and we stepped out of the thatched mud shack and walked towards the path which led through the jungle to the inlet. The path was less threatening in the morning sun, and most of the jungle animals were nocturnal creatures. I twirled around once to gaze back on the shack, and rubbed Annapurna's rear lovingly recalling our night and morning together, but she cut me off.

"You can not do that now."

"I understand," and I knew she meant it, and she was right. The wall of the Sunderban jungle with tigers and water buffalo patrolling the perimeter like sentries had put a spell on us last night, and made Annapurna think she had behaved like the Western women she was trying not to be. She had difficulty admitting that she had enjoyed the frolicking and the sex, because she had been taught that those nights were for procreation. And then she remembered staring up at the hundreds of carved stone figures from the Mahadeo temples at Khajurahori detailing acrobatic sexual positions. Wanton sex was in India, her adopted county's history too.

Annapurna was a proud woman, and she walked straight, upright, never behind the man, as was the custom in India. She looked aside at me, and liked my long sandy brown hair and blue eyes. She thought I was so American. Last night she had taken a chance, and so far with God's understanding, she had not been punished.

4

"Chiii, chi," whined a vendor, like the baying of a cornered animal. At Lakshmikantapur, where we boarded the train on our way back north to Calcutta, the noise of the masses at the station was a cacophony of sounds matched by hundreds of pairs of hands from beggars with out-stretched arms hopping for a few pence to be thrown at them from slow moving railway cars. When the train pulled out late arrivals shoved their children and bags through open windows as they trotted along side barking directions. This wondrous chaotic generosity of mankind kept amazing me and must have kept India's modern decay from turning violent.

The train ride brought us back to daily reality in Calcutta. On arrival at the Howrah Station, the celebration of the Vishnu God of Snakes was over, and a new religious celebration dawned tomorrow for a Babu family across town.

Annapurna and I moved quickly, not bothering for small talk, not even feeling like we had made special love last night. She stopped at a vegetable cart for red tomatoes and red peppers and green celery. I was thirsty again for a coke. Instead I found a vendor selling tall cool glasses of water with a slice of lemon floating in them, I bought one glass, drank it, then another and overpaid the old man, feeling like I had done a good deed.

"Your stomach is not yet used to the bacteria in our water," Annapurna warned. "You should stick to coke and tea."

I knew that of course, but in my reckless fashion, I was thirsty, so I quenched my thirst.

.   We moved off the platforms and out of the grand glass-domed structure of Howrah to the streets. "You see that," Annapurna said, pointing to the red graffiti of the Naxalites. "That Communist slogan was not there yesterday. They are getting braver every day and no one will stop them."

I thought to myself, but your friend Nandalla is a Naxalite.

She quickened her pace and I followed. Around another corner and another corner, a bump there and an unintentional push there, and I got a whiff, and I knew we were getting closer to The Rooster Palace.

Turning to Annapurna, and half trying to explain to myself what happened last night and why I was here in Calcutta to begin with, I said what I surely must have read elsewhere. "Without experience we are just readers, never really feeling, never really suffering." I ran my hand down her hand, trying to be honest with my feelings.

I could tell Annapurna was thinking 'not now.' She was concerned about her flat, and worried that she shouldn't have left. She was sure she would be punished. Her room would be robbed, or Chaleea gone with all her possessions. She walked faster, and I too stepped up the pace thinking of the bathroom down her hallway. My stomach was churning, and I was not sure I could hold on. It must have been the water.

When we got within sight of her building across the Square, I awkwardly ran ahead of Annapurna, through the vestibule crowded with workers getting out of the noon-day sun, smoking their triangular Beedes. I bounded up the stairs three or four steps at a time. Don't let it be occupied, please. It wasn't. I sat and exploded into the toilet. There is a God. What would I have done without a toilet?

Feeling thin and relieved, I tapped on the door of Annapurna's flat, and Chaleea greeted me with his gawky smile. "What did you do while we were gone?" I asked. Before he could answer, I went on "And King Rooster? Is his cage ready? Have the placers tried to carry him up yet?" Was The Fat Man working today?

Still smiling, he answered no to the last questions, while tilting his head from side to side, swiveling it like a parrot, enjoying the attention. "I did nothing but watch parades and dodge firecrackers down the street from the Chinese," he sneered. Like most Indians, he resented the Chinese who took over the restaurants and shops so quickly, claiming a sector of Cal as their own.

"What did you do all night?" Chaleea asked bravely, tapping a finger on my chest. He caught me off guard, and I looked quickly to Annapurna, but she was opening the shutters out to the balcony.

"At night I had the best rest," continued little Chaleea. "And I played dominoes."

"And the package, it's safe?"

"Right where you left it."

Did you eat?" I asked absently.

"Not much, Sahib Jack. And you can check her closet. All the food is still there," he said proudly. "But I am hungry now. I'll take you to the market." He grabbed my hand and pulled me back out the door.

"Annapurna, okay?" I called back.

"You do not have to ask permission," she scolded. "I am not your wife, and I have work to do, so be gone. But bring back some tea and some nuts."

IX

Calcutta Streets

Once we hit the streets, the game began. I was in no hurry and had time to smile and laugh and push off the beggars. One white-haired woman carried a skinny baby in her arms. Pointing to the baby's face, she moaned, "Backshish Sahib, Backshish." One of the baby's eyes was pure white. From my wad of rupee notes, I flipped one out of my pocket and held it towards her. She shook her head no, and motioned me away.

"Too little," she said, "too little."

With my right hand in my pocket gripping the bills, staring at the baby, wanting a bunch of babies myself some day, I nimbly peeled off another rupee. Of course in U.S. dollars, two rupees were worth only about 22 cents, but here, you could get something to eat, a meal perhaps, for two rupees. Or for 12 rupees you could spend the night at the Salvation Army Guest House just opposite the more expensive Taj Hotel.

Begging was a game of percentages and she had already improved her lot 100 percent by resisting my first rupee. Now there was a trailing group of mothers and children walking behind us, some deformed - one

girl with only one arm, some normal but starving with rib cages protruding.

I thrust the two rupees into the hands of the Untouchable woman,
and said "That's all. That's all."

Without touching me, she managed to extract the notes. I quickened my pace to get rid of her, as she called out, "More, more." The
other mothers, wrapped in pinkish cloth, the Hindu mark on their fore-
heads, clustered around her examining her earnings.

Meanwhile, a worshipped and wizened bull, doing as it pleased,
with a lay of pink flowers dangling from its small horns, ambled through
the crowd on just another morning on a narrow, dusty, Calcutta road.
An old tanned man with a white cloth wrapped around his head for a
turban and a long crooked stick in his hand for a staff, strolled a few
yards behind. The old man smiled at me, the foreigner. I nodded back,
appreciative of a normal gaze of questioning recognition from a
stranger.

The uncertainty of each day was dangerously seductive. I thought
back to a conversation with my Dad about hitchhiking across the country. He said he didn't like the uncertainty of it, of not knowing where
exactly he was heading, or when he would arrive. We were different
there.

Dodging the thickening human traffic cascading towards us, two
street-savvy kids, a boy and a girl, popped up on either side of us.
Chaleea knew them. They were twins, younger than he, named Sanray
and Sumantha.

Chaleea started grunting, and with exaggerated motions cleared
and pushed other beggars and street hawkers aside as we neared the
congestion of the outdoor Houghly market. A bearded man with one leg
and a crutch hopped in front of us, and the kids barked at him and
made some menacing gestures. I thought Chaleea and the twins were
going overboard, so I grabbed a hold of Chaleea's long white shirt tails
and yanked him back before they toppled the bearded beggar.

"We're protecting you, Mr. Jack," Chaleea admonished. "Yes, and you pay me," he stated with authority.

I saw some wisdom to his strategy. Part of Chaleea's job, as he saw it, was to keep all the street hawkers and assorted riffraff away from me, so that I could walk through the bazaar without being surrounded by a group of skinny backshish-begging boys and wrinkled old ladies carrying emaciated babies. Chaleea thought he had done well, and I liked the protection he provided. Plus I liked his company. Up until now I only had been paying for his meals. I gave him three rupees. He shrugged, and stuffed one bill somewhere inside his flowing white shirt. He gave the other two rupees to the twins who dashed off never to be seen again.

In my naiveté when I first arrived, I gave away a coin to one angular boy, and instantly a crowd of boys surrounded me preventing me from moving in any direction. I became trapped, padded down by dozens of beseeching hands as if I were being nibbled at by crabs.

Those were in my early days in Cal when I still wore bluejeans and snap-button western shirts. I learned. Now when I was out in the bazaar, which meant anywhere in the city, I wore white Indian garb, which camouflaged my Western ways and was cooler.

Looking around, I felt the exotic intensity of Calcutta. Sheep baaaing, cows crossing the streets, withered men hauling vessels of drinkable water, plump lipsticked Babu princesses commanding their weary rickshaw wallahs.

We meandered by waves of colored silks, past a stall selling leather bags and snake skins, past flower stands, and into tents peppered with glistening golden and silver scales for weighing any of the hundreds of teas. We bought a mixture of loose Assam and Darjeeling teas.

Chaleea proceeded to pull me in a new direction past a whole row of men selling nuts carefully arranged on colorful clean silk cloths, with silver, shimmering scales for weighing. I wanted to stop, and the vendors observed my hesitation. Two stood motioning with their hands, beckoning me over. Chaleea tugged on my sleeves in the other direction, but I didn't move. Careful not to show too much money, I pulled out two crumpled rupee notes and pointed to the plain pistachios. Back in the states pistachios were always colored red, because red was supposed to be more marketable. The vendor watched me as he started piling the nuts on the scale. When the mound looked like as much as I wanted, I told him to stop by slicing my hand horizontally back and forth, like I was playing blackjack and didn't want another card.

"How much money?" I asked in Hindi. The vendor looked quickly at my guide standing straight by my side, and said in Hindi an amount I didn't understand. Chaleea grabbed my fist and uncurled my fingers, took out one rupee and gave it to the man. The vendor quickly emptied the mound of blond pistachios into the thinnest of small brown paper bags. The vendors to the left and right sat cross-legged and tight-lipped, probably envious of the sale, wishing this white man was buying from them. I was ready to leave but Chaleea refused to move and waited.

Chaleea stuck his hand out. "Change," he said firmly in Hindi. "Change," he demanded again of the street hawker. Now a small crowd encircled us. Maybe the Indians sensed an incident developing with this foreigner. The vendor, squatting on his haunches, like a collapsed folding chair, with his own legs the same thin diameter as chair legs, appeared to be busy separating the nuts into precise piles. I was still interested in the other nuts, particularly the cashews. But I knew I could stop on almost any busy street in Cal, and find street vendors selling nuts.

Chaleea wouldn't budge, and it dawned on me that the vendor must owe me some change. With one eye the vendor looked up, and then snapped down a coin into his Chaleea's flat outstretched hand.

Bravely and quickly Chaleea said "More." Again with the coin still sitting in his open palm, Chaleea repeated the word "More." The crowd swayed and a murmur arose. The other vendors felt we were pushing far too much. The puchkawalla was annoyed. He flicked one more coin into Chaleea's hand. As he did so, Chaleea yanked on my sleeve to get moving. The vendor stood up from his folding chair position, got up off his haunches, and was standing, yelling, not so much at me, as at Chaleea who had pressed for the lower local price. The two of us trotted away from his shouts, until the incident was just another transaction in the market place. We were soon enveloped and hidden by the milling throngs, the way the multitude of green leaves in a rain forest covers its creatures.

We wove our way deeper into the labyrinth of the market. Chaleea shooed away other beggars and walked proudly by my side, showing off his American prize. My almond-eyed young boy smiled and looked up at me, reaching to put the two coins in my pocket. Before he could drop them in, I said, "No, you earned them, you keep them." He lowered his eyes and tucked the coins within the folds of his pajama-like garment.

Occasionally in the crowded market, handsome, bearded Sadhu men, wrapped in a distinctive orange cloak that only religious men wore, padded quietly by like the puff of a warm afternoon breeze or sat cross legged like a bright toadstool in the shade of a vendor's stall. They, at least, never openly stared at me. Rather in their eyes, they preached a contentment, an acceptance of the world, an acknowledgment that one day the foreigners would come, intrigued with the poor and the otherness, searching for the spiritual.

The day when this version of American's best and brightest would be trekking through India, searching, had arrived. Some Americans wore dhoti or saris or another chosen Indian garb; some took the time to learn and speak the Hindu dialect of the ruling party; all were young and fed up with the materialism and constant quest for wealth in the United States. We were an invading army of willing converts ready to experience almost anything.

While I was pondering the tenor of the times that had brought me here, the street crowds magically opened up for two soldiers, shoulders back, rifles pointing straight up next to their red epaulets. Their uniforms were the same color green as my Army surplus sleeping bag. For a moment, the soldiers appeared startled to come upon a foreigner in the back alleys of Native Town. They looked straight at me and my young Indian guide. I smiled back while Chaleea looked down at the packed dirt and hurried me along.

X

The Fat Man Makes A Move

Returning to the Square from the rush and buzz of the Houghly market, Chaleea and I did as the Indians do. We draped our arms over each other and strolled towards the lingering crowd around the flat, smooth rocks. We sidled our way to the front of the pack. The Fat Man, his bald head an easy target for the sun, settled down to work under a white umbrella. Using his hatchet and wood chisel, he shaped and notched and bent the vines and the debarked branches, while he barked out commands. He was constructing the largest cage ever built for the one and only King Rooster.

The Fat Man scanned about, his eyes fixing on me for a moment, then moving on. "You," he said pointedly, "you, come here." Chaleea and I turned to look behind us to see who in the crowd The Fat Man wanted. "You, little girl. It is you I need." She was one of the street urchins who played in the Square chasing rats.

"No, this is your day. Come here," commanded The Fat Man. And the crowd silenced, wondering what was up with the crafty Fat Man. He was a controlling sort of man.

"This young girl is about the same size as King Rooster. We will construct the cage so that it can hold the girl. We will build the cage around her," the Fat Man pronounced to the crowd.

"No, the rooster is bigger," one woman declared while balancing a circular basket of fruit on her head. Others in the crowd took up the cause. "Yes, the rooster is bigger. The girl is too small," they called out.

Seeing that he had miscalculated the crowd's notion of how big this rooster was, he shooed the girl away. Bewildered but relieved, she brushed by us to the back of the crowd. Just as quickly, though, The Fat Man recovered and pointed directly at Chaleea, while bellowing, "You, you are the lucky one then. Come here."

When he realized The Fat Man wanted him, Chaleea shrunk back. I saw no harm and nudged Chaleea forward to The Fat Man who was seated yoga-style like a Buddha. Now Chaleea had the mixed blessing of the shade of The Fat Man's umbrella.

The ragged crowd looked to their market lady with the basket of bananas on her head for a sign. She stood straight, adjusted her sari, touched the diamond in one nostril, and said, "Yes, now you have it. This boy is more the size of King Rooster."

"It's decided , then, " proclaimed The Fat Man. "You are my model, and I am the sculptor. You are my prize pupil." With a gleam in his eye, he slid his huge paw-like hand through the boy's hair. "You must stay here," he commanded. "It will take me all afternoon to finish this grand cage."

"But I'm hungry," said Chaleea while glancing at me for some sort of signal. He was not sure he was ready for an all day commitment. The Fat Man, who was always hungry, snapped his fingers and from his tent, wearing just a loin cloth, a young boy about Chaleea's age emerged and ran up to his master.

"Go to Kwality and bring back a hot dish of Mughlai," barked The Fat Man, and off the boy tore in the direction of the market. "Now you will have supper," The Fat Man said matter-of-factly to Chaleea.

Putting my hands together in prayerful fashion, I called out, "Chaleea," and bowed slightly towards The Fat Man. I gestured with a quick wave of my hand for Chaleea to come here.

"All right," declared The Fat Man.

Chaleea and I stepped back from the thinning crowd to talk. "It might be fun," I said , "and I won't be far away," pointing to Annapurna's flat at the edge of the Square. Chaleea stood silent with a frown. Finally he shrugged. "I'll stay, but be sure you're back to get me before it's dark. And don't get lost," he said smiling weakly.

Chaleea went back to the stage of stones, and I needed to get out of the heat. I didn't want to stay at Annapurna's place all day. I would drop off the cashew nuts and the bag of loose tea at her place and then be gone. I didn't want to be perceived as too available and commonplace. But where to? I would go to the Broken Plate Cafe to arrange to drop off the package,

The apartment was empty and I wondered where Annapurna was and who was with her? After debating whether or not to take the package with me, I decided to leave it at her apartment. I headed out, determined to find my way back through the fingered, crooked streets to the Broken Plate Cafe. The narrow twisting alleys were not packed like this morning. The street vendors chanted with less urgency.

A deformed Kali beggar sat cross-legged under a yellow umbrella with a dotted, white face and a third, leathery hand sticking out of his ribs. He looked at me beseechingly, chanting a mantra, but it didn't phase me. Amazingly how quickly I had become hardened to beggars' hardships. I didn't want to stare. Then I would have been obliged to toss a few coins into his brass dish.

After maybe fifteen minutes, I stopped and asked directions to the Red Shield Hotel. I thought I might remember the way to the Cafe from there, and its name aroused no suspicion.

"You're almost there," chuckled a pleasant man hobbling in the streets. I was traveling on a stretch of crooked, dirty streets typical of

Native Town. In the distant sky, I caught sight of the onion-shaped domes of Nakhoda Masjid, a landmark I recognized.

With my thumb I felt the excess space between my bluejeans and my waist. I was getting thin; something I wanted to do. I liked being thin in sympathy with the Indians.

I passed a billboard for the Bombay cinema showing a bare backed dancing girl being embraced by a dashing man dressed like a pirate. Then I saw the Hotel. I turned down Gariahat Road which eventually led to the alley that led to the three descending, concrete steps of the Broken Plate. The door was unmarked, but I remembered the faded yellow outside wall covered with political slogans and posters of Lenin and Marx.

After I was inspected again through the slat, the heavy wooden door swung inward, and I felt the relief of cooler air, maybe 75 to 80 degrees. Inside the regulars were holding court. They gave me a cursory look and proceeded with their discussions.

"Come," one said to me, who had been speaking in animated conversation to three others, younger than him. "Come here, sir. Please sit. You are an American. Right? Now, what are your impressions of Calcutta? Really, what are they?

Self-consciously, I approached. "Thank you," I said as someone placed a satin cushion on the cool, rug-covered, earthen floor. "I love this place; I'm dazzled by it," I said truthfully.

"He's lying," said one of the younger listeners. Quickly with a hand to my arm, the older man patted me as if to say, don't take offense, my young friend is just making a point.

"Calcutta is dying. It's going backwards. Its only attribute is this silly, elegant decay the intellectuals talk about," said the younger man.

I nibbled on the biscuit before me as the young man continued. "No sewers but what you see in the gutters along the streets. No phone system to speak of. The only way to get a message across town is to send a messenger."

"Yes," said the older man, "but do we want to be like other cities. There is only one Calcutta. That's why you're here, isn't it?" He looked laughingly at me, trying to elicit support for his side of the discussion.

"Tell me, the cities of the United States are violent, aren't they? Calcutta is not violent. We have the Naxalites, but they are political."

I noticed a slight shifting and uneasy looks at the mention of the Naxalites. An alert young waiter seemed to stiffen and smile extra hard as he feigned concentration on his task of emptying the hand-carved mahogany ashtrays.

A man with a wide streak of gray running across his black, matted hair, and a wider smile, said quickly, "Tell us about New York City. It is violent, isn't it? Ordinary citizens are violent, not for political reasons. Yes?"

"Yes," I conceded, "New York City is violent. Mostly poor people robbing others for money. And drugs. Heroin is a big problem. Remember I'm from the countryside; a mountainous region of New York State called the Adirondacks."

"Ah, ha," said one. "At night. It is dangerous? In the City of New York?"

"That depends where you are; in what part of the city you are," I said.

"Same as here," said someone from the back. "See Calcutta is like New York."

"Yes, but there is one big difference, " I said. "A lot of people own guns. A lot of the young hoods have guns, and carry them all the time."

"No, they really carry guns on their body? Then there is violence." Turning to a friend, the Indian said, "See Patnode, you don't want New York. Better to embrace the beggars of Calcutta. Even the Naxalites leave you alone in the daylight and prefer daggers to guns."

The waiter stared silently in the direction of our conversation, his pile of wooden ashtrays teetering in his hands.

"Why?" asked the older man. "Why go there? Unless you have to for business?"

"He doesn't know about business," remarked Patnode. "He is a hippie; aren't you?"

I shrugged. " I guess I am. I'm here in India for the city, the jungle, some adventure and some spiritual soul searching."

Patnode zeroed in. "How old are you. How do you make your money. It costs money to cross the ocean. And to bring a woman with you, like most of you do."

"Yes and these white women are all whores," yelled the waiter from the back of the cafe.

"It is not your place," snapped the older man to the waiter. But I could tell what the waiter had blurted out, the rest of the men believed. Indian women were covered and chaste until marriage and then dutiful and true to one man for life. I was told a Muslim woman could still be shot if she were unfaithful to her husband.

"In the U.S.," I said, "women are the same as men." With this comment they all rolled their eyes as if I had said the most preposterous thing. "What about your ruler," I countered. "What about Indira Gandhi?"

"Again, that is political," said the old man offhandedly. "And, of course, she is the family of Nehru-Gandhi. Much like your Kennedy's. We are full of contrasts." He poured some more tea. "And you must come back, and tell us more about New York City. Patnode wants to go there so that he can get shot." With that they laughed uproariously.

"In Calcutta, you can only get stabbed, and only at night," said the old man as an afterthought.

"Yes, we still like our daggers," commented the waiter winking at me with a wry look on his face.

The others stirred and rose. The noontime gathering was over. I had been dismissed. But I had one last important question. This one for the waiter.

"How can I get in touch with a man called Nandalla?" No one responded. Silence. "He may have been here the first time I visited this blessed sanctuary."

The waiter sauntered over, his arms folded across his chest. "If it is important, he will find you," he said, staring straight at me. "Come back some evening, after we close, and I will show you some things." Brushing his waist with one hand, he said, "There is a struggle here in Calcutta, a darker side, which a foreigner like you, probably knows little about, " and then he disappeared through a back room.

I left scratching my head wondering what to do next and how to deliver the package. I leaned against a wall for a while, watching life on the streets. Near one of the low crumbling clay brick buildings, a man squatted at the corner with a studied look of nonchalance, white garb around him like a tent, while he urinated. Few public bathrooms existed, so he made his own couple of feet of privacy.

I yawned and headed towards the heart of what Chaleea told me was the New Market, where the more established merchants set up shop. Instead of simple buying and selling, the merchants talked of commerce, of importing and exporting. The stalls were permanent, not taken down each evening and set up each morning. Some stalls were wooden, with red and green striped canvas curtains covering the front to be rolled up when business was open.

I came upon one emporium which sold white, shirts without collars, a little fancier than the common Indian man wore, a little more color, a weave of red and blue embroidered through the chest. I decided I wanted one, and for the second time I saw two other foreign women, Europeans or Americans, I couldn't tell, rummaging through the shirts while the storekeeper nodded appreciatively at their sides.

Two sandy-haired girls, my age, in bluejeans, already wearing the white Indian shirts were absorbed in shopping. I walked right up to them, really happy to see others like me.

"Hello," I said.

They both turned and smiled. "What do you think, 35 rupees?" they asked.

"Hey, I don't know."

"Where from?" they asked.

"Well, off a freighter from L.A."

"Ayee, that's different. I'm Rebecca and this Heidi. We're from Calgary."

"Calgary?" I questioned.

"Canada, my boy. You know the largest country in the world."

"I've heard of it," I said sounding as I laid back as I could. We were casual, but we checked each other out. I knew any women traveling on their own in India could take care of themselves. Canadians, along with the Australians, were known to be voracious travelers especially to the remote spots of the world.

"Do you want a treat?" Rebecca asked.

I nodded my head yes.

"Meet us at the Hungry Eye around 5:00. They make the best banana milk shakes and fritters, and it's a hang out for travelers. It's off Chowringhee Road, four streets back from the Maidan, the big park, on Wesseley Street."

Before I could respond they walked deeper into the stall. The Indian shopkeeper drifted behind them smiling, happy because he was about to make a sale and delighted to be between two pretty white women from North American. Though they were breaking Indian custom by flaunting their uncovered white shoulders, this shopkeeper had long since stopped taking offense and started to enjoy the titillation and the sale.

Maybe this emporium was one of those shops designated in some off-the-beaten-path guide as the place to buy a genuine Indian shirt. More likely it was word of mouth. My head was already abuzz with possible long range destinations for myself. Goa for the beaches and nudity after spending Christmas in Kathmandu. Time was no problem. I was here to slow time down. To get away from the rat race of my father.

I stood watching the two girls appear now and again, like blooming white flowers between the hanging shirts. And each time I saw them, the shopkeeper's dark face, of southern Indian descent, probably from Madras, popped up between the shirts with a big smile quoting the price.

"Only 40 rupees for you. Or 30 each if you buy all." He would get his sale, I knew that.

Seeing me standing there, Rebecca, the one with long braids and freckles, called out "Hey Sailor, see you this evening," while she continued to barter. They were reaching into their orange and red, handmade shoulder bags like the one I carried.

Go with the flow. Maybe I'd make it to a rendezvous at the Hungry Eye. But I had done that before, busted my ass to get some place on time, only to find the other person didn't show. Go with the flow.

2

I smelled the stench of The Rooster Palace before I saw it. I walked to the center of the smooth stones, which were unoccupied, looking for The Fat Man and Chaleea. I entered The Fat Man's tents and found his servants there, lounging, enjoying their leisure time.

"Your friend is out with our boss, somewhere. He'll be back soon," they snickered. "Sahib, are you from America?"

"Yes" I said curtly. I was concerned about Chaleea. Maybe I had left him in the company of the wrong man. I tended to be too trusting sometime. But I had to be, otherwise I made no headway. And usually, when I showed trust, the other person reciprocated. "Where did they go?"

A man outside one of the tents, under The Fat Man's umbrella pointed to an alley-way at the corner of the Square, and I marched off, determined to find Chaleea.

This dirt alley was particularly narrow; only rickshaws could fit down it, and only one at a time. A cow, its ribs protruding, wandered out of the shade of the alley into the sunlight of the Square. I brushed away some beggars, young kids Chaleea's age, and felt a skinny hand reach in and out of my back pocket of my bluejeans.

"Hey, get out of there!" I yelled. Off they ran cackling and pointing at me. I made a move, as if to go after them, but I wanted to find Chaleea. Instinctively, I patted my pouch underneath my shirt. My passport and money were still there.

The alley had a dampness to it which I welcomed. A small stream of liquids pooled and flowed ever so slightly in a concrete gutter. In a doorway a man sat hunched over, smoking a Beede cupped in his hands. I always felt light headed and strangely happy after puffing on a Beede. Other travelers had told me marijuana was mixed in with the tobacco.

Indians were certainly interested in our cigarettes, especially Marlboros. Above a wall of graffiti I had seen a torn billboard of the Marlboro man in his red shirt saddled on his brown horse, blue sky in the background, looking healthy and rugged. If I had had a carton of Marlboros to trade, I'm sure I would have had a pocket full of silver by now.

I didn't know exactly what I was looking for, but I was hunting, sniffing the air for clues. From a side alley dust swirled around a man who stood still and silent, watching me. He was Jean Paul, the turbaned, raconteur from the Broken Plate.

XI

The Package Gets Delivered

He radiated easy assurance. I learned later that he was waiting for nightfall and notice of the Naxalite's next secret meeting. With lizard quickness, he grabbed a banana from a passing cart. The cart pusher looked at him but said nothing and moved on. Someone, sometime would hand him a Beede, and when he unrolled it, a time and place would be written on the inside. He didn't know how, but they always found him, even near the congested markets bordering The Rooster Palace Square.

He puffed on his Beede, flicked the butt and ground it out with his size 14 sandal. He had been watching me search for Chaleea. "Mr. Westerner," the man called derisively. "Where are you going?"

He wore the odd combination of a turban and a cut-off tee shirt. He had a body builder's upper body and leaned casually against the shaded alley wall. His gold chain and pendant glittered in the hairs of his chest. He seemed less refined than when I had met him in the Cafe.

"I met you at the Broken Plate. My name is Jack Hamilton. And you're," I hesitated, "you told me Jean Paul." He didn't say a word, except to have an annoyed look on his face. So I continued. "I'm looking for a young friend of mine, an Indian boy."

"Perhaps I can help," he paused. "Is he with The Fat Man?"

Of course now I was interested in what he had to say. "Yes, he is with The Fat Man. Did you see him?" I was still cautious. He swiveled around and between the white folds of his robe protruded the ornate ivory handle of a dagger.

He didn't answer. He saw what I was staring at. "Yes," he paused again scanning the intersecting alleys, "You are interested in my dagger? Perhaps you're a collector." He didn't wait for an answer and adjusted the dagger back under his garments before beginning his rather one-sided negotiations.

"Let's proceed. First my street name is Nandalla. Second, you have a package of mine, I believe. Delivery of the package and a trivial sum of money for my troubles, will help me find this . . . waif of yours," sneered Nandalla.

I was focused on finding Chaleea and took his revelation in stride, recalling that I was suspicious of him at the end of our first meeting. "The package I have, as you know; but not on me. It is yours though, and I know where it is and I intend to fulfill my promise to deliver it. But how much money are you talking about?"

"One hundred rupees and I will tell you where he is. Two hundred rupees and I will lead you there."

Digesting his bold request for money, I asked. "Is he in danger?" Nandalla roared a hearty laugh in response. "This is Calcutta, my friend. You are in danger right now. We all are in danger of dying from a lack of order." Nandalla spat and growled.

"Okay, I'll pay you 100 rupees. Fifty now, and fifty when I find him."

"You drive a hard bargain, you Americans," he said with a sinister wink of his eye. "Let us go find my package."

I walked back to Annapurna's pad, and he followed me without being seen. I avoided the more conspicuous balcony entrance and entered through the back vestibule and up the creaky stairs. As I went to knock, Annapurna pulled the door open and greeted us with clenched teeth and pursed lips. I don't think she was happy to see the two of us together.

The package was rolled up in my army surplus sleeping bag. I yanked it out and remnants of the frayed newspaper floated to the floor. Nandalla and Annapurna were locked in an icy stare. I prayed Nandalla knew nothing of our jungle tryst.

The sight of the package broke the standoff, and he grabbed it from me and was about to march out. But his mind was working and he spun about. "My dear lovely, Annapurna, and you my American friend, come closer, I have something to share with you. You are conspirators. You are part of the Naxalite movement whether you like it or not."

As he spoke he put the package in front of us and ceremoniously, unwrapped layer upon layer of newspaper and twine, until what lay before us was a ten-inch long package of shimmering dark green felt. He stopped and eyed each of us, and then with a dash flipped over the last fold of cloth.

All of the sunlight in the dimly lit room seemed to be drawn to the object sparkling before us. It was the most magnificent encased, be-jeweled dagger I had ever seen.

Nandalla's eyes gleamed, and he looked around triumphantly, thrusting out his chin and showing his yellow teeth. "You fools don't know what this is. This is a nineteenth-century ceremonial dagger from the princely state of Hyderabad, now rightly in our possession. It had fallen into the hands of a greedy American collector, who knew nothing of its spell. He had bought it on the black market after it had been sto-len from the Jang Museum."

"Any Sikh, high or low caste, who unsheathes this dagger, who draws it from its scabbard, must in turn draw blood. And the second half of the spell is, he may kill without fear of reprisal, since he is under the ancient aura of the Hyderabad dagger. Only three exist. This one will fulfill a special mission."

I froze in awe of the gleaming jewels on the handle which ended in a golden tiger's head turned to the side its jaw open with red tongue and great sharp incisors ready. Nandalla's face went white and he clasped his hand on the diamond and emerald encrusted handle.

"No, Nandalla," screamed Annapurna, as she stumbled back.

Nandalla savored the moment and loosened his grip. "You fools, I would not waste this treasure on you."

Annapurna sat, breathing heavily. Nandalla seemed to come out of his ancient trance. "It's a powerful legend, which we can and will use," he warned Annapurna. "And now both of you know the legend and have seen the dagger."

Nandalla quickly wrapped the felt around the dagger, and tucked it inside his long coat near to his massive chest. He rose and the color returned to his face.

I didn't realize how close to danger we had just come. But obviously Annapurna did, and later she told me the history of Nandalla and why those who know him fear him.

He was leaving when I had the presence of mind to ask, "What about Chaleea?" He stopped and his frame loosened, as if he was back to a mundane task.

"Give me the rupees then," he said ever so softly.

I didn't want to have to open the thin leather case which around my own hairless chest. Thankfully, I had just enough rupee notes in my silver money clip and placed them in Nandalla's large outstretched hand.

"Meet me at dusk on the corner where you found me," said Nandalla with stern finality.

After he left her flat, Annapurna succumbed to a smoke to calm herself and slowly she told me the story of Nandalla.

XII

The Story of Nandalla

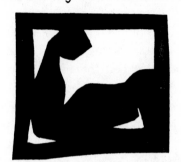

Annapurna puffed on her sacred American cigarettes, and told me what she knew about Nandalla's background. She said in and around Native Town, Nandalla was respected and feared, much like Americans revere a former athlete. He was taller than most Indians, and heavier in the chest. So by Indian standards he was big and imposing. People stayed out of his way because of his mercurial, stinging nature and his history.

When he was Chaleea's age, his first job was sweeping a cinema floor. He kept an eye out for dropped rupees and one time he found a working watch. But mostly he watched the movies. When his employer showed a Western movie, he watched the fist fights, and he learned how to throw a punch, how to smile and disguise his evil intentions.

In his room a long mirror leaned against the wall, with a silvery crack down the center. In front of that mirror he would raise his arms to the side, bend his elbows, make fists and tighten his muscles. After flexing like this day after day, like he had seen Johnny Weismiller do in the Tarzan movies, he discovered that his muscles were growing noticeably harder and larger.

In India boys seldom fought, and if they did, no one really knew how to box. Few kids had ever seen a punch thrown. They did like their mothers and fathers occasionally did to them; they slapped with open hands. When Nandalla threw a punch, not only did it devastate his adversary with its crashing impact, but it was like a brand new weapon of destruction.

An Indian boy in a fight with Nandalla would find himself stumbling up off the ground with a bloody, broken nose, wondering what had happened, where the blow had come from and how he had delivered it. His opponents fled beaten and baffled.

In school he established his tough reputation quickly, and the rest of the boys feared him, and either stayed away or befriended him. They would lend, well, really give him their extra rupees for lunch money.

Unlike most large boys Nandalla was comfortable with his size and well coordinated. In the combination Hindu-English school he attended, they played the Indian games of cricket, field hockey, soccer and some tennis. Boxing was only known about because of Muhammed Ali's heavy weight victories all over the world. Both Muslim and Hindu Indians were convinced a God watched over Ali, and that's why he was unbeatable. American football was not played. If they played football Nandalla would have been the fullback, and on defense he would have been the middle linebacker. There was only one Indian sport left that interested him, and that was Greco-Roman wrestling.

In Greco-Roman wrestling you can't use your legs. You face the opponent standing, and you try to throw him to the mat and gain points for a fall. The coach had approached Nandalla in the eight grade inviting him to participate on the team with the older boys. The coach told Nandalla he must change his eating habits. He needed to eat more than just vegetables. He must eat meat to gain weight. Nandalla agreed. Though he was Hindu, he didn't feel bound by the religious dictums about avoiding meat. But money to buy the meat was a problem. Like most Indian families, his had no extra money, and certainly none for him to use to break the family's religious customs. His father worked at the Howrah Railway Station as a ticket master. He made the equivalent of $46. dollars a month, just enough to feed their family of four, and pay for one cinema a month. So Nandalla began to steal, mostly at night from the Bangladesh refugees whom he resented. He stole a few rupees, a pair of shoes, or maybe the meat itself. No one knew.

Nandalla gained weight and strength, and in a short time he became Calcutta's premier heavyweight, Greco-Roman wrestler. His favorite move on the mat was to bear hug an opponent, lean way back, and twist and lift, heaving an opponent in the air down onto his back with all the weight of Nandalla landing on his chest. Wrestlers knew of Nandalla's bear hug and throw and feared it. Many times the opposing wrestler got hurt. The match usually had to be halted because the impact of Nandalla crashing down on the opponent's chest as his back hit the mat knocked his wind out, or broke ribs and in one case broke a collar bone.

During tournaments, the other heavyweights would meet and talk together, probing to find Nandalla's weakness, to find a strategy to beat him. But they seldom succeeded. Nandalla had other winning characteristics -- he was mean and he hated to lose. If his school was wrestling in Calcutta, the bleachers would be jammed and the crowd would all stay to the last match, which was the heavyweight match, no matter what the team score was. Nandalla had a reputation on and off the mats. The fans may not have loved him, but they loved to watch him. Before a match, Nandalla imagined he was invincible. He saw himself wrestling with a man-eating crocodile, wrapping his arms and legs around the beast, squeezing the life out of him.

Nandalla swarmed with ideas, much like the way he wrestled. But he was always desperate, never satisfied. Those who knew him thought of him as a dangerous imposing physical specimen, one who was used to getting his way on and off the wrestling mat. He made no empty threats.

As Nandalla grew older, he was not satisfied with his size, or his state in life, or with India in general. He yearned for a better place to live, and for a better India. And he was used to taking direct action to achieve his goals.

Annapurna met Nandalla three years ago in her days in the Peace Corps. At first he was idealistic, hoping to achieve change in the spirit of Mahatma Gandhi, through peaceful agitation of the existing convoluted democratic system. Nandalla acknowledged that in the present democratic state the peasants were free. But free to do what? Free to relax and sing, yes. Free to stay poor and diffused in energy and thought, yes.

Nandalla and his Naxalites came to believe that the only way for the peasants of India to rise economically was through a Communistic system based on a strong central government where the rampant corruption and bribery of the decadent British civil service system would be eliminated.

Annapurna had joined his underground political organization, and they became devoted to each other and the cause of the Naxalites. Without him she felt vulnerable, with him she felt protected. But as much as she tried to disguise herself and erase her own imperialistic roots, she was still an American, and being an American she couldn't and didn't develop the same fervor for his cause of improving the economic plight of the peasant.

Like most idealists once his attempt for meaningful change failed, he became bitterly cynical and turned to violence as the catalyst for change. She had loved him in his fiery idealistic phase, now she feared him. Increasingly, she was bound to him by her knowledge of the organization and its illegal and violent activities, which she was having difficulty justifying.

The Naxalites operated through a loose political collection of cells of three or four dedicated activists working together. The members of each cell were unknown to other groups or cells within the same larger organization. Since one cell did not know what the other was planning, a degree of secrecy was preserved, and the chance for infiltration by a government agent was reduced..

His dedication to the importance of the overthrow of the government had grown beyond his concern for Annapurna or even himself. In the growing violence and the cry for change coming from the decay of Calcutta, he contemplated grave acts.

XIII

The Hunt for Chaleea

Outside it was twilight, and I left to keep my rendezvous with Nandalla. As I walked back to the alley, I couldn't help but be worried because of what I had learned and jealous because of the relationship he had with Annapurna. Whether they slept together or not, I didn't know. She warned me that he disliked Westerners and resented their freedom, which he labeled ultimately destructive.

He was there, at the designated corner and led me back out into the streets where he gave directions. "The Bain Kunth Temple on the north side of the Square. It's a Shiva temple. Three streets meet there. As you face the Temple take the one to the extreme right. There is a silk shop on that street. A clerk will try to entice you in to buy. Behind the shop is a money-changer. Tell him you have dollars and want rupees."

"Be careful," he continued, "the black market is illegal." He laughed to himself. "You tell him Nandalla sent you."

Nandalla rolled back his sleeve and revealed a small tattoo of an unsheathed dagger. "Look closely and make sure you can describe it to the money changer. Otherwise you are there only to change money.

After you hand him your dollars, ask the man where your missing boy is. He will tell you."

Nandalla looked up past me. A group of soldiers were approaching. He scowled and walked slowly down the street taking the first alley out of sight.

I knew the temple, I thought proudly. Off I ran, brushing by the knot of soldiers, weaving around the veiled women and twisting away from the street hawkers.

I wore a white Indian dhoti and had been out in the sun, so I was not so easily marked as a foreigner. I was enjoying a breath of anonymity. For me the greatest insult was to be called a tourist.

As I danced sideways to avoid a puchkawalla and his lunch cart of kobi and tomatoes, I spied the blond hair of a western girl. I chastised myself for having frivolous notions at a time like this. I dodged ahead and could see the temple. I wondered if Nandalla was telling the truth?

Faded orange flowers hung on the rusted wrought iron fence. The panes of glass were gone from the arched windows. High above, the golden dome glared magnificently, reflecting the blinding sunlight. Swiveling around, I counted the merging streets: one regular street, three alleys, and one pathway. Five, not three as I had been told.

Confused about which way to go, I stopped. I wanted to chug a cold bottle of coke. Instead I bought a hot cup of tea, creamy white with goat's milk. The tea was too hot to drink and the cup belonged to the merchant. I wondered if drinking hot tea in hot weather cooled you off. I stared down the last alley through the swirl of humanity and for a moment I thought I saw Nandalla.

I blew on my tea and gulped. It was strong, an acquired taste, much like getting used to beer - a necessary adolescent rite in America. I took another gulp, swirled the remains in the ceramic cup, and finished the dregs. As long as everything was boiled I thought, I won't get sick.

"Namesti." I returned the cup with a quick prayerful bow to the mustached tea merchant dressed all in white with baggy, billowy pants, as cool as a man could be in this oppressive wet heat.

I tugged at my newly acquired loose Indian sleeves, and darted off down the alley on the farthest right, on the lookout for a silk shop. A Sadhu man, dressed in the bright orange, with long black hair and beard, looked me in the eyes as he strode defiantly down the center of the street, chilum in hand. He gestured to me, offering me a toke through a moist cloth, and I hesitated, not sure if perhaps he was a messenger of the money changer. But no, the Sadhu man was simply curious about a Westerner, probably looking for a conversation or something material in return for some spiritual knowledge and heavenly ganja. I only paused. The Sadhu man was not insulted. He wrapped his chilum in a wet cloth and took a long toke himself.

I trotted forward, my eyes darting to the stalls on the left and right. I almost tripped on a black cat darting between my feet. I didn't like that. I had grown superstitious since coming to Calcutta. I patted my chest where my embroidered leather case hung about my neck. That thin case was with me 24 hours a day. At night I either slept on my back, or stuffed it way down in my sleeping bag.

A boy approached with arms out like a scarecrow, draped with beautiful silk scarves, billowy and dream-like in the hot Calcutta breeze. "You like? You want beautiful Indian silk scarves? Come with me. Yes, come."

And I followed. I now began to think and plan. My goal, I reiterated, was simply to get Chaleea back. I felt like I was responsible, like I owed Chaleea his safety.

Luxurious silken waves of red and yellow flowered scarves hung in front of the shop. I followed the boy to the back of the stall, waving aside the scarves which softly caressed me. The storekeeper was busy placing embroidered pillows on the high shelves. The smell of sweet incense and the silk scarves swaying in the hot breeze, set a sleepy, luscious mood.

"Rashid" the boy called, "This traveler is interested in silk." Rashid slowly got down off his rickety ladder, put some coins in the boy's hand, who scampered back out to the action of the street.

I began quietly, "Yes I am interested in silk. I have a girlfriend who needs a scarf."

"We all have girlfriends who need scarves," the chubby storekeeper remarked, smiling. "Yes," I continued "and I would like to change money." The storekeeper, Rashid, frowned. "And what makes you think you can change money, here?"

I spoke up. "Nandalla sent me here." The storekeeper, Rashid stood still and said nothing. Then I politely grabbed a piece of paper and pencil off his counter, and sketched Nandalla's tattoo, the dagger in its sheath. I passed the drawing to Rashid, who looked around his shop, called for another to watch the goods, and motioned for me to follow.

Changing money was a common piece of black market business, but it was against the law. Young foreigners seemed willing to take the risk. If they went to the bank they could get maybe 11 rupees to the dollar. In the black market, they could get 16, and if they bargained well, took their time, knew some Hindi, enjoyed the process and the money-changers, they could get even more.

I followed Rashid, pushing aside some heavier canvas-like material, stepping across a dry path into a small wooden structure. Once inside I went up narrow stairs through a trap door to a second floor where it didn't seem like there would be room for a second floor. The ceiling was only inches from my head. Rashid handed me over to a veiled woman, and with a trace of uneasiness, looked around the room and left.

"Good day" pronounced the woman, with a slight nod. I instinctively responded with my hands pressed together as if in prayer, and mumbled the Hindi, namesti.

"Would you like to change money?" she asked.

I nodded yes.

"Do you have American dollars?"

I nodded yes.

"May I see some?" she asked pleasantly.

I fumbled around for a second, reached in my soft leather pouch for bills in the money clip, but remembered they were all rupees. I really didn't want to reveal my leather case, in front of her, a stranger. But I felt I had no choice. I would have to take off my new Indian shirt, which pulled up over my head.

"Just a minute, I will show you." I leaned over and tugged at the back of my shirt behind my neck, and succeeded in sliding it off. I stood, bare chested, singularly white, shirt in hand, with my leather case hanging down around my neck. I flicked the case up over my head, and I stood naked from the waist up.

The veiled Indian woman's eyes widened in mild shock. For the first time in her life in such close surroundings, she gazed at the healthy white body of a foreigner. She was flustered.

Just then from behind her, a small panel in the wall slid open, and her bearded husband emerged. His eyes popped, and he demanded, "What the hell is going on?"

"American dollars, American dollars, he has American dollars to trade," she said frantically. I hurriedly put my shirt on and held my leather case firmly in my hand. The man turned from his wife and feigned a smile at me.

"Gentleman," he cooed. "Please come with me. And please Sir," looking at me, "In my home keep your shirt on."

I was about to babble on, but thought better of trying to explain and said, "Yes, of course."

I prepared to follow the husband through the sliding panel. I assumed I was on my way to the hidden room where they changed money. Leaning over I brushed by the veiled woman with her silk sari clinging to her, and a little man-woman chemistry passed between us. I understood that I had broken some taboo. I turned back and looked into her almond-shaped eyes, heightened in intensity by the veil and found myself winking. She stared backed at me serenely. But then I was sure her eyes brightened, twinkled maybe, in a flirtatious moment between us, that she could never otherwise admit to.

I repeated to myself why I was here to rid myself of my drifting state of mind. Maybe it was the running through the market and the heat that left me feeling light-headed and silly. Or the Indian women with the almond eyes. Sometimes I thought it was all a dream.

I actually did need to change money and wanted to get a good rate, but I knew my first mission was to find Chaleea. Carefully I wedged through the opening which led to the narrowest of winding stairs, much like in a lighthouse. Below on a carpet of blue and gold, sat a young Indian man cross-legged wearing bluejeans. Without a word my guide, now fully composed, plopped down into the lotus position, his loose shirt dropping around him to the floor like a parachute.

I knew I would have trouble sitting like that. My ankles would hurt and after a few minutes I would have to switch positions. But etiquette demanded I sit. From my yoga classes back in the Adirondacks, I had learned two other choices. I could squat down, resting my arms on my knees. But Indians who went to the bathroom in the streets assumed that position, so I figured that wasn't appropriate. What I did was to kneel and sit back on my heels, a position I could comfortably hold.

The smoke from a few sticks of sweet-smelling incense in a small copper vase rolled up against the ceiling. From a carved wooden box the size of a briefcase, the younger man pulled out bundles of rupee notes and stacked them in front of me. The young trader also rolled out rich brown clay-like bricks with grooved sides.

"Go ahead. It is yours. Pick one up."

I gingerly handled one of the malleable and earthy bricks. It had a musty, pungent smell. I knew I was holding the biggest chunk of hashish I had ever seen. I couldn't help but think of its value back in America.

"It is the best. And we will give you a good price," the young man smiled. It was the young trader's belief that all young Western travelers wearing bluejeans craved hash.

"Well" I started, while glancing around, "I don't have enough use for this much hash, though I might want to buy some later. If it's still available."

The young trader, cocked his head, "Here, try some." He started to prepare a chilum, and twisted off a thimble size corner from one of the bricks.

I held up my hand and protested with a smile. If I smoked even the least amount of hash, I knew I would be worthless in any money-changing negotiations. For as the California hippie travelers would say, 'This stuff was for sure dynamite.' But I didn't want to insult my adversary by not considering his offer. "If I smoke now, I'll be no match for you," I said, trying the direct and friendly American approach which had always served me so well. "Look, could you give me that," I asked pointing to the piece of hash between the man's thumb and forefinger. "As a gift." The young man looked at the older man, who shrugged and nodded approval.

"If you like, yes." He handed it over to me, and I took the smidgen of hash and placed it in my pouch with the leather drawstring running through the holes in the cross section of a deer's antler. I had probably lost any advantage in the money changing or the negotiations for Chaleea, since I now owed them a favor.

I broke the silence. "I do want to change money. And I have plenty of dollars, but I am also looking for someone, a young boy named Chaleea."

I watched the eyes of the money changers for a flash of recognition, but I detected nothing. "He was with Ali Kahn from The Rooster Palace -- The Fat Man." Still no reaction.

I fidgeted, then spoke. "Nandalla with the dagger, said you would know where he is. I am here under his authority," I said speaking rapidly. "Yes," I emphasized, "he has a tattoo of a dagger on his left arm. On his foreman." I shoved my left sleeve up, and pointed to my own forearm. But it wasn't necessary. The traders knew exactly what I was talking about.

The traders sat with complacent smiles. "Yes we can help," they finally admitted. "But first we change money." With that they loosened up again, eager to begin bargaining.

Really I had little control or leverage in the negotiations. My only recourse when they wouldn't even give me 15 rupees to the dollar, was to say I was just interested in changing ten dollars.

The traders laughed at that amount, with a trace of real concern. "We are here to do real business. This is not a game," the older man stated crossing his arms on his chest.

"Fine." I said. "I know 16 rupees is the going rate. I will trade two hundred dollars at 16 rupees, and even then you know you are winning." With my final offer on the table, I slid out two hundred dollar bills from my case, and placed them on the carpet. For a moment the two traders were transfixed. They had twenty dollar bills, but it wasn't too often they had seen hundred dollar bills. That's what I was counting on here in the back streets of Calcutta. I slid the bills the three feet across the carpet to my Indian adversaries.

"All right," they smiled "You drive a hard bargain." Which I knew was not the case today. Both traders reached for the bills, but the man who had offered the bricks of hashish, cocked his head, and waited for his partner to release his hold on the bills, which he did, slowly. They counted out 3200 rupees into a shoe box, and handed the box across to me. I picked out 100, carefully folded the bills in half, slid my silver money clip over them, and dropped it into my little leather pouch.

I counted "3100 rupees." I'm sure it was the most rupees either of us had ever seen and touched. I stuffed the them into my leather case, which I was barely able to snap shut and awkwardly hung it back around my neck, under my shirt, where it bulged conspicuously. Finally, I looked up and said with as much coolness as I could muster, "And Chaleea, the boy?"

The traders were closing their wooden strong box. They both cocked their head to one side, and from behind curtains, stooping to avoid hitting his head, Nandalla appeared.

"My Western friend," he said with his arms wide apart in an apparently friendly gesture. "There are things you don't know about in Calcutta. You are naive." As he spoke the traders packaged their paraphernalia and with bags under their arms, slipped out the way Nandalla had entered.

"Now listen," he continued, "You will follow me and you won't chatter as we walk." I sat with an ashen face. I knew I was outmatched and I noticed even the money changers, who were of higher caste, had deferred to Nandalla.

Nandalla crouched lower and went out the back. I collected myself, wondering what was next, hunching over to follow while taking a last look around the tiny room, wooden surfaces polished by eager travelers like myself rubbing against them, everything with a purpose, compact and cozy like the captain's cabin in an ancient sailing vessel.

We stepped up and outside to a platform under a leafy cocoa tree, and followed a sandy path behind shacks. I hit my shoulder on a protruding shower head, a sign of some wealth. After brushing through tall weeds under overhanging roofs, we emerged onto the streets of Calcutta.

As that now familiar candied urine smell filled my nostrils, I flashed back to the blond Western woman I had caught an enticing glimpse on my dash here. I decided I needed to talk to other Westerners soon, just to anchor.

The two of us walked with a purpose through the dusty, crowded streets. I had to adopt an exaggerated stride to stay with Nandalla, who strode mightily through the white, silent heat. I felt tense. My breathing wasn't relaxed and in the heat I feared a wave of dizziness.

I tried to get a sense of where we were going. I was looking left and right. At one intersection of alley-ways, I saw the domes of the Nak-hoda Masjid in the distance, but we turned, and now the busy market was behind us, and in the noon day heat, the number of people dwindled. A coolie and his rickshaw angled towards Nandalla, but with a scowl he waved him away.

This was a part of the city I had never been to. I felt a breeze and detected some coolness. We turned on to a wide promenade, called Strand Road, a part of which was cobblestoned, and there was the Hooghly River, a tributary of the sacred and mighty Ganges. Along the banks of the river women and men stood in the water up to their waists, washing clothes, cooling off; a man even stealing a glance at his favorite young Hindi girl in wet clothes, able to see her figure for once, knowing unless he married her that would be as far as he could get.

A brown barge packed with families from the north floated down with the current. The pilot tossed a ragged rope to his boy on shore, who wound the rope around a wooden stanchion in a figure eight. When the rope stretched taut, the force lifted the stanchion and the at-tached wooden planks. The whole dock, groaning and creaking, sounded and felt like it was about to be pulled apart, and one day it would. But today it held, and like a pendulum, the barge swung slowly closer to the dock, until it hit and squished the lashed rubber tires. The families scrambled ashore. The ferry captain held his money in one hand and waved with the other. The children tossed bundles onto the dock, where the alert mothers piled the possessions close to them-selves, wary of strangers stealing something. Once a family gathered intact, they headed for a shoreline banyan tree and staked out a spot in the shade. The youngest was then sent to buy orange ice to suck on.

Why Nandalla had brought me here, I had no idea. On the shores of the historic Hooghly River were Hindu burning ghats, the now vacant summer homes of jute merchants, and the once prized bordellos of the French Colony. Nandalla pointed up river to what looked like a tender or tugboat churning towards us at an angle. He cupped his hands, and gave out a resonating rooster-like call. Clearly the tug was heading towards us and the pilot hollered to the boy at the stanchion to be ready to grab the line.

When the rope was tossed, the boy snapped to and looped it over the stanchion, whipped the rope around many times, and again the whole dock we were standing on raised a few inches with the pull of the tug. The engines rumbled, a gush of brown bubbles and whirlpools played at its stern. The pilot, dressed in a clean white shirt, saluted Nandalla. From below a large man, wearing a red turban came up on deck. Flipping my finger, I pointed from my waist, and whispered to myself, "there's The Fat Man."

"Where's Chaleea?" I demanded of Nandalla. With a silent, knowing look, Nandalla directed my attention to the tug and up scrambled Chaleea from below. He leaped over the railing, hopped over the ropes, and ran to me, hugging me and laughing hard.

"Did he hurt you?" I asked. Chaleea looked down at his callused bare feet for a moment, before he said, "It was a great adventure. He's a rich man."

I held Chaleea by the shoulders, and asked, "You're all right?"

"Yes, I'm fine. Thank you." And he politely hugged me around my waist.

Now I looked to Nandalla and The Fat Man, a bit puzzled to find Chaleea so seemingly happy. The two men were absorbed in an animated conversation in Hindi.

"What did you do Chaleea, all the time you were with The Fat Man?" I asked.

"He played with me and fed me, and took me to his mansion near the sea." Chaleea looked out across the Hooghly. "And he bathed me. And he asked me a lot of questions, some about you."

"He bathed you. What do you mean, he bathed you?"

"He never touched me," Chaleea said with firm lips quivering.

I dropped the subject, and looked to Nandalla and The Fat Man who were still talking face to face. While patting Chaleea on the back, I grabbed his hand and motioned for him to listen to their conversation.

What's up Chaleea? What are they talking about?"

"Politics" he answered. "The assistant minister of finance was killed two days ago while he was having tea. They are talking about the results of that, and then Nandalla said he had to go see a woman."

Nandalla acknowledged us, and with an impatient wave of his hand, motioned for us to go.

"Leave," he said.

I undid the drawstring of my pouch, and with my fingers pulled out my silver money clip and the folded 100 rupee note it held. I unfolded it, and keeping my half of the bargain, handed Nandalla the note.

He took the note with a shrug, as if the money meant little to him. Then he faced The Fat Man, his eyes narrowing. The Fat Man opened his arms, palms up.

"Chaleea," Nandalla called. Chaleea walked over, warily. "This money is for you. A gift from Nandalla and the Naxalites." Chaleea bowed in appreciation. "Dhanyabad," he said.

I could tell Nandalla was pleased playing Robin Hood. "Let's go," I said. The Fat Man called good-bye to Chaleea, but Chaleea did not even turn his head. Chaleea and I walked hand in hand. I knew we would talk later.

Once back in the alleys, Chaleea turned to me and said, "The Fat Man asked a lot about you. He thought you were a military agent pretending to be a traveler. He couldn't understand why you would hang around The Rooster Palace."

"I told him you were just a curious man. Another lost Westerner," chimed Chaleea.

It was great to be together and happy. Chaleea was certain he knew the way back, but first we celebrated with two cokes. We sat in the shade of the Writer's Building near B.B.D. Bay, its facade chipping away, and through white straws sipped on our treasured green coca colas.

I had learned the hard way not to drink the water. My diarrhea was gone, thank God. I had fought it the only way I knew. I simply had stopped eating. I pinched my waist, and got nothing. By now, I was probably below 150 pounds.

Chaleea said he was hungry too, so we went to the Gariahat market to find a puchkawalla selling some cooked, river fish. Chaleea insisted on paying with his 100 rupee note.

I ran my hand through Chaleea's thick shinny black hair, but he yanked his head away. Chaleea always used to like it when I rubbed his head with affection. I suspected something bad had happened to Chaleea.

"Chaleea, what happened with The Fat Man?" I asked as I followed Chaleea to the market. He didn't answer. I shut up, feeling guilty about my probing questions.

While we ate I took a few moments to think, which was something I didn't consciously do that often. I thought back to what Chaleea had first told me, about being bathed. My mouth tightened, and I lost focus on my immediate surroundings. I understood now that The Fat Man must have in some way molested Chaleea. A rare seething came up from my gut and settled in my head. Thoughts of revenge and hatred pulsated there, new thoughts for me.

We took our time eating, not saying much. I looked at Chaleea and figured he needed the comforting touch of a woman, his mother. But he had no mother. Annapurna would have to do.

Interrupting my thoughts, a street beggar, shirtless with a toothless smile, rushed up to me, "Sahib, backshish." I shoved him away. Then I immediately felt guilty. I had never done that before, and I was surprised at my hostile reaction. I was angry and disillusioned.

"I'm sorry. I don't have any god-damned backshish," I yelled in explanation.

Onward the two of us strode, back to Annapurna's and the vast Square of The Rooster Palace which was now in shadows from high clouds. Soon the Square was in sight. Once inside her crumbling brick building, we stepped over some Untouchables sleeping on the cooler tile floors, and taking two and three steps at a time, headed for her door.

"Be there, please be there," I mumbled to myself. Chaleea knocked and knocked, but there was no answer. I raised my finger to my lips, signaling for him to be silent. We heard some rustling inside. Maybe she was taking a nap, an afternoon siesta. "Annapurna, it's Jack" I said, but not too loudly.

We waited. Then the welcome clicking and unlatching of the door, and the final sliding of the bolt. Annapurna stuck her head out. "You'll have to come back," she said matter-of-factly, but then her eyes went to the floor and I heard movement behind her. "Come back in an hour," she said to me. Seeing my puzzlement turn to hurt, she added a long whispered, "Please, I will explain."

Chaleea knew the score and was already half way down the stairs. I followed, much like a lost puppy. I didn't know where to go. Walking passed the dark-skinned Indians, out onto the yellow heat, for the first time, I sensed I didn't belong here. I felt vulnerable. Chaleea grabbed me by the sleeve.

XIV

Enter Sadhu Ricki

"I know where to go. We'll go to the tent of Sadhu Ricki and wait there." Chaleea said.

"I'm not going back to see her," I said defensively.

"Oh, yes you are," commented Chaleea. "All your belongings are there." I was silent. Chaleea was right. But we would go back only to get my things and leave.

With a wrinkled forehead and sad blue eyes, I looked to Chaleea and then for a moment lost concern for myself.

"Chaleea, whatever happened to you, you had no control over. He is a grown man, and you were trapped. You could be dead now. I know whatever you endured was unpleasant, bad, maybe unspeakable, but there's evil and there's evil people in the world." And, in a new voice, a voice from a part of me that was just starting to grow, to germinate, "We will get our just revenge."

After a moment of silence, I asked where we were going? "To a Sadhu man, he will help you," said Chaleea with a hint of authority.

We were heading towards the outskirts of Calcutta again, away from the now welcome stench of The Rooster Palace - a smell which no longer bothered me. I tried to stop my mind from churning. I had no right to be jealous of Annapurna, but I was. How else was she able to support herself in the poverty of Calcutta. She was a whore. Or was that Nandalla? I heard her get up from bed. Why am I always the innocent lad? Get me out of here. I prided myself on fighting off depression, but I felt lonely.

Sitting back home in my family's living room asking Dad if I could drive the silver mustang to get an ice cream cone, sounded awfully good right now. What was I doing here anyway? One month was long enough; it was time to leave, or at least get on the hippie trail and head to the mountains of Kathmandu.

"It's not what you think" said Chaleea, as we waited for a tired wallah man, his calling bell ringing, pulling his rickshaw and a Kali women resplendent in purple and red saris. We dashed to the center of Chowringhee, avoiding a trolley coming in one direction and a moped in the other.

The sights distracted me from my silly broken heart and brought back my love for adventure. But I did need a woman for a traveling companion. That way I would be an island, self-sufficient, and self-indulgent, I thought mockingly.

"What is it then, Chaleea?"

"She will explain, when we return." I knew it was useless to press for more information, and decided to try to suspend my judgment until I spoke to her, until I touched her in some way. I needed to be reassured that she cared for me.

We headed across the street for a vacant lot, which in America would have been cluttered with debris and paper. In Calcutta everything burnable was used for fires to keep warm and dry on damp winter nights; scraps of metal were used to cover leaks in their make-shift roofs; chewed gum to patch bicycle tires. The field was brown grass and dusty soil. Chaleea said the lot used to be a cricket field for a now-closed English prep school.

"It's still used on weekends, by the club teams. I can play cricket," Chaleea said quietly.

That was the first time Chaleea had volunteered some information about himself since his ordeal with The Fat Man, and I smiled and patted him on the head, brushing my hand through his long black hair.

"I'm good. My position is wicket keeper. Come and see me play," said Chaleea proudly. We were away from the traffic and into the dust of the fields and the side roads, permanently rutted from the pounding rains of the monsoons.

Shielding my eyes from the sun, I decided a hat would cheer me up. Otherwise I would have to heed the Indian custom of staying inside from noon to two. 'Why not stay inside and have a conversation and even close your eyes. It's too hot outside,' the merchants would say gathered in their favorite cool hideaway, where nobody moved and a breeze through the windows was a gift from the Gods.

Chaleea pointed to a worn gray canvas tent at the crossing of two dirt paths. "That's our Sadhu man," he said. I stood by covering my eyes while Chaleea called to the tent.

From inside a voice said. "Yes I hear you. I knew you were coming. So I am here."

With a look of relief, Chaleea waved for me to follow. The flap opened, we entered crouching. "Yes I have been expecting you. Please sit down." He pointed to two faded orange pillows with tiny mirrors the size of buttons embroidered on them. They were carefully placed directly in front of him.

The Sadhu man sat cross legged, as though he had been sitting there comfortably for weeks, his bright orange robe wrapped about him. He held his hands up together, fingers touching in steeple fashion, bowed his head slightly and introduced himself. "My name is Swami Randasstar. My Western friends call me Ricki."

"Namesti." I took the liberty of kneeling on the pillow and sitting back on my ankles, I just couldn't sit cross-legged for even the shortest time.

"Please get comfortable. I am comfortable." giggled Swami Ricki.

Chaleea introduced me and started to explain the rigors we had gone through, but Ricki held up his hand, and motioned for him to be still. "You know," said Ricki, "I spend a lot of time observing and then contemplating what I observed. I can see the two of you are troubled for different reasons. You Mr. Jack have wrinkles on your forehead that shouldn't be there. And you Mr. Chaleea should look up. Look at my pictures."

Behind him were paintings of sunsets and sunrises. Some were hung by coat hangers and others were propped on top of wooden sea-faring trunks, or held upright between suitcases. But all were visible in their dazzling colors. Sunsets and sunrises over Mt. Everest, over the Ganges delta, over the temples and palaces of Calcutta, over the Grand Hooghly Bridge.

Chaleea stopped looking down at the worn carpet on the cool hard-packed earthen floor and gazed at the paintings. A small smile appeared on his mouth.

Ricki's tent was crammed and cozy. It had a sweet smoky smell. Some air circulated through an open flap at the rear peak of the tent away from the dirt paths. It was cooler inside the tent than out. Heavy blue and gold silks were attached to the canvas walls. Stacks of leather bound books held a cot up off the carpets. Two candelabras, covered in pink wax were beside Ricki. Knapsacks and suitcases were piled in the corners with name tags fastened to them by safety pins.

Right now I wished I had a tent to call home. Other than what was around my neck, all my belongings - my duffel bag, my sleeping bag, my carved Buddha, silk scarves and my Puma knife, were back with Annapurna.

"Give me your hand, Mr. Jack."

I was unsure of what was going on, but I was certainly willing. Sadhu Ricki took my hand. He closed his eyes and rubbed my hand with his thumb and fingers, feeling my palm. He opened his eyes and looked closely at both sides of my hand and then at me. He gently released my hand and began to speak.

"You come from outside the city in the United States. Your hands are soft. So you are not a laborer. You have only slight calluses. You have no scars. Your family is of the ruling class, white collar, as you say. You're upset now. I see that in your face. You're not married. You wear no ring."

He paused and looked serenely at me "You are upset because of a woman. She might be an Indian woman. She might be an English woman. But in fact you are full of self-pity and have no right to be upset. You have done no wrong but neither has the woman. You must learn to be a man."

I arched my back, to speak in my own defense, but also impressed with what this palm reader, this fortune teller, this painter of sunsets and sunrises had said. How had he known, I wondered?

"Mr. Jack, please do not speak. I want you to think about what I have said for a few days, and return here. And then we will exchange goods and have our own celebration, and you will feel better," he laughed. "I promise. But only if you do not give up."

I was absorbing his words and the power this canvas tent contained. I liked this Sadhu Ricki, and I told myself I would return.

"And your hand," Ricki said to Chaleea. Between his fingers he felt Chaleea's bony hand and looked closely at Chaleea's downcast face.

"Who am I?" he asked Chaleea, casually. "Yes, who am I?"

"You are a Sadhu man," said Chaleea looking questioningly at me.

"Yes, I am. I have respect. People simply give me food. Travelers give me their most precious gifts to watch over." He pointed over his shoulder at the backpacks and suitcases piled in the corners. "I have never lost one item. Never has one thing been stolen."

"When I was a boy, I thought I was bad. But then, with the help of a God and my mind, I discovered only men can be bad. Boys can not be bad. They can do bad things, but they can not be bad. Now it's different with a man. A man can do bad things, and he can be a bad man."

"So now you know, because I am telling you. You are not bad, but you met a bad man. You too can not give up. You are lucky you have a foreign traveler with you. He will help you. In return, you know the streets and you will help him. I want to see you again. And, you will be smiling then. With God's help."

Sadhu Ricki uncrossed his legs and stood. He was short. His head and its bushy black beard with a diagonal streak of gray, dominated his upper body, as if his mind needed to be housed in a larger container. His was a big head on a small body. His teeth were straight and white, his skin healthy. His black hair was slicked back to his collar. His age was a mystery. He could have been 33 or 63.

"Please rise, I'm tired, and I must take a walk. You will return in a week, a few days," he said, tossing a twirling hand up towards the heavens, "and we will talk of your progress. And if you need to store some things while you go off to Nepal to trek and smoke," he giggled, "I can keep them for you. As you can see other Western travelers searching for themselves, have trusted me and are grateful for my watchful presence. These two," pointing to a dark brown leather suitcase with a large silver buckle and a green backpack with a climbing rope, "are way behind schedule, I'm afraid. It has almost been a year, and I have yet to open them. But when a year comes I will see what's inside. Then they become gifts to me. This sleeping bag," pointing to it spread out on his cot, "is one that never returned. He sent me a post card from Hong Kong. He's a banker now, and he said to keep the sleeping bag. It's pure goose down, the best," said Ricki chuckling. "Thank you, I hope I have helped. I have tried," Ricki concluded.

I was filled with a teary gratitude to this Sadhu Ricki, and I took his hand in both my hands and held it for longer than a handshake. "Thank you, I'm thinking about what you said."

Once out of the tent, even though the clouds covered the sun, I had to protect my eyes from the brightness. Chaleea turned to Ricki standing outside his army surplus tent, and asked, "Did you paint all those pictures?"

"Yes, of course, my son. I will teach you sometime. By the time you return, I will paint another."

Chaleea said bravely to Ricki, "I want to watch you paint. I want to learn to paint."

"See progress already," laughed Ricki, before changing his tone. "Chaleea, you be careful. You are not a man yet. The streets of Calcutta are no place for you after dark. At night you should be in a bed dreaming of rainbows."

Chaleea only smirked. He had no home but the streets.

On our return to Annapurna's, we passed through the Jaggu Bazaar area off Bhowanipur and walked by the Salvation Army Red Shield Guest House where I had spent my first night in Calcutta. I remembered having been ushered in at night by flashlight through a curtain of beads, I slept on my back the whole night, not moving, with my hands clasped over my leather case on my chest. Bewildered, I waited for dawn to find out who was making the breathing and snorting and purring noises next to me. When I awoke I saw I was in a unadorned room crammed with two rows of four cots each, all occupied.

Today I strode more confidently through the nearby Sir Stuart Hogg market that I had been warned not to go to after dark, because the Naxalites were killing government officials, and who knows, maybe Westerners like me would be next.

XV

The Storm

This time, having been hurt once, I let Chaleea knock on the door. The door opened and I looked up from the hallway.

"Come in, come in," Annapurna said offhandedly. She was sweeping, but she was dressed in a yellow sari with azure trimmings, and a matching blue ribbon in her hair. She looked almost regal.

I couldn't resist a bitter remark. "You got dressed, I see."

Annapurna didn't reply. Instead she offered Chaleea some chapati and curry. "Jack would you care for some too? The water for the tea is boiled, and the curry is fresh."

"Yes I'll have some food." The two of us ate quietly as Annapurna served the tea. "It's monsoon season. The rains will come. Let's just hope it's not too bad. Out on the Bay, they'll get the real cyclones," said Annapurna. She looked at me with a warm glow in her eyes. "Near Sunderbans, and the Royal Bengali Tigers, cyclones strike."

Yes I remembered. I knew we had made love. I hadn't forgotten the shack in the field, and the jungle and the threat of the tiger. That's why I was melancholy now. I had taken possession of her. The thought of Annapurna sleeping with another man was gnawing at me. I closed my eyes and tried not to think of the details. I looked over at the faded maroon couch she used as a bed, and felt sick to my stomach. All of sudden I wasn't hungry. I stopped eating and instead inspected my belongings.

I reached for my small Buddha, the size of a thumb, carved out of brown ivory, tucked in a side pocket of my duffel bag. I had bargained for the Buddha at the Tiretti Bazaar in Calcutta's Chinatown. A tiny channel was carved through its back so I could wear it tied to my belt. It was a good luck charm that kept the bad spirits away. I figured I needed something like that, a little outside help, even though I always thought I could get by alone. Maybe I wanted to do more than survive; maybe I wanted to thrive, and to embrace just one woman, who wanted just me.

Chaleea was totally immersed in eating. With the Chapati bread, Chaleea wiped his plate clean of any moisture and returned our plates to the sink. He curled up on one of the large embroidered pillows on the floor. Good for him, I thought, maybe he's putting the incident with The Fat Man behind him.

An unusual coolness and a slight stirring in the air brought a breeze, and Annapurna opened the shutters. The sky was a twilight purple with puffy clouds on the horizon to the south. Annapurna smiled and placed her comforting hand on the back of my neck. I craved her soft skin which reminded my of a puppy's belly. We both knew we needed to talk. Chaleea's head slumped down. He was asleep in the corner.

Annapurna and I stood near the window looking out. I broke the silence. "Are we in for a storm?"

"Yes. Let's hope it's not too serious." She felt me standing behind her and turned to face me. "I'm sorry," she whispered placing her head on my shoulder. "But I have a life here. I was here before you came one month ago. And I will be here after Christmas when you leave, won't I?" She looked up into my eyes.

"Yes, you're right," I said flatly. I was looking for a way to feel better. I did not like feeling sad, and I needed an explanation so that I could play the lovesick fool and keep seeing her.

"Who was the man?" I asked, ready to break and cry like a boy beaten in his first fight. "Someone I have known a long time, who knows about you, and who I will see when you are gone." She paused. "You don't really know me enough to love me. I'm just part of your adventure. Just like a log in a storm at sea. You will cling to me until you drift to shore. And then you will walk away happy to be safe on dry land. You won't even look back as the next wave washes me out to sea."

After she spoke a gust of moist wind blew the curtains across her face, and the first drops of rain clattered and rolled off the tin roof. The sky was a deep purple. I brushed the curtain back from off her face, and gently kissed her on the lips, tasting her jasmine lipstick.

"This storm will be good for the city and good for The Rooster Palace," she said. "The rain will take the stench away. We need a storm to clean Calcutta."

And to clean her soul too, I thought. I was emotionally exhausted and wanted her; but with Chaleea in the room, it wasn't right.

We saw the distant wall of clouds and as she reached to close the shudders, I pictured the saltwater jungle haunting in intensity like the intensity of this coming storm. The fear of the tiger and my own vulnerability had heightened the risk and excitement of making love in the shack in the jungle.

I wrapped my arms around her warm waist. "You remember our night near the jungle," she began. Having spoken the perfect magical words, I put my hands on her hip and turned her to me. I craved her touch and slowly rubbed my lips back and forth across her full mouth. I reached through the furrows of satin and silk and found her bare skin. She held me close, her strong soft hands on my back, and I kissed her neck and pressed my Irish red cheek against her Indian brown skin. I was lost in the present moment, where there was no future time and no future hurt, where there was no past, and no past mistakes. I wanted this heavenly zone.

Outside black cumulus clouds piled up over the Bay of Bengal. The sky darkened and wind-driven rain rattled The Rooster Palace. We pulled back from our embrace and stared. The shutter Annapurna had latched shut, popped open, and we could see men bent against the wind, running to find cover. The rain pelted the tin roofs and the clatter grew. Directly across the Square, the faces of others who had been watching the storm retreated behind shutters and doors as the intensity increased.

The noise woke Chaleea. He sat up, fuzzy headed, and clung to Annapurna, his little arms clutching tightly. "This is a cyclone," he said knowingly. We watched two tin shingles fly through the air like deadly saucers, capable of taking heads off. Bales of hay tumbled and jumped through the Square. The vibrating wind and the cascading noise trans-fixed us.

Suddenly the rain was coming in sheets driven horizontally by the wind. Roosters in their cages were tossed about like dice on a table, rolling and tumbling, until they came up against an immovable object and shattered. One splintered against a concrete culvert catapulting a rooster to safety inside the pipe. I thought of King Rooster and wondered if he were safe.

The sky was a yellowish black color. The dark purple clouds were upon us. Annapurna tried to push the shudder closed and was thrown backwards, hitting Chaleea in the head. She held Chaleea in her hands and spoke tender words to him. Then Chaleea and I pushed our full weight against the shudders, wide-eyed at the force of the wind. Chaleea sobbed softly.

"Go under my bed. It's the safest place. It has an iron frame and nothing can move it." Annapurna nudged Chaleea in the direction of her maroon couch but Chaleea wiped his eyes and stayed next to us.

Annapurna stood up, but was knocked back down by Chaleea who was thrown by the wind from the other shudder which had again popped open. Holding our hands up shielding our eyes from the stinging, driving rain that was now in the room, we looked out the window one last time. Annapurna called out.

"The flag. What color is the flag? Is it yellow or red?"

"Where is it?" I demanded.

"In the middle of the courtyard, where The Fat . . . the cages."

I couldn't make out all her words through the roar. I tried to peer through the ferocious rain. I could see one man still in the Square. He was hammering a slab of wood over a window. But he gave up and ran for cover, just making it inside before the wind spun the slab lose and flipped it in his direction.

The roar of the storm was tremendous, and Annapurna feared this was no ordinary storm. Usually the cyclones quieted down once they hit the warmer land. This felt more like the devastating storms she had heard about on the shores of the Sunderbans.

"Chaleea! Find the flag. You have the best eyesight." A fire still flickered in the courtyard under an overhang, but no peasants hunched nearby. Even the chickens had scurried for cover under the sheds. The courtyard was filling with water.

I could make out a crouched figure near the stones clinging to the base of the flagpole. He was visible and then lost in the whitish waves of water.

"I see him" Chaleea said. "He's trying to lower the flag. It's down now. But it's ripped. It's yellow. He's taking it down and raising . . . " He paused. By now Annapurna knew the answer. "He's raising a red flag."

Annapurna had never before seen the red flag raised. A yellow flag was a warning that a cyclone was headed in this direction and would probably reach here. A red flag meant that a cyclone of major consequence, a mother of a typhoon, would hit head on, full force. Many people didn't live to tell the story of a red flag.

"We must close these shudders," commanded Annapurna. All three of us leaned against the shudders. "Hold them."

"Use your legs to push" I yelled, switching positions.

Annapurna darted to the corner near the gas stove and pulled out two long wide boards. "Prop these up against the shudders."

As we did, a banging came from the door to the hallway. Annapurna rushed over not knowing whether it was the wind beating on the door or the homeless from downstairs. She squinted through the peep hole.

"Go away" she pleaded. "It's not safe up here. Go to the cellar. To the cellar."

"We must bolt the door too, somehow." She hollered.

Chaleea and I had jammed the boards in place against the shudders. I leaned against the door while Annapurna appeared with a slat of wood and a large stone. Wildly, she was looking around for nails. Chaleea held out his hand and unclenched his fist which held two long brown rusted screws.

"Where did you find those?"

"From the hinges in the window," he yelled.

The noise level was like a dozen diesel trains rolling into the Howrah station squealing and scraping to a halt. We all yelled to be heard.

Annapurna looked at her ceiling which was shaking and undulating. I grabbed the screws from Chaleea, and the stone and slat from Annapurna and in a frenzy started pounding the screws in the board first on the floor and then I tore it up from there and slapped it diagonally across the door, banging the screws into the wooden frame.

The gas burner still worked, and Annapurna was trying to think ahead and boil some water for drinking. She knew the water supply in

Calcutta would be worthless and disease-ridden for at least two weeks. She managed to start a fire under a large caldron of water.

"Chaleea, get under the bed," I yelled. Then the floor started to roll, as if we were fighting this storm at sea in a freighter full of jute, and our cargo had just shifted. Chaleea fell and I pushed him under the bed and he pressed his hands against his ears.

Air charged up from below us and the gust lifted the flames high off the propane burner onto Annapurna. Her sari was burning. She stood there frantically patting her chest. I tackled her and smothered her with my body. Her sari had melted in places and turned to ashes in others.

"You all right!" I hollered. She nodded her head yes. She was only out of breath. The floor and the ceiling heaved, moving together like a living beast. The pot of warm water slid off the stove and landed on our legs. We tried to save at least a few inches of water, and quickly turned the pot upright, keeping a splash of good water.

Annapurna, speechless, stared at the burner which was now roaring flames. She pointed to the knob near the propane tank, and I knew it had to be turned off. I lurched the few feet to the corner and kneeling, thought counter clockwise, and turned it off. The flame died. As I crawled back to her, something exploded. But it wasn't the propane tank.

The wind had hurled a full bale of hay through one of the shudders, splintering the wood, sending dust and thousands of pieces of straw flying. The wind and rain whirled wooden spoons, shudder slats, and torn clothes around the room.

The storm had hunted us down and found us, thought Annapurna. "Please Kali, I don't want to die. It is not my time yet."

I was screaming in her ear, "Under the bed, under the bed," shoving her there. We didn't fit, but somehow we got under wedged next to Chaleea. I pressed against her, tried to be one with her, and held my arms up over my head to protect myself. My back and my butt stuck out. And there we huddled together, powerless.

XVI

Dawn

Dawn broke on a ruined city. Calcutta had gotten a wash all right, but the Gods had gone too far. The Hooghly River flooded over its banks, making muddy canals of nearby alleys. The silk shop where I had gone to find out about Chaleea had collapsed. The hidden room behind the shop for changing money remained, though no longer hidden. The building which housed the world at noon was now without a roof. The stalls of the city's bazaars were scattered from Calcutta to the Sunderbans. And the inside courtyard wall of Annapurna's brick and plaster building had come crumbling down, balcony and all.

Early morning fires crackled throughout the city, sending spirals of smoke into the patchy blue and gray sky the day after the cyclone. Men mourned and women wailed at floating funeral pyres where they cremated those the storm had killed. The deaths were in the hundreds but not the thousands; so the tragedy, as tragedies go in India, was more of a destruction of property than a loss of life. The survivors laughed at being alive. They screwed doors on, hammered thin sheets of pliable printer's metal onto roofs, searched for the heavy rocks that had been blown off, and prided themselves on going back to work - collecting train tickets, pulling rickshaws, and selling copper pots needed to carry potable water from the wells to replace the contaminated city water.

Men dressed only in leather gloves, loin cloths, and sandals made of worn tire treads, shuffled around, staring at the damaged buildings surrounding them on the edge of the vast Square of The Rooster Palace.

A gaggle of men were arguing over how to save an overhanging bed with three people clinging to it, from sliding down off a shattered second floor apartment with no outer wall. When a loose board would slide out, or a brick tumble down, they would yell up, "Don't move. Don't move. Stay still. We will help."

The stairway inside Annapurna's building was smashed into firewood, so they couldn't reach us that way. I was slipping in and out of consciousness. Above my waist a doorknob from the dislodged door stuck into me, and something felt painfully wrong inside of me. My chest stung every time I took a breath. Probably broken ribs. Just as long as a lung wasn't punctured.

Chaleea and Annapurna were bruised, soaked and shivering. But if they got out of here, sleep and hot tea would restore them.

"We must find a ladder," said one man down below in the crowd.

"There's nothing solid to lean it against, you monkey," said another.

The sun started to shine on what remained of Annapurna's flat. All three of us were being jabbed by the springs of the couch. Chaleea was on the downhill side of the slanted floor, the closest to the edge which hung in the air like a wooden slide, and he started to squirm.

"I'm hungry," Chaleea moaned.

"Stay still. They will find a solution," counseled Annapurna.

But Chaleea was not himself this morning, or maybe he had changed. The cyclone and The Fat Man had changed him. They ,had sucked away his sweetness, and in the wake, Chaleea was forming a distrusting personality, which relied more on his own instincts.

He pushed off with his foot against Annapurna, who was miffed at his recklessness. Chaleea groped for something to grab with his hands to pull himself up towards the doorless frame. He needed traction. He grabbed on to some tangled, water-soaked sheets, which were laying on the slanted floor caught inside the collapsed closet.

The men below, those standing at the back of the crowd in the courtyard, had enough of an angle to see his maneuvering and yelled out advice and warnings.

"Try to get higher."

"Be careful."

Chaleea was out from under the bed. All Annapurna and I could do was to watch and see what happened. He held onto the sheets in one hand. His foot was braced against the foot of the couch, and he looked like he was getting ready to lunge to the only corner of the apartment which hadn't disintegrated. If he made it there, the crowd below could raise a ladder for him to climb down.

He pushed off the couch and lunged for the corner, swinging on the tangled sheets, using them like a jungle vine. But the sheets didn't hold. They popped out of the closet as he slid down the floor a few feet before he tumbled off the edge, falling the fifteen feet through the air into the crowd below.

Three men tried to catch him. With arms cradled, yelling nonsense, the tangled group crumbled down to the muddy ground, breaking Chaleea's fall. Chaleea rolled off them and popped up. The men, who were surprised at their own spontaneous attempt to catch him, got up, muddied, but grinning. Everybody was fine. A cheer went up.

Chaleea called up to Annapurna. "You can do it. Just slide off. It's not that far."

"Gather the hay," said one of those who had caught Chaleea. Within minutes a dozen of the loose bales were in a pile forming a mound of hay.

127

"Ready Annapurna," called Chaleea with a sense of accomplishment and self-importance.

Annapurna was hesitant. She had a problem. She was Hindi, and she was nearly naked from the waist up. The men would stare, and her reputation would plummet even further.

"Go ahead," I moaned. "I won't be able to jump."

"We'll get you out, don't worry," she said.

But I could tell she was worried about me, the jump, and the men below. She hadn't recognized any voice she knew, and now the crowd was almost in a festive mood.

She looked down at her tattered clothing, but decided there was nothing else she could do. She hitched up her bra to cover as much of her breasts as she could, and then listened to Chaleea, now the newest expert on sliding off a careening, second floor over a crumbled brick wall into a pile of hay. She knew she wasn't as agile as Chaleea, but she prided herself on her strength and toughness. With difficulty she squirmed out from under the couch onto the slanted floor. She pressed her body against the floor, concentrating on surviving the fall without injury, Her bra was being pulled down, and pieces of glass and grains of rice were scraping against her tender skin.

Glancing down, hoping she was aimed right, she flipped over to her back, sat up, and with her hands pushed off the floor to gain enough momentum to land beyond the bricks and onto the stack of hay. Rather gracefully, and without screaming, she slid off the wooden floor, caught some splinters, and fell chest first into the soaking hay.

She had the wind knocked out of her, and was wheezing for air. Finally she held a hand up, as if to say I'm okay. She stood, took a deep breath, and looked around for Chaleea. The circle of men surrounding her had wide-eyed, frozen expressions. Her bra was barely on. Scratch marks shown red and spots of blood appeared above her nipples. A few men turned away. Some stared wantoningly at her. Most were married and had probably never seen the breasts of a another woman.

Chaleea looked around desperately for anything, a piece of cloth, to cover her with. Quickly he took off his shirt. Annapurna spotted him behind the men and moved a step towards him. But the circle of men didn't part. She had no choice but to push through, and as she did a hand grabbed her breast. Chaleea was right there with his shirt, and she made the wise choice to disregard the pawing. Leaving the crowd, she buttoned every button, stood up straight and looked up at me and what was left of her place.

The crowd of men were blathering, staring with dark, quick eyes at Annapurna. But now that she was covered, she felt safer. To preserve a smidgen of dignity, she decided she had no choice but to stride back to the men gathered around the pile of hay.

"Thank you citizens for assisting today, after this remarkable storm in our grand city of Calcutta." She said in her best, most educated English. Indians respected education, which someday might rival caste in determining ones standing. The crisis of the flesh was over with. She put it out of her mind, and really excused the men. They were so like a flock of goats.

"My friend is injured. He will not be able to slide down. And he will need a doctor."

"I will run and try to find a doctor," said one.

"You will not find a doctor today," said an older man. "Everyone's hurt. All over the city."

"I will try," said the younger man, and off he trotted.

Exhausted, but taking command, she took a long look upwards at her apartment. "We must find another way," she said shaking her head while she scraped one foot side to side in the dirt, fighting off tears. She was not looking forward to another new start. She was tired of it all.

The sounds from below told me everyone was safe, and I could hear Annapurna's voice. I was aware that the roof of Annapurna's apartment had been blown off because the sun was in my eyes, making me squint. My face felt warmer but my body was still cold. The weight of the couch kept me from shivering.

The sunrise and the reassuring crowing of the roosters reminded me that we had made it through an awful night. I accepted, reluctantly, that I needed help. When I moved even an inch, I felt stabbing pains in my chest and a faintness in my head.

The crowd below was busy discussing options. "We must find two ladders," said one.

"No, better we build a scaffolding," said another.

"No, you monkey. He'll be gone by then."

In the midst of this dialogue one of the roosters skimmed overhead and managed to land next to me and my tilted couch. He must have been the scout, for soon another and another followed, desperate for food, and free of their smashed cages. They clucked about, pecking at the scattered rice on the cluttered remnants of the apartment floor.

The sight of the roosters was a welcome diversion, but my eyes kept wanting to close. The shaded area for the crowd below was becoming narrower and narrower as the sun rose drying off the city. The roosters now filled the apartment. The crowd stood perplexed and began to lose interest.

"We're not birds. We can't fly up. He must come down to us," said one man, appealing to logic.

"He's hurt," responded Annapurna. "He can't move on his own."

Chaleea searched his mind for a solution. Staring up at the collapsed second floor apartment, his eyes rested on the rickety floor below.

"If we can't go up, he must come down," he repeated to himself. "The building must come down," he blurted out. He was looking at one sturdy pillar directly below me. It looked like it was holding up the entire remains of Annapurna's second floor apartment. Chaleea figured if the crowd could somehow remove that pillar, then the apartment with me in it would come tumbling down.

"Find a rope. A strong rope," he yelled. "I have a plan." He explained his idea to Annapurna and the men milling about.

"It will kill him," said one.

"No," said the monkey man. "It's the best idea." He ran off, and called over his shoulder, "I have a rope."

The crowd moved in, stepped over the bricks and gathered around the wooden pillar. It was round, made of pine and about fourteen inches in diameter. One by one each man touched it with his fingers, or ran his leathery palm across its smooth surface.

"It's possible," said one.

"It won't move," said another skinny man as he jammed both hands against it.

"Be careful," someone yelled, and the crowd jumped back a foot or two. The building had seemed to shake, but what really happened was more roosters had landed above.

Out of breath, but with a broad smile, the man returned with a rope which must have been used to tether barges on the Hooghly. He was dragging it through the Square. It was thicker than his arm.

Fastening a knot around the pillar was not easy. They argued about what kind of knot to tie and finally succeeded in tying one that didn't slip. The rope ran back about fifteen feet just beyond the strewn bricks and their pile of hay.

Annapurna called up to me, trying to sound calm. "Jack, Jack."

I moaned a reply.

"Brace yourself. Hold tight. The building may collapse."

Chaleea found an inch or two of rope to grab, closer to the building than the others. Pulling became a tug of war between the post and the crowd. And the crowd saw it as a contest, and momentarily forgot why they were trying to pull the post down or what would happen if they won.

"One, two, three pull. Pull!" yelled a one-legged man on the side-lines, who flexed his facial muscles as the mighty rope snapped straight. The building creaked and groaned.

"Pulllaa." he chanted rhythmically. "Pulllaa."

From all over the vast Square people trotted over to help. Even The Fat Man walked over. If they couldn't find a bit of rope to hold on to, they grabbed someone by the waist and pulled on him. At first The Fat Man simply observed. The post held.

The Fat Man sized up the situation and yelled for them to stop. The one legged man ceased his commands, and the rope fell limp. The Fat Man walked side to side, his feet facing out, over to the end of the rope.

"Give it to me," he demanded. The two men who had been pulling on the end, let the rope drop and walked away. The Fat Man looked around in disdain, reached down over his huge belly, grabbed the end, wrapped it around his waist and tied a firm knot. Looking directly at the one legged man, he said, "Proceed."

The rope was tied about two feet from the bottom of the pole. The Fat Man backed up a few steps waiting until the rope rose off the ground, and then looking at the crowd in mocked astonishment, he asked "Well?"

Everyone rushed in and grabbed the rope leaning back the way The Fat Man leaned back. The Fat Man puffed out his cheeks and nodded in the direction of the one-legged man.

"Pulllaa" commanded the one-legged man. The building shuttered. The roosters in the apartment cocked their heads and stood erect, feeling the floor beneath them quake.

"Pulllaa" he exhorted. "Use your legs!" he implored.

Without warning the post swung out from its base and flipped up in the air sending thirty men back on their buttocks, eyes fixed on the fly-ing timber, scrambling to get out of way. Chaleea who was closest, fell backwards, but the pillar flew over him. It landed inches from the one legged man who was laughing hysterically at all his fallen comrades spread before him.

At the same time, a wrenching groan and creaking of wood arose, and Chaleea and the fallen men scurried backwards on all fours. Above them roosters flapped upwards as the floor below them gave way.

The smaller vertical timbers snapped and splintered, and true to Chaleea's prediction, the building came tumbling down, with me frightened to death, clinging to the legs of the couch. The floor twisted away beneath me, and for a second, the couch and I were together falling through the air. I knew if I landed beneath the couch on something hard, I would be seriously hurt.

Maybe because it was heavier than me, the couch turned and cartwheeled, crashing down first on its end, snapping off an arm, and toppling over upside down, with me embedded in it like a tick on a dog. Chaleea rushed in through the mushrooming cloud of dust and undid my hands from around the curved legs of the couch finger by finger. My back was bloodied. My ribs were broken. I was in shock.

I decided I did not want to speak. The young man who had told Annapurna he would find a doctor led a white-haired man in through the crowd followed by two shirtless boys carrying a Red Cross cot.

"I'm a doctor. Please give me room. Thank you." In silence the doctor examined me. He took my pulse. He looked at my eyes. He tore my shirt to examine the cuts on my back and to listen to my heart. The crowd waited for his verdict.

"He may have some broken ribs or other internal injuries. The blood is nothing, some punctures. Stitches will do." He paused for dramatic effect. "He will survive." Looking at the crowd, he announced, "You've done a good job."

A roar of clapping and yelling went up as the men congratulated themselves. Annapurna was kneeling by me, holding my hand, gently rubbing my head. The two boys put their stretcher on the ground next to me. I grimaced and moaned when they moved me.

Annapurna walked by me side, while Chaleea jogged off on his own to explore the damage from the storm. Annapurna looked back over her shoulder at what used to be her prized apartment, and rubbed her eyelids with her fingers wondering where the Gods had been.

2

During the storm rooster cages had been flung about and smashed, and some roosters had perished. But most simply found themselves uncaged and free, and were spending the morning in search of food.

A woman with a black cane picked grain from her basket and spread the kernels out on the flat stones of the Square. A few rats scurried about nibbling the grain. A pack of boys raced around throwing stones at the rats, occasionally stunning one long enough for a boy to pick it up by its tail to cage it.

The head of the cage builders, Ali Kahn, The Fat Man, waddled towards the ageless stones, oblivious to all but himself and his entourage. The Fat Man approached, stopped and cupped his hands to his mouth, the way boys in the country do when putting a wide blade of grass between their thumbs in preparation to blow a high-pitched sound. The Fat Man twisted his beefy hands close together and trumpeted a commanding cock a doodle doo, cock a doodle doo. From all around the Square the roosters and chickens perked up and twitched. First one, then two, then in groups of six and seven the roosters flapped themselves back to the Square and the bait of the grain.

Maybe the storm had been good for The Rooster Palace. Cleaned it, knocked a few tiers down, and the birds had twenty four hours of exercise. The cyclone separated the strong from the weak. The weak would be dead by now, chewed apart by the rats, or boiled in a pot for a family dinner.

What was particularly worrisome to The Fat Man was that he had found King Rooster's cage with only minor damage but with the door unhinged and King Rooster gone. The beast was to be the main attraction for the upcoming festival and auction. Already word of his size and ferocity had spread to the ruling classes. The handlers were hoping for a good turnout of Babus and wealthy merchants and a record price for King Rooster.

Some buyers reportedly considered him for cock fighting. Others argued that he was too rare a rooster to risk being clawed to death by a smaller, faster, well trained fighter with sharpened steel claws. Most of King Rooster's admirers thought a loss in the ring was impossible. Because of his sheer size, they argued, one kick from him would pulverize any opponent. Such was the talk which had gone on in the Square. But now King Rooster was missing, and his handlers and The Fat Man were worried.

Again The Fat Man overlapped one hand in the other, cupped them to his mouth, and between his thumbs, crowed his rooster call as only he could do. The handlers were ready when one by one the roosters returned and pecked at the grain. The handlers walked up from behind, grabbed the roosters behind the neck with one hand and with the other gloved hand held the roosters' shanks above the claws. Right behind each handler stood a boy with an empty grain sack and into each sack the handler stuffed one rooster. The boys jogged over to where The Fat Man was assembling his team to repair old cages and make new ones.

Soon a row of tied sacks bounced and danced like immense jumping beans, as the roosters flapped upwards in futile efforts to escape. A couple of the more energetic birds actually succeeded in having their bags go up in the air and fly a few feet. The men smiled and pointed and the boys laughed hilariously, particularly if it was a rooster they had personally bagged. "A flying bag, a flying bag," they shouted.

The procession of reclaimed roosters continued throughout the day, but King Rooster did not return. Cage by cage the pyramid of The

Rooster Palace rose again, slowly but methodically. The process was a classic division of labor. The workers wouldn't get paid unless the pyramid was totally rebuilt enabling the bartering and buying and selling of roosters to flourish again.

Even though many people knew someone who had died in the storm, on the day after such a dramatic event, the boys working on the pyramid were happy. Death in Calcutta was viewed as a daily occurrence, and the survivors mumbled stoically that we all eventually died anyway. Every ten year old boy and girl had seen a dead body - a beggar in the streets who had simply expired, or a child crushed in a stampede, and a few had seen the body from a political killing by the Naxalites.

The Fat Man's expressions grew grimmer as the day wore on. He worked feverishly, demanding more pliable branches, roping the corners together, making cages at a faster pace than ever before.

"Where is King Rooster? Where is he?" he lamented to no one in particular. Then he stood and cupped his hands like a megaphone. "A 100 rupees to anyone who brings back King Rooster, alive and unhurt. A 100 rupees," he bellowed.

All over the Square people stopped picking up bricks, stopped putting stones back up on their tin roofs, stopped mending their carts, to listen to his pronouncement. Inwardly, no one was too impressed with what he had to say. They didn't like The Fat Man. They didn't trust him to pay.

"What does unhurt mean?" muttered one woman sweeping garbage off her porch. "You won't find an unhurt rooster after last night. Not after a storm like that. I don't care how big he is."

The Fat Man's bellowing for the return of King Rooster was the last I heard before the boys carried me out of the Square to the white-haired doctor's temporary hospital.

XVII

Where Am I?

The storm had knocked me out and sent my mind twirling into the hazy past as I lay in my cocoon waiting for my strength to return. Relieved of the pain in the right side of my chest by a shot of something, I drifted in and out of consciousness, as if I were watching white puffy, clouds float by.

I had never felt further from home and my family and friends back in the Adirondacks, but I dared not dwell there. That was too far away. I wanted the present. I fought for the present. It kept me young.

I woke from my sleep-walking world of review, satisfied that I could recall how I had got here to another cot in Calcutta. The storm was over and I was alive. Annapurna was hunkered down next to one of the other men lying in cots all in a row. The other man was Nandalla. He had been trapped in the back kitchen of the Broken Plate Cafe when a brick wall collapsed onto him, like an angry mob raining fists on his back, reprisals for his nighttime work.

Nandalla was thrashing about yelling out commands at anyone who passed. Annapurna felt like a nurse, listening to his tirade then getting up to go down the row of cots to visit me and hold my hand. Annapurna told me he wasn't yelling because of his wounds, but at the failure of one of his plots. Finally a tiny bespectacled doctor walked over and told Nandalla he would get no shot of morphine if he didn't control his temper.

Both Nandalla and I got some extra attention from the tidy doctor. I was a Westerner, and the Indians liked to prove themselves to Westerners. Though Nandalla was suspected of fermenting illegal activities, he was popular with the people to the point of being an outlaw hero of Native Town.

Nandalla and I were separated by five or six heavily breathing patients on cots. The walls and the slowly turning blade of the ceiling fan where all that I could easily see. The walls were a chipped plaster painted a sickly green. Four framed fading photographs hung above me, and two of the subjects surprised me. I expected to see Mahatma Gandhi and Indira Gandhi. But next to them were pictures of President John F. Kennedy and the boxer Muhammed Ali. Of course Ali had converted to the Moslem faith, which was the second largest religious group in India behind the Hindu, and both Mahatma Gandhi and John F. Kennedy had preached civil rights and been assassinated.

I heard Nandalla yell for the doctor. The doctor tightened his jaw when he examined Nandalla. "Beyond the morphine, there is not a thing I can do for you without taking an x-ray."

Nandalla reached out with his long muscular right arm and grabbed the doctor by his pointed elbow and pulled him towards him. "You have contusions and cuts on your back," continued the doctor in a state of distraction.

"I know about cuts. I have cut other people," spoke Nandalla inches away from the doctor's ear. "I want a supply of morphine," he whispered clearly into the doctor's ear. The doctor stared at Nandalla until he let go of his elbow.

"The typhoon has left many persons injured, more seriously than you, and we have no extra morphine." With that he turned and left to work on the next patient.

Annapurna witnessed Nandalla's demand, and could not figure out why he wanted morphine. Nandalla, of any man she knew, was capable of enduring pain, so the morphine must have been for someone else. She thought the situation might present an opportunity to make herself useful.

When the doctor, now almost falling asleep as he worked, came to check on me five patients later, she was there by my side. She explained that I would be traveling by train and rickshaw to the Nepalese border and then by overland truck in order to arrive by Christmas in Kathmandu. The ride would be long, painful, and bumpy. Could I have as much medicine as the doctor could spare, she asked, while discretely passing one of my American ten dollar bills into the doctor's hand.

The doctor looked at her with raised eyebrows and down-turned mouth challenging her for a moment while recognizing the large value of the bill in these difficult times. He blinked his eyes closed and walked away to return with a bottle which he handed to her. "I hope it gets him through the journey safely."

She nodded appreciatively and tucked it in her sari, as I looked on with a drug-induced smile.

The doctor took a step to leave and turned back to her, "He has two broken ribs, numbers three and four and a general soreness from the fall."

She looked down for fear she was blushing. Probably the doctor knew the morphine was really intended for Nandalla's purposes. She curled my fingers around three of the plump pills before walking to Nandalla who was sitting up in the cot holding the side of his hairy chest. "Why do you want extra morphine?" she asked directly.

"We have wounded who don't feel it would be wise to come to a hospital."

She knew the 'we' meant the cause, the Naxalites, who might be wanted in connection with the death of a politician. She dug in the folds of her sari and put her hand around the clouded plastic bottle with a yellow top holding a dozen plump pills, and placed it in his hand.

He read the label out loud and was pleased with her resourcefulness. "Thank you," he said genuinely. "Help me up. I need to go." She helped him and looked around at Chaleea who had returned from exploring and was fast asleep with his head on the end of my cot.

My eyes were half shut. I made a semi-conscious decision to abandon my drug enhanced dream state, and opened by bleary eyes wider. Once I realized Annapurna was leaving with Nandalla, I was not about to be left behind. I shook Chaleea awake by rustling my feet under the covers and knocking his head off the bed.

"Chaleea, " I said, turning my head towards our departing friends, "I have to leave too. Help me up."

Chaleea hesitated, rubbed his eyes, and looked around for the doctor whom he didn't see. "Yes, Sahib Jack, rise up so you don't lose sight of your princess Annapurna."

Chaleea grabbed me around the waist and we found our way out of the temporary hospital determined to follow.

"I have to go to the bathroom. Here, help me up." I was afraid of the pain in my side. But I only felt a stiffness. The plump morphine pills were still doing their job. I hobbled up, steadied by Chaleea, and made my way to a make-shift bathroom. The putrid smell convinced me it was best to leave today.

On my way back, the doctor came by. "Are you leaving us?" he asked.

"Yes he is," answered Chaleea, respectfully.

"Well, make sure you sign out. We can't be responsible. Your ribs are not healed, and it is still possible one of your broken ribs could puncture a lung." I went wide-eyed. The doctor observed my alarm, and added, "But it's unlikely. Just don't get yourself shoved. Stay away from crowds."

In the background between the curtains, the doctor watched us leave in the dim evening light, and for the third time turned his new American ten dollar bill over in his hands wondering about the American president on the bill.

As Nandalla and Annapurna made their way arm and arm through the washed and battered streets, people stared. He was injured and limping, so what at first seemed like a daring show of affection from Annapurna, could be justified as cane-like support for him. Public displays of affection were not permitted in India, except when carved in stone at ancient erotic temples.

Chaleea and I tagged along hardly noticed.

"Nandalla, you all right?" called out one of the poor street beggars, his teeth red and his mind high from chewing on too many betel leaves and smoking too many Beede's.

Two young boys on a mud-caked bike, one on the handle bars, wove through the clog of humanity drifting around, happy to be alive after the latest mother of all typhoons. "Nandalla!, Peace!" shouted the boy riding the handle bars, holding up the V sign of the western hippie travelers. Nandalla acknowledged them with the peace symbol, and the boys basked in the recognition. "He's a gangster" said the boy proudly over his shoulder to the rider who was peddling as fast as he could while avoiding crack-ups.

Somehow Nandalla got away with being seen with more than one woman. Other Indian women eyed the couple disapprovingly, but if Nandalla fixed his stare back at them, they invariably lowered their eyes. He was one of the kings of the street. He could have become a merchant or a banker, but he stayed in the streets, and Calcutta's poor respected him, and at times hid him in their hovels.

Sometimes soldiers, who were the city's policemen, would venture into the squalor and exotic decay of the back alleys, usually in groups of three and four. The downtrodden characters of Native Town gawked at them and the contrast they presented. Wearing mirrored sunglasses, dressed smartly in different shades of green, standing straight, a saber on one side and a club or rifle on the other, the soldiers strode through these shanty towns taking liberties. As a result of Indira's President Rules of 1969, imposed to fight the Maoist threat of the Naxalites, soldiers could roundup and relocate groups of street people at whim. They arrested anyone they deemed a suspicious character.

Like tugs plowing through the Hooghly, the soldiers caused a wave of commotion in front of them and a wake of reaction behind them. When soldiers were spotted, runners, boys on bikes, and occasionally even a storekeeper on a phone, if it worked, broadcast ahead that soldiers were coming. Contraband disappeared from shelves, money changers folded up their card tables and disappeared like marauding tigers into the jungle. Just as the soldiers would round a corner of a dusty alley, the lone prostitute was now squatting down well wrapped up, selling pistachio nuts. The black market money changer displayed fine silk scarves over his arm for the soldiers' wives, and a known gangster like Nandalla was hustled away into hidden rooms by helpful strangers.

"Where are we going" asked Annapurna of Nandalla, her arm stretched tightly around his waist, his chest leaning on her shoulder.

"To the Broken Plate. Only the back part of the kitchen is damaged. The rest of the building withstood the wind. I will lay down there."

"Nandalla" she said softly. "I can't stay with you."

"I know that," he said impatiently. "I'm useless right now anyway."

Still wanting to explain, she continued, "I have to get back to the Square, and collect what's left of my apartment."

"Why don't you speak the truth," he answered, "and tell me you want to go and take care of your American hippie. That's all he is, right? Nothing but another hippie traveler," he said with an edge to his voice.

He was taunting her and her typically American taste for bluejeans, but he was also interrogating her about my political leanings, and she knew she had to be careful how she answered. Plus she suspected that Nandalla was jealous.

She took the offensive. "Listen Nandalla, I've told you basically he's an innocent traveler. He wants to stay around for the festival of The Rooster Palace and then he is leaving for Nepal, like they all do," she said with a touch of derision. "But I will still be here, Nandalla. Why, I'm not sure, but I will."

For some reason, in private conversations she was able to best him. Nandalla, who admired verbal dexterity, was apt to be quiet and listen when she talked to him. For the moment, he was satisfied with her explanation. She was discreet, he thought. She knew never to mention the word Naxalite when others might hear.

They reached the familiar three blue stone steps leading down to the door of the coffee house. Nandalla grimaced and lowered his head to get through the doorway. He needed to lay down.

She held his hand for an extra second, squeezed his fingers while looking at his scruffy face. "I'm leaving now." Without waiting for a response, off she trotted.

She passed by us, but didn't say anything. I don't know if she saw us or not. She headed towards The Square, and we meekly trailed behind. The storm had washed away the stench.

The peasants couldn't afford the luxury of refrigeration so they collected and cooked the dead chickens without waiting. To start the fires they picked up the smaller pieces of wood tossed around by the typhoon. Those that had lost a friend were full of sorrow and ate in silence, alone, but happy today for their stomachs. They knew to cook the chickens well.

Annapurna thought of herself and this life she had sought out. Underneath her Indian attire she was full of cultural uncertainties. How dedicated to Calcutta was she? Should she turn and head north to Nepal with me? Should she take care of me? It was her natural tendency to do so.

Now was her chance. Her apartment was destroyed and most of her possessions had been flung about the Square. She looked around, surprised at how quickly life returned to normal after a storm. She felt weary and went to brace herself against a wooden post, when she saw pieces of hay, like the long needles of a cactus, imbedded in the post. The wind had actually driven the hay with such velocity that single pieces stuck in the wood like arrows. The Fat Man sat across the Square watching her.

She wandered over to where her room used to be and in an absent-minded fashion wondering if she should try to climb up and look for some of her things. Staring blankly upwards, a messenger tapped her gently. "Mademoiselle, The Fat Man would like to see you."

The touch stopped her reverie. She looked over the head of the messenger across the courtyard and focused on The Fat Man who sat next to the largest rooster cage she had ever seen. What does he want? She thought she better be prepared to negotiate. Once in front of him, she stood straight in an attempt to conceal her exhausted, dreamy state. With a small sense of alarm, she noted that she could have fit into the cage; it was that big.

She took the initiative, and spoke first. "Have you found King Rooster. Or rather has he returned?"

"No," The Fat Man scowled, "and I'm at a loss of what to do. I owe many workers money - the cage builders, the placers, the hawkers, the poster-makers - the list goes on indefinitely. King Rooster was our big attraction."

"I'm sure he'll turn up, but maybe dead." she said blankly.

"Yes, I'm afraid of that. He's probably being roasted right now over a giant spigot down Chatawala Gully to feed all the Chinese left in Calcutta for their New Year's Eve festival." He said with black humor. "I need some luck, or maybe I need you." His eyes narrowed. "How would you like to dress up as a rooster, just for a day." His belly shook as he cackled and grabbed one of the bamboo corners of the cage.

But Annapurna wasn't laughing. She found herself stepping away from the open, roped-on door to the cage, glancing over her shoulder for his henchmen, whom she feared might even push her in. The Fat Man was dangerous and unscrupulous, and she was taking no chances.

She deftly edged away. "Maybe my dear friend Nandalla can help you find your rooster." And now her temper rising, she said, "Or maybe you want to wrestle Nandalla and the loser gets locked in the cage. That way you can get a free ride to the top of The Rooster Palace."

The Fat Man scowled and guffawed at the same time, unaccustomed to such impudence but enjoying the repartee. "I was just joking Mademoiselle, but we do need an attraction, if King Rooster is gone. You are attractive." He paused while Annapurna's indignance grew.

"I see now your are in need of some things. For instance, a place to stay. I offer you my palace across the muddy Hooghly." As she glared at him, he added, "Of course, I guarantee your safety. Unfortunately, I won't even be there to look out for you. To see your beautiful skin. You will be safe and comfortable."

Calmer yet desperate to rest and clean-up, and so sure of her own instincts for survival, she almost said yes. But she had learned the ways of many men and had hardened herself. She politely declined his offer.

Turning, she saw the quick movement of a boy behind the post with the pieces of hay stuck in it. She walked towards the post.

"My palace is better than the cage," The Fat Man yelled after her with a big belly laugh.

XVIII

The Search

Behind the post and around the corner, Annapurna found Chaleea. I was laying down in the background in an amorphous, groggy state. She frowned at me but smiled at Chaleea. "I thought it was you. Do you have any ideas on where we can stay.?"

"No I don't Mademoiselle," he said with delight in his eyes.

"How is Jack?" she asked.

"These pills are wonderful. I don't feel a thing, " I said.

"He's trying to keep up with you," Chaleea said. "But guess what I've discovered?"

"Well, I have no idea" she said pleased with his happiness and momentarily distracted from her own grief from the loss of her possessions and uncertainty from her tango with The Fat Man.

Chaleea took the liberty of standing close to her, tiptoed up to her ear, and after a furtive look in both directions, whispered, "I know where King Rooster is."

"Really?" She pulled back to look at him to see if he was lying or not. "That's marvelous," she said, confident he was telling the truth. And now her mind started to spin with plans. She just couldn't believe it. "You're sure?"

"A friend is with the King Rooster now, guarding him."

"Far from here?" asked Annapurna.

"Best you do not know, Madame. The Fat Man really wants him back for the festival and no telling what he'd do."

"Yes, you are right. No telling. Is he safe for tonight?"

"Yes, I think so."

"Let us go now," she said looking back at the gigantic empty cage. "We need to find a place to stay tonight and figure out what to do." Chaleea kneeled down and attended to me. "We'll come back here first," she said reassuringly. She grabbed his hand, and he glowed inwardly at this.

Chaleea had this confused feeling of affection for Annapurna. He loved her like a mother but then sometimes he fantasized she would one day be his girlfriend, out of reach now only because he was too young and she was too old. Either way he liked holding her smooth creamy hand and long cherry-red finger nails.

Chaleea was feeling like a man in charge tonight. He had the one secret The Fat Man was desperate for, and a place to stay had popped into his head. "I think I know where we can stay tonight," he said proudly. He was thinking of Ricki and his tan, army-surplus tent on the back paths behind the Marble Palace.

Chaleea started to mention something about The Fat Man and then his voice trailed off, as he thought of his confusing experience at the hands of The Fat Man. Annapurna skipped over Chaleea's reference to him and decided now was not the time to ask questions about what had happened at The Fat Man's palace. She realized The Fat Man had in some way taken advantage of a boy, her friend Chaleea.

Instead she plotted to so some damage to the unctuous Fat Man. She shuddered, thinking just moments ago she had actually considered accepting his invitation to stay at his palace. Annapurna was confused but emboldened by thoughts of retaliation. Revenge was foreign to her, but she was in a foreign land. She wasn't really Indian was she? She wanted to rip her Sari off and grab her bluejeans. This was one big crazy experiment, and she was scared now, wondering what the hell she was trying to prove?

Then she thought of it. Her escape hatch. Her passport. Where was it? Oh no, she remembered, it was back in the rubble of her apartment. "Chaleea," she said, "I have to go back to my flat. I have to get something." She was even afraid to admit to Chaleea that the something was her passport.

"Annapurna," he said sweetly, "there's nothing left of your flat."

"There's something I have to look for."

"What is it?" he asked.

"It is . . . " she hesitated.

"Tell me," he insisted. "This is my lucky day. I've already found King Rooster."

"It is my passport!" She blurted it out, almost crying.

First Chaleea shook his head, no. Then he slid his hand out of hers and demanded quietly, "So you are leaving us."

She spun Chaleea around and held him by the shoulders. "I do not know. I do not think so. But, Chaleea, I do not know what is going to happen here. And I do have a family back in the United States." The tears were tumbling down her cheeks.

Moved by her crying, Chaleea said what he had heard Nandalla say, "Don't worry, I'll take care of you," and he grabbed the fingers of both her hands in a gesture that surprised even himself.

Now she was sobbing. "Oh thank you." And she hugged Chaleea, adding a blessed moment of sensual comfort to his blossoming confidence. In a flash, he forgot his own accusation of her running away and was now helping a friend he liked very much.

"Let's go. I will help you find the passport. He gazed across the vast Square at the collapsed wall. "But we'll have to be careful. It's unsafe up there."

149

All that was left of her emotional breakdown was a sniffle. And within two strides of their change in direction, she had wiped her tears away with the end of her Sari, and was again the responsible adult.

"Stand up straight, Chaleea. You are slouching." Chaleea was perplexed by the fast change in emotions. "There," she said standing straighter herself, pointing, "there is a ladder we can borrow." She was back in control and Chaleea was thrust back into the role of the obedient street boy, He shrugged and trotted over to drag the ladder up to Annapurna's place while there was still light from the sun.

"Annapurna," he said with a fading taste of the authority he had felt a few moments ago when she was crying, "We should carry a candle with us."

"Yes, Chaleea. You are always thinking, you are," and she padded him on the head, affectionately swishing his black curly hair. He sighed and accepted her praise, breathing slowly and happily. He tucked away those other moments of welcome luscious confusion to contemplate later when alone before going to sleep. He leaned the wooden ladder securely against the crumbled wall.

Chaleea climbed up first, testing each wooden rung before resting his full weight. He held onto the ladder with one hand, stepping slowly, carrying the flickering candle in the other hand. At the top where the window used to be, he put the candle down and turned to help Annapurna.

Across the Square the sun was setting and the sky was red. The Rooster Palace was being rebuilt in the evening coolness, and soon it would only be missing its crowning rooster, the apex of the pyramid, King Rooster. Chaleea mouthed the words 'King Rooster' from his perch high on the ladder. Ah, the glory he felt. His hair was blown back by a passing wind, the welcome vestiges of a colossal storm. The men working like army ants swathed in a gentle evening breeze and a deep orange sunset, brought a sense of poetry to him.

"Mademoiselle" he said gently, helping her up. "Look, it's a beautiful evening." In certain situations, to entertain himself, and show off the few French words he knew, he liked to call pretty ladies in the market, "Mademoiselle." She looked oddly at Chaleea. These Indians, she thought, they find tranquillity wherever they need to.

She looked out over the Square, but was preoccupied with watching where she was walking. She knew she had hidden the passport underneath the top of her only bureau, slid under a supporting wooden runner for the top drawer. She found the bureau tipped over, and some of her clothes, soaked. The passport wasn't where she had put it.

Had others picked through her apartment, she wondered? With the stairs gone, yet the apartment so visible to the Square, she prayed they hadn't.

"I hid it in here, Chaleea."

Chaleea looked around with the sharp vision of young boy, and saw clothes and a bra, lacy and black. He was drawn to the feminine contraption, but he resisted. Instead he moved to the stove, still upright. He squatted down and flicked around some broken china at the base of the stove. He really didn't know where to look for the passport.

Standing, they both poked around carefully with their feet, kneeling down every minute or so when they spotted something of promise. Annapurna nudged the crumpled Ajax can where she had hid her money. She picked up a frazzled wicker picnic basket and started putting in things of value or just memorabilia. She was quiet again, and he sensed a hurt about her.

"Do you want this?" Chaleea had found one jade earring.

"Oh yes, thank you. The earrings were the first gift I bought myself when I came to Calcutta." They poked around some more. "Bring the candle over here." She had found some photo's, but no passport. "These are my parents and me and my older brother."

She showed the pictures to Chaleea, but he didn't want to be reminded of her other life. So he only pretended to look.

Before Chaleea leaned up against one of the two remaining walls, he kicked it to test it. "It doesn't look good Mademoiselle."

"Please, Chaleea, you are lucky at these things, please keep looking. Soon it will be totally dark."

What did he think, he asked himself. Probably someone had already been through the apartment and found the passport, and it had already been traded on the black market. U.S. passports were sought after, very desirable. With a few changes, and for a few thousand rupees, an Indian women with connections could start a new life in an American suburb, like Chappaqua, open an Indian restaurant, and pine for her family and country the way Annapurna was starting to pine for her home.

Chaleea hopscotched over debris back to the bureau. He tilted the candle and let the melted wax fall onto the side of the bureau, and stuck the candle there. In the flickering light, Chaleea was drawn to the bra again, which to him symbolized modern western sex, something he knew little about but wanted to know all about. While Annapurna was preoccupied squinting at her family photos, he reached down and from a small pile of wet underwear, picked up the tantalizing symbol of the unknown. His temperature rose and he felt hot and guilty, holding in his hand one of the few contraptions in Annapurna's apartment that had survived in perfect shape. He wondered if Annapurna was wearing one now.

Enough, enough, he thought, and went to put it back. Something blue and gold from the pile, under where the bra had been, spoke to him. He squatted down and uncovered a thin blue book, with gold letters. He couldn't believe his luck; it was the passport. With the speed of a viperous snake, he snatched the passport and stuffed the bra in his pocket. Holding the little blue book triumphantly above his head, he thought, from now on the bra is my lucky charm.

"Mademoiselle" he said with a twinkle. "I have something for you."

With a sigh, she placed the photos in her basket and was drawn back to the reality of Calcutta. She thought maybe he had found the other earring.

He waved his arm in circles holding the passport, smiling from cheek to cheek. "I found it."

"Ah, Ohhhh, Chaleea. You're wonderful. Ohh." She took the passport and looked it over as best she could. It was damp, but otherwise undamaged. "I knew you could find it, Chaleea. Where was it?"

"It was over here, under your clothes, your underwear." And he pulled at the tangled bra and waved it in the air. "Under this."

She was so happy to have her passport, she barely noticed that he had pulled her bra from his pocket, hardly cared really. "Give me that" she said smiling while blushing pink. "Give me that, you little boy." And she snatched it from him and hugged him dearly, and he felt so good. Good not to be punished for his naughty interest in her underwear. Good to feel hugged.

"I'm nothing but a success today," he beamed.

"Yes, you are Chaleea. You are a big success." she declared ruffling his hair. With calculated nonchalance and a well-concealed touch of embarrassment, she dropped the fancy French bra in her basket, tucked the passport securely under her sari and carefully made her way to the ladder.

Chaleea picked up the stub of the candle and held it for them as they descended the ladder down to the Square. "We must hurry now, Mademoiselle. It's dark. We must rescue Jack and be off the streets."

"I've never been bothered before."

"But tonight there is still some looting from the storm. People are in a lawless mood. And you know about the Naxalites," Chaleea ventured. "I know you know Mister Nandalla, but there are many other Naxalites that don't know you." And then he added quickly and reassuringly, "But if they think you're an Indian woman, which you look like in the darkness, I see no problem." And finally, "I'm taking you to a Sadhu man's tent. He is trustworthy."

XIX

The Sadhu's Tent

Watching from afar, waiting patiently, with my back propped against a warm clay wall, I struggled up when Annapurna and Chaleea approached. In silence each took an arm, and in earnest now we careened through the back alleys, across the broad Chittaranjan Avenue, dodging a trolley and a rickshaw, across a cricket field with small fires smoldering and what looked like bundles strewn about. At first I thought the bundles were cattle, but when we stumbled around the middle of the field, I realized they were low caste Indians, many of them Untouchables, curled up in their tattered garbs for the night. The ground was still damp from the pounding rain of the typhoon, so there would be little comfort for them tonight. Others simply squatted for hours huddled around the fires, or if they were lucky enough to possess dry straw mats or cardboard, they slept on them.

Chaleea was careful to take only the safe, familiar shorts cuts. He veered away from the Hooghly waterfront where he knew thugs hung out in the Dakshineshwar park looking for unsuspecting foreigners who were mesmerized by ancient riverside temples and the last glow of the Indian sunset.

"This way Mademoiselle. Hurry," he said. There were no street lamps, and only the wealthy hotels with uniformed guards out front had lights, usually running off their own generators. Two or three times Chaleea and Annapurna bumped into unsuspecting stragglers shuffling slowing through the night, almost sleepwalking, looking for a better patch of earth on which to lay down. I was wincing the whole way. They were not including me in any conversation, disregarding me as if I were a sack of fish they were lugging to the market.

A fog had risen, and moisture, or was it sweat, covered our faces. I was looking waifish, as thin as I had been my sophomore year in high school, seven years ago. I liked having a flat stomach, but I felt weak. In the mornings, my eyelids were crusted shut with some kind of cold. Here in Calcutta, I would have felt guilty waiting in the long line to see a doctor for something as trivial as an eye infection. Did I have two arms and two legs? I did.

Chaleea was walking fast now, taking big strides. Annapurna flung her shawl up and around her mouth and chin, so only her eyes were visible. We saw fewer people as the darkness descended and the hum of the crowds subsided.

In her one free arm she carried the dilapidated picnic basket with photos, an earring, some clothes, one fancy bra, and gem-stones that were precious to her because of the bartering she had done to get them. With her elbow, she patted her side in the darkness and happily felt her passport, and locked hands with Chaleea's around my waist.

"Sadhu Ricki is very close now," said Chaleea. "I first came here with Sahib Jack, and we stayed here one night. He is a good and honest Sadhu man, and he shares my secret Mademoiselle."

Annapurna wasn't sure what secret Chaleea meant, but she genuinely felt respect towards the few religious men she had meant in India. Somehow they appeared happy and healthy in their bright orange robes.

"The tent is there. Be careful, there are trees here. He gets some shade that way." Annapurna was exhausted and in the blackness of a clear and moonless Calcutta night, had no idea where they were. She squinted to make out the shape of the trees, and between two of them she thought she saw the shape of something large and alive.

The outside tent flaps were closed and roped down. In the darkness, Chaleea was confused for a moment. During the storm the tent had been blown down. Sadhu Ricki resurrected the tent at a spot a few feet away but faced it West so he would have a different view for the next six months. Being a painter, views were important to him.

From the dark large tent, a calm voice said "Welcome, and may God protect you. Now go around to the front of the tent."

"It's Chaleea," he said. "And I have a new friend, Mademoiselle Annapurna, and Sahib Jack who is not well."

Sadhu Ricki opened a flap, and a held up some candles in an ornate, bronze candelabra. He collected himself for a moment, decided he was pleased to have visitors, and when the light flickered over her face, suspected she wasn't an Indian. He painted a picture in his mind of Chaleea, me and now this woman.

I insisted I could make my way into the tent alone. With the help of Sadhu Ricki's wiry arms, I collapsed with a groan flattening the pillows. Annapurna bowed slightly, her hands together as if in prayer. Sadhu Ricki, bowed in return, and announced, "Please sit down, a friend of Chaleea is a friend of mine." She ducked her head and he gestured to a carved round three-legged stool with hundreds of colorful beads pressed into the wood. She sat and sighed. Chaleea sauntered in smiling and bowing. This was his night and he knew it.

Annapurna spoke. "Like many others in the city tonight, my apartment was destroyed in the cyclone. Basically, this is all I have now," she said, opening her hands in the direction of her picnic basket. She was taking a chance trusting this Indian fakir, a stranger to her.

157

Sadhu Ricki observed her, her face, her Indian garb, her totally covered body. He knew that she had helped Chaleea. "You are welcome here. It's late now and we will talk in the early morning. Here comfort yourself on these two pillows and just rest there," pointing to right where she sat.

As she began to feel safe, her body gave way to a deep emotional and physical fatigue. "Namesti, Namesti," she said rocking her hands in a prayerful motion. A Western woman, an American, had never before spent the night in Sadhu Ricki's tent and he was rather excited by this turn of events.

"And Mademoiselle," he said chuckling and looking at Chaleea who eyes were twinkling like the brightest stars on a winter's night, "Don't be frightened in the morning if you're awakened early by something loud and thunderous."

But Mademoiselle Annapurna was fast asleep and never heard Sadhu Ricki's friendly warning.

2

In the early morning the blue nighttime sky had turned gray in anticipation of the Asian sunrise. Wonderfully moist droplets of dew covered a spider web which had been spun on the tent in the still of the night. Inside Chaleea slept an enchanted sleep on a pillow next to Annapurna.

A stentorian "Cock a doodle, doooo, cock a doodle, doooo" startled me awake from a deep sleep.. At the second crowing, I clamped my hands over my ears amidst the suitcases and silk and Indian pillows. In a corner wearing coral beads and an orange T-shirt, Sadhu Ricki sat upright in locust position, his eyes softly shut, a peaceful look on his face.

Again the rooster crowed, and the tent flapped in a pre-dawn breeze in unison with the magnificent and frightening trumpeting. The noise sounded like it was right outside the tent, yet Sadhu Ricki and Chaleea appeared oblivious to it. Only Annapurna and I were roused by it. My eyes adjusted to the waning darkness, and I could see better and think better. With a sparkle, I realized what I was hearing. None other than the crowing of the missing King Rooster.

Annapurna sat upright and looked down at the face of Chaleea under a thin gray blanket. He had been secretly watching her through the slits in his eyes. Finally he couldn't contain himself, and grinning, winked at her. "Yes, it's the King Rooster and we have him," he whispered.

Happy that Chaleea was the one who had found King Rooster but still tired, she slumped down back to her pillows and delicately moved a few inches away from Chaleea, ready to cover her ears again.

She had seen something between two trees last night, some huge lump. That must have been King Rooster. And so it was, tied between the two banyan trees.

Chaleea said "He's done, Mademoiselle. He only crows twice."

"Thank you, Chaleea" she said sardonically. "Now back to sleep." Chaleea was already crawling out on all fours through the tent flap to go to the bathroom somewhere nearby in the field.

I was drifting off when another foreign but calmer sound began. It was a mumbling-like chant. "Momboly, bumbobly, momoboly, bumb." It was gibberish to me, but mesmerizing nonetheless. I opened one eye to watch Sadhu Ricki, who had a thick black beard, swaying slightly in a circular motion chanting his mantra. I felt as if I were intruding; yet still I was intrigued. Did he pray each morning? Then I wondered if he was so disciplined that he was able to sleep sitting upright the whole night? Or was he sitting only because there wasn't room to lay down?

I felt privileged to be listening to this morning ritual, and forever treasured the memory as exotic and so apart from the rushed mornings of my Western upbringing. I took one last look and listen to absorb as much as I could and, lulled by his chant, drifted back into a second and rare deep sleep. "Momboly, bumbobly, momboly, bumb."

Chaleea crawled back into the tent. He had been busy feeding grain to the prized King Rooster, and chewing on some himself, trying to soften up the kernels by swishing around prodigious amounts of saliva in his mouth. The experience was like eating popcorn without popping it. Probably there was some nutritional value, but Chaleea would have preferred two eggs scrambled.

That's when he knew he had to find some hens. Outside the tent was the largest rooster in Calcutta, and he needed some hens to give King Rooster purpose and to give himself eggs. He put on his flattened leather sandals which seemed to stay on his feet through friction only, and went back out looking for a hen. Just to borrow, he thought. He did not want to walk all the way back to The Rooster Palace.

Instead he headed towards Chowringhee where the original spice merchants and tea traders first built their mansions. A few descendants still carried on in the streets behind the newer hotels as if they were wealthy traders. Pretending kept their station in society, and allowed them to enjoy some of the frivolous pleasures.

On the way there, four women stood in line at a pump, while two boys pumped vigorously to start the smallest trickle of water. One by one the women filled their ceramic vases. Waiting patiently in line, two street hawkers pushing carts carrying an assortment of things from old copies of National Geographic to skeleton puzzles, wakened themselves by wetting cloths and then patting their proud faces.

A brown puppy, with a white spots on his hind legs, looking like a cross between a hyena and a dog, lapped up some spilled water and padded towards Chaleea, who took the time to reach down and pick up the mutt, petting him, feeling his ribs against his fingers. "Nothing I can do. I'm hungry too." Chaleea put the dog down and opened his nostrils to see if he could smell chickens.

He knew that somehow Sadhu Ricki would provide for them, at least for a day or two until the Festival of The Rooster Palace. Now that Sadhu Ricki had found King Rooster, they certainly were entitled to something. Some money maybe. Surely Providence must have guided the wind to blow King Rooster into Sadhu Ricki's tent, knocking it down, enabling Sadhu Ricki to capture King Rooster by tethering him with a rope. All this Sadhu Ricki accomplished during the storm with no harm to himself or to the rooster. Now it was up to them to use King Rooster to help themselves. They must try to sell him back to The Fat Man.

Where are the chickens? I need to find some hens. Then we will have eggs, thought Chaleea rubbing his stomach. In a few minutes of poking around the sheds behind the old mansions, he caught the feathery scent of chickens.

With his head down, Chaleea ran quickly after a scraggly orange hen. The desperate hen squeezed under the floor of a collapsed shed and turned around underneath to face Chaleea's hand, beak first. Chaleea gave up and crawled out backwards in search of another hen. He strode along on a former servant's path parallel to King's Road.

Some chicks scattered across the path, and he slowed up waiting for a hen to appear. This time he pretended he wasn't interested and instead found a few pieces of grain in his pocket and tossed them in front of a white and orange speckled hen, plumper than the first hen he had chased.

While it pecked at the grain, Chaleea swooped down and grabbed it from behind and wrapped her up in his shirt. He ran bare chested back to the tent, his blinded prize quiet in his arms.

First he knew he would have to make a cage or collar for the hen, place it within range of King Rooster, and then in no time at all they would have eggs for breakfast. He slowed to a walk once he saw the army-green tent and looking down at his loose sandals, formed an idea. He took one off and easily tore off the worn leather strap. Holding the hen between his legs, he tied the leather strap around its neck. Care-

161

fully he approached the banyan trees and King Rooster. His heart beat faster as he got closer, and he talked quietly to the huge bird assuring him he was a friend.

"Yes, King Rooster, I bring you a gift. A friend so you two can make a few eggs for us before the festival. Yes, King Rooster, be still."

Using the frayed twine from King Rooster's rope, he tied a six foot length onto the hen's collar he had just made, and underneath his shirt working with both hands and all fingers, attached and tied the collar and string around the neck of the hen. King Rooster was only three feet away and Chaleea was well aware he and the hen were in striking range - Chaleea's bony back exposed to the claws and mighty red beak of King Rooster. But King Rooster sensed a friend and stood statue-still waiting.

Chaleea unveiled the hen and retreated. King Rooster perked up and strutted around in a circle, as if he were parading to marching music.

The rare smell of honey from the tent drew Chaleea back inside. He had seen a rooster mate with a hen before, and he had learned nothing except to see feathers flying for a few brief seconds. Sadhu Ricki, who had a stash of English tea biscuits and honey, was boiling water on one of the stoves he watched over for other Western travelers.

"And where did you find the hen, my wise one. Not in this neighborhood, I trust," queried Sadhu Ricki with a twinkle.

"On no Ricki," he said. Sadhu Ricki knew he was lying but appreciated his ingenuity and recognized the boy's thievery was from an empty stomach.

Annapurna looked happy munching on her biscuit and she asked Sadhu Ricki to reveal how he captured King Rooster. He was delighted to explain to her. In his high-pitched cackling tone of voice, he told of a great wind and water spout during the storm which had delivered King Rooster unharmed with a crash through the branches of the banyan trees while Sadhu Ricki was feverishly praying for his own safety. "A gift from the Gods," he concluded.

We sat around softening-up biscuits in our mouths, sipping tea with goat's milk, aware of the moderate early morning temperature and a giant prized rooster copulating nearby. I rubbed away the crust clinging to my eyelashes and quickly found something to say to distract from the rustling outside. "Well Annapurna, you seem in better spirits today."

"As long as I do not think too deeply," she said. "What is our plan for King Rooster?"

"We will all proceed to the Square with the magnificent one," answered Sadhu Ricki gesturing towards the banyans which provided his tent precious shade from the tropical sun.

Chaleea chimed in. "Sundown, then. We'll meet at sundown on the smooth stones where The Fat Man makes his cages."

"Yes, but you must demand money from him first before you show up with King Rooster. Otherwise The Fat Man will just grab the beast, and the show will be his," said Sadhu Ricki. "First we should leave the rooster tied here, and go to bargain and secure some form of payment for his appearance at the festival tonight."

Annapurna paused before she spoke. "I know one man, Nandalla, whom I think can help us deal with The Fat Man."

Sadhu Ricki held up one finger as he spoke. "Oh, Nandalla and I are good friends. But be careful, when it comes to business, he can be ruthless. And you know he has brainwashed himself to sacrifice for his Naxalite cause. He is too serious now. I do not know if we should include him," he said, shaking his finger sideways.

"Well, we'll see," said Annapurna demurely.

After a moment's silence, I declared, "My goal is to extract something from The Fat Man, my pound of flesh if you will. Chaleea and I have a score to settle."

"It is about time you took some control," said Annapurna to me.

"Let us prepare to go, then," said Sadhu Ricki throwing up an arm as if leading a charge into battle.

"May I leave my basket here?" asked Annapurna.

"Of course. You see the rest of my collection. Just make sure you return. Otherwise I'll take payment in your goods."

"Oh, there's nothing valuable there," she sighed.

"Nooo," he crooned. "You don't know. I know what's valuable. Anything you have touched is valuable," he said flirting with her.

She didn't take offense. He seemed honest and open. Coming from him, words did not offend.

"First let us give thanks to the Gods, Siva and Vishnu," Sadhu Ricki said. He reached out with his arms and Chaleea, Annapurna and I instinctively held hands and formed a diamond, all sitting cross-legged as he chanted a prayer in Hindi. Then in English he asked that the mighty rooster who was blown our way bring us good fortune, and ended with more of his early morning incantations.

With my eyes closed, I breathed in the sustenance and warmth of the moment - in a worn canvas tent on an unused cricket field in the teeming city of Calcutta with a mammoth rooster about to be paraded through the streets of Calcutta to inaugurate the Festival of The Rooster Palace.

"Amen" I offered. Annapurna rose, looking prettier than ever, and in a matter of seconds magically tied her long black hair in graceful swirls, interwoven and wrapped in a red silk scarf.

"Jack and I will go ahead," said Annapurna. "He is still wobbly. We will meet you there."

I swallowed my last pill and pulled myself up. With a captivating curtsy from Annapurna, off we went, leaving the smiling Sadhu Ricki with her basket in his lap.

3

Annapurna was convinced random events were buffeting her off course, blowing her nowhere. A woman with no home, no direction of her own, and no man of her own. She felt for her passport near her breast. Thank God, she thought. After a year and a half maybe it was time to leave. Yet she was wise enough to know, having returned once, that she would have to start all over again back in the States. People in the States wouldn't know, and if they knew, only a few would care what deeds she had done or where she had been. Even if she wore her travels in her dress, in her manner, again she would eventually be heading towards a lonely canyon.

Jostled by some beggars in the street, she grew unruly, "I have nothing. Can't you see. I'm just like you." But she knew that was a lie. She had a whole other life. She was cheating, she thought. But then she was here, wasn't she. She had managed to find her own place to stay, to get from airplane to railway car to rickshaw in a country were women traveling alone were examined and questioned. She had learned to be stared at and not to care. Not to look down, not to change one step, not to change one intention.

"I'll remember," she declared to me. "I'll remember Calcutta, I'll remember Sadhu Ricki, and I'll remember you Jack, my happy American."

Together, arm in arm, we walked onward, just as she had with Nandalla. Before I took a sip of the coke or peeled a banana, I gave Annapurna a kiss on her hair. "You're my savior," I cooed. The comment did her good.

XX

The Standoff in the Square

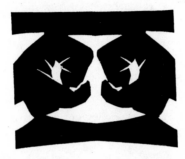

As we walked, pleasantly dazed in the blistering heat, I touched my forehead and felt no sweat. Left turn, and straight and then right and then I spied the Square. I had no idea how long our walk had taken us and didn't think to ask.

Back at the Square, The Fat Man was in a raunchy mood. His grand cage for King Rooster was complete. He joked, "Maybe I should get in the cage." In fact if he sat, he could have fit. His mood worsened, as was his mercurial nature, and he grew furious. Pounding his blubbery fist on the stone, he yelled in the air, "If he's not alive than where is his body? Find his body!"

A few of his servants scattered, but only to run out of his sight, huddle together, puff on a Beede and mimic their master's tantrum. In the meantime Annapurna and I, with her arm around my waist, were joined by Sadhu Ricki and Chaleea at the end of their trek to the cobble-stoned Square. I immediately veered off for the shade of one of the few remaining porches and a wall to lean on.

The other three marched forward. Once they saw The Fat Man across the Square they changed their pace to an amble to disguise their singleness of purpose. As the threesome crossed the Square, The Fat Man watched Annapurna.

"I know you," he yelled out. "Come here." And when she got closer. "What are you doing back here? Your place is in shambles. You refused my hospitality. You're lucky to be alive." He paused, and flicked his open hand in the direction of one of his servants. Immediately a servant reappeared with a large metal vessel containing a mixture of lemonade and orange juice. Yellow flowers, and sliced lemons and oranges floated on the surface. The servant poured four cups on a copper tray and offered them to all.

"Sit down," commanded The Fat Man. "Why are you here? And where is King Rooster?" he bellowed, not expecting an answer. All the time he gleamed possessively at Annapurna. Young Chaleea saw this and an anger grew inside.

Chaleea and Annapurna looked quizzically at Sadhu Ricki. With a tilt of his head as if he were trying to think of the answer to a math problem, Sadhu Ricki smiled, "Yes, we know where King Rooster is."

The Fat Man was silenced. He glanced around at his servants. He was trying to figure out if Sadhu Ricki was telling the truth.

"And is he alive?" he asked matter-of-factly.

"Yes, he is alive." responded Sadhu Ricki.

"Then where is he?" he blasted.

Annapurna took her turn. "We have him in a safe place. Do you want him?"

"Do I want him? Now my pretty," he said with teeth showing and his evilness surfacing, "You know I want him."

I had been watching from the porch, holding my side, more or less aware of what our goal was and that some sort of negotiations were going on. I didn't notice a tall dark man until he sidled next to me, silent like a jungle snake. The man was Nandalla and he had a contorted look on his face.

"Do you like her?" he asked looking across the Square at Annapurna.

"Yes I do like her."

"Do we have a problem then, my friend?" asked Nandalla mockingly. And as he asked that question he slid his powerful wrestler's arm directly around my rib cage, and like a python with its prey, squeezed.

I was frozen in pain, and moaned, "My ribs!"

Nandalla was sending a rather direct message. He released his arm. I was limp and in shock. I involuntarily slid down the shaded wall until I collapsed in a heap, barely conscious.

A few of The Fat Man's servants had spotted Nandalla's stealthy entrance into the Square and were alarmed. His appearance in daylight sent worried rumors from one servant to another. Nandalla knew that The Fat Man's men had observed him. He stared intently back at them.

Unbeknownst to The Fat Man, two of his own servants were at a midnight meeting with Nandalla and were as dedicated as he was to the Naxalite cause. One of them had taken care of an errand for the Naxalites. Errands were the Naxalite's expression for acts of violence committed at night.

Nandalla calmly stood up over me observing the negotiations from afar. In the background could be heard the occasional crowing of the roosters while workers repaired old cages or built new ones for the restacking of the storm-tattered tiers of the pyramid of The Rooster Palace.

The Fat Man was now convinced that Sadhu Ricki had in fact captured King Rooster, or at least knew of his whereabouts. The Fat Man was willing to trade. "What do you want. Name your price . . . within reason."

Chaleea and Annapurna thought of revenge. "We want you."

"You want me? What do you mean, you want me." The Fat Man looked around at his servants and forced a nervous belly laugh. "You want me?" he repeated.

"Yes, it is a trade, the King Rooster for you," said Annapurna, in a calm and measured voice. Since Sadhu Ricki, who was known throughout Native Town, was by their side and echoed their demand, The Fat Man was, for the moment, stymied.

"Yes, but I need to be at the ceremonies," said The Fat Man, stalling for time to think.

"Yes, you can be at the ceremonies. They have some religious significance, I'm sure. But then afterwards you must come with us," responded Sadhu Ricki.

"And what if after the rooster festival, I decide not to come with you?"

"Well then we'll come looking for you," declared Annapurna, and she surprised herself by spitting on the ground between them.

"The three of you, and your hippie friend against the wall there?" When The Fat Man gestured with his head and hand to across the Square where I was sitting, still dazed, he squinted at the other man next to me, but apparently couldn't make him out in the glare of the sun. Seeing his momentary puzzlement, the servant holding The Fat Man's umbrella, leaned over and whispered Nandalla's identity.

This turn of events didn't please The Fat Man. Was Nandalla aligned with Annapurna? Was he here as an enforcer? He knew all too well of Nandalla and his political organization, the Naxalites, and had supported them financially so that he would be left alone. The Fat Man did not want to get overly involved in the serious, sometimes fatal West Bengali politics of Calcutta. He was doing fine running the Square and The Rooster Palace.

Annapurna had followed The Fat Man's eyes across the Square, and she watched The Fat Man react nervously and pull at his collar. He was sweating more, looking left and right, squirming a bit. "Why do you want me? What are you going to do to me?"

Annapurna stepped forward. "We want you because you molested Chaleea. We want to pay you back. I don't think Chaleea intends to kill you."

The Fat Man's large bald head popped up off his fleshly shoulders. "Rubbish," he mumbled, preoccupied.

The Fat Man was concentrating. Of course he didn't seriously contemplate giving himself over to anyone or any group so that they could extract some sort of punishment from him. He would laugh in their faces when they came for him. The only face he couldn't laugh in was Nandalla's.

But The Fat Man worshipped money, and there was no festival without King Rooster. The big rooster was his main attraction. He was his Bengali tiger, his King Cobra, wrapped into one. Never before had anyone seen a rooster so big. People would travel from miles around to come to the Square. It would be like a religious pilgrimage coming to see this giant. To see him in a cockfight. To see him mate. To hear him crow from on top of the pyramid of The Rooster Palace before he was sold. Sold to some tottery Maharaja for the diamonds and emeralds at the bottom of his trunk that his regal grandfather had accumulated during the heyday of the Raja's rule of India.

The Fat Man collected himself. "Now first," he continued in a business-like tone, "I did not touch, or molest Chaleea. He's dreaming that up. A pat on the head, an arm around the shoulders, yes. But that's all. I swear to the almighty Vishnu, that's all." Sadhu Ricki looked imploringly from Chaleea to Annapurna, who was thrown off balance by The Fat Man's convincing denial.

Chaleea spoke up, perplexed but pleased with The Fat Man's words. In his innocent confusion he wasn't sure what really had or hadn't happened between himself and The Fat Man. He had felt guilty; that much he knew.

171

"All right we will promise your safe return. But then we want three thousand rupees for King Rooster," said Sadhu Ricki.

"Three thousand," repeated The Fat Man loudly as if it were the largest sum of money he had ever heard. Now The Fat Man was on familiar territory, bargaining, haggling over a few thousand rupees. "One thousand five hundred and not a rupee more," The Fat Man shot back.

Minutes later, they agreed to a price of two thousand rupees, and The Fat Man appeared very sullen as if this merry band of pranksters had really taken him. Sadhu Ricki insisted on a payment of half now, guaranteeing The Fat Man return of the money if they didn't produce King Rooster. Reluctantly The Fat man handed over ten, one hundred-rupee notes.

"You still have to come with us after the ceremony," reminded Chaleea bravely.

"Yes of course," waved The Fat Man, as if he were swatting away a large mosquito near his head. "Now, I'll have the remaining rupees for you all in good time. Where's King Rooster?"

Sadhu Ricki shielded his eyes, and looked at the sun. We'll bring him here at sundown this evening. Make sure you have all the money, and preparations for a few days or so with us afterwards," he said twinkling his eyes at Annapurna and Chaleea.

They got up to leave and crossed over to get me. I was right where they had left me, except I was sitting and suffering instead of standing. Nandalla had disappeared like a slithering snake.

Annapurna filled me in on the gist of the negotiations. "What the hell do we want him for? What are we going to do with him, kill him?" I was upset.

"He molested Chaleea. We should punish him."

"Are you sure that he molested Chaleea? I know something un-pleasant happened, but Chaleea never told me that."

172

"Well, put two and two together then. He's a disgusting man with no morals," she said.

"Unless Chaleea has told one of us specifically that this guy, The Fat Man, touched him where he's not supposed to, or whatever, we can't be sure," I said.

I thought for a moment. "And let's say Chaleea does in fact say that. Then what do we do? We keep him away from The Fat Man, that's what we do. We don't know what trouble we're getting ourselves into."

Annapurna was angry and confused now. "Okay let's just let him go. Do nothing. Give him an award. While Chaleea suffers for the rest of his life."

I reached out for Annapurna, touching her waist, forgetting for a moment the pain in my side. "Annapurna, these are street kids. They're tough. He'll survive."

Annapurna was emotional. She knew they couldn't go to the military police with this. It was just one powerful person's word against a street urchin's. "These kids have souls too, you know. Just because they don't have a home, doesn't mean they don't have feelings. Doesn't mean their dreams don't get crushed by a foul, filthy incident like this. I know he did it, that shit." She was almost crying now. Ironically she was homeless now too.

"Come now," Sadhu Ricki gently interrupted, "life is imperfect, and you must smile through it. We will go back to the tent to get our treasure. Two thousand rupees is a wonderfully large amount of money. Thank the Gods for the storm," he chuckled. "We don't really want The Fat Man. What would we do with him? He'd eat too much."

"You, Chaleea, you. You did an excellent job of negotiating," Sadhu Ricki said fondly. "I never dreamed we would get that much money."

"And," speaking solemnly to Annapurna, "you said what was on your mind to a powerful man. He will stop and think now. He knows he has done wrong. And we at least know to keep children away from him."

Both Chaleea and Annapurna took solace in Sadhu Ricki's words. I shuffled along at the back of our pack, which had now been joined by the same spotted puppy Chaleea had picked up before. We wound our way through the alleys in the noon sun back to the cricket field for a siesta and a visit with King Rooster.

Physically my body was calling for something to drink. Mentally I was preoccupied, thinking about Annapurna and Nandalla. I shrugged off the thought, too groggy to concentrate. After all, in less than a week, maybe I would be gone, traveling by rail and truck to Kathmandu for Christmas.

What I really should do is talk to Annapurna about why Nandalla had threatened me today, nearly squeezing the life out of me. Right now I wanted a coke in a thick, greenish, chipped glass bottle.

2

Even now, as we wandered back to Sadhu Ricki's tent, others drifted towards us heading to the Square for the festival of The Rooster Palace which was to begin tonight. These early arrivals were mostly lower caste. The merchants and the storekeepers and the bureaucrats were still at work. At nightfall all layers of society would be there to witness the vicious cock fights, to watch the spectacle of King Rooster atop The Rooster Palace, and to show-off by buying a rooster for some ungodly price.

The Babus and the Raja's tried to function as the last remaining royalty of India, vestiges of a bygone era. They showed up in old polished black and silver Rolls-Royce's left behind by the British. Or they promenaded in native luxury, women sitting ramrod straight wearing feathery silk in golden rickshaws.

In the distance Chaleea saw the aerial roots of the banyan trees above Sadhu Ricki's tent, a welcome sight on another stifling afternoon.

Shade and a cold soda were all I wanted in life right now. I was feeling giddy.

"I'll go for some soda," I said, grabbing one of Sadhu Ricki's canvas broad brimmed hats. I went in search of a street hawker, and suddenly I had a craving for a banana fritter. I was glad to have the hat to protect me from the sun, a hat which I mistakenly thought served to disguise the fact that I was a Westerner.

Aided by the sun, my mind drifted back to the States. I wondered what my friends, Travis and Jeffrey were doing back in the States, probably in Ohio or more likely at a demonstration in Washington, D.C. I yearned to see my two brothers, and my parents. I was lucky and proud that my Dad tolerated my world wanderings, even though he worked hard as a successful magazine publisher.

Usually here in India, I hadn't reminisced like this. Most days I was simply worrying about diarrhea and where the bathrooms were, or rather where a cluster of bushes were. Or I was intent on bargaining down an Indian merchant for a few rupees over a blue silk scarf, or listening to a fellow traveler on how to buy rubies cheaply in Ceylon. I pushed back my long straight hair parted in the middle, and looked down at myself. I had never been this thin. Never been this self-sufficient.

"Where's the coke, man?" I said to myself. It was noon, that was the problem. All the puchkawallas had retreated out of the sun. Two boys no taller than two feet tugged at me.

"I need something to drink," I said to them.

"Come with us," and I gladly did. I was feeling light-headed again. They brought me to a cart pushed back under the shade of a kiosk crammed with everything from matches made in India, to light bulbs and British biscuits.

A beautiful auburn-haired women wrapped in a pure white sari and a red mark of the Hindi on her forehead, sat quietly, reading a magazine about the Bombay cinema. Behind her, hanging from a wire were

175

painted political pictures for sale - of Nehru, India's first prime minister, Indira Gandhi, India's current prime minister, and the Russian leaders Lenin and Stalin.

During this quiet, languid time of the noon siesta the beguiling woman was left in charge of the soda carts. I haggled for three cokes, and bought a box of tea biscuits of which they had numerous varieties. I ripped into them immediately and started munching. I didn't realize how hungry I was. And now thirsty. When she looked up again from her magazine, I asked the woman if she didn't mind if I shared her shade to drink one coke.

"Of course, it's no problem" she said. I sat down on a folding chair and drank.

3

Back at Sadhu Ricki's tent the others napped except for Chaleea who was feeling guilty about stealing the hen. He made a quick dash within range of King Rooster and grabbed the near-lifeless hen, ripping her frayed leather leash apart. No eggs yet he thought. He slid the hen a bowl of water and she pecked at it. He wrapped a damp cloth over her head so she couldn't see and that calmed and cooled her as he carried her back to her dusty neighborhood off Kings Road. He felt better already, undoing his theft.

When Chaleea walked back across the cricket field, I was weaving towards him, waving my shirt, a bit unsteady. Probably a combination of the sun and the pills and my cracked ribs.

"Thank God for these blessed trees," I said as Chaleea helped me gingerly sit against the trunk keeping a baleful eye on King Rooster, who like us, had absolutely no intention to move a feather in this heat.

Chaleea sat next to me. "Sahib, Mr. Jack, are you all right? You shouldn't be walking in the noon heat."

I nodded, breathing shallow quick breaths, and handed Chaleea one of my prize cokes. Chaleea generously gave me the last swig. We sat listlessly until our eyes fell on the motionless beast, King Rooster.

Chaleea asked. "What is he thinking?"

King Rooster was a glorious sight, and he knew it. His breast was broad with scars that only enhanced his image of a hardened warrior. His killing claws protruded from shanks the size of a man's ankle. Bony spurs like armaments projected from the back above the orange claws.

We could only guess whether The Fat Man would attach sharpened metal blades to the spurs, so that he sliced up his opponent when he kicked. Metal spurs, or gaffs, were supposedly illegal in the ancient sport of cockfighting. With a gamecock this size you probably didn't need those killing slashers.

XXI

The Procession

Sadhu Ricki appeared from inside his tent, giving Annapurna time alone to dress for tonight's grand rooster festival. Sadhu Ricki's hair and beard were carefully combed and greased, and he wore his cleanest bright orange robe. Chaleea wore a pair of my rolled-up blue-jeans, which were prized by the ever Westward leaning youth of India.

When Annapurna emerged the three us stopped talking and stared. She was after all a young woman and she looked heavenly, wearing a long blue and white sari falling to just above new leather sandals which wound up around her calves. She had tied one of Sadhu Ricki's gold scarves around the Sari and her slim waist. What stopped us though was the olive skin of her shoulders and neck which was plainly visible because she had put her hair up in a barrette. She knew she was walking the edge of breaking Indian customs, but for this festival, she was willing to take the risk, and beside it was cooler. She had the long graceful neck of a young swan, and once we stopped gawking, we complimented her.

"You're trying to outshine King Rooster," began Sadhu Ricki with a broad generous smile.

"Annapurna, you look beautiful," I said. I had the most to lose or gain in a relationship with her, and I was verbally clumsy.

Chaleea simply said "Wow," and Annapurna gave him a big hug while I twinged with a touch of awkward jealousy.

She radiated confidence and appreciated the compliments, particularly because she knew they were spontaneous.

"Onward," said Sadhu Ricki as he clapped his hands together signaling the start of our procession to the festival. Chaleea and I carefully attached another rope to the neck of King Rooster.

Chaleea, meanwhile, knowing how well his wet cloth had worked as a hood to calm and cool the hen, was wetting down a black towel with a hole for the beak to place over King Rooster's head. Chaleea and I each wore a tattered leather glove. Sadhu Ricki held the two ropes for us, like the reins of a horse, and stared down the rooster while singing his morning chant. King Rooster stood transfixed as if hypnotized, while Chaleea and I tossed the black make-shift hood over King Rooster's dazzling crown. King Rooster even seemed to bob his head downwards to help us line up the hole with his beak.

Sadhu Ricki ceased his chanting and holding a blond cane, assumed the lead position. Our procession was ready. Behind him, ten feet back, walked princess Annapurna, a dazzling and daring cross between Indian and Western cultures, who would make the younger Raja's salivate. The older, ruling Raja's would outwardly voice disapproval while looking wistfully upon her and inwardly coveting her. Directly twenty feet behind her, King Rooster strutted at the center of our parade with thick ropes out to either side held taught by Chaleea and me.

As soon as our procession crossed the cricket field, street beggars tagged along sensing the beginnings of something. Sadhu Ricki became serious, and in Hindi warned them to keep back, not to touch, that the rooster was valuable and violent. With King Rooster held at bay stretched between us, our procession took up the entire width of the side streets. To prevent from being trampled and to allow this procession, strange even by Calcutta standards, to pass by, the street merchants closing up their shops were pressed back to the walls and the women selling pistachio nuts and Beede cigarettes on the red blankets were forced to unbend and unfold from their squatting positions. The black towel serving as a hood over King Rooster's head accentuated the demonic quality that his immense size evoked.

The storekeepers murmured that our procession was a genuine event. Something exciting and unplanned was happening around them, which is why many villagers had come from the poverty of countryside to the poverty of the city -- just to escape the repetitive boredom, and partake in the activity and uncertainty of a once proud city. This too was one reason why Annapurna and I had traveled to such a chaotic land. The youth of the West yearned for the unpredictable and the unplanned, so alluring to the young in the short run, and so deadly to a society over time.

Our procession marched onward. And even Sadhu Ricki with his sense of ritual had not envisioned the crowd and the uproar that would surround us. Bengali's stirred from their somnambulant afternoon state to witness our passage. We formed the magical arrowhead of a slow-moving, ever-lengthening spear, our serpentine tail growing in numbers at every tiny intersection as the gawkers and hawkers joined in behind King Rooster to see how close to him they could get.

As our primordial procession neared the Square, the crowds thickened. News of the King Rooster's arrival preceded us. Realizing that we were really part of a parade now, Annapurna and Sadhu Ricki, Chaleea and I adjusted our outfits and took a last look at ourselves before coming within sight of The Rooster Palace and entering the Square.

I felt dizzy. I wasn't sure if my feeling of faintness was the pain of my ribs resurfacing or just too much action too soon. In my pocket I had one round lemon-drop-like morphine pill left, and I popped it into my mouth.

As we turned the final corner, the way narrowed and the crowd thickened and threatened, pushing inward. Some in the crowd tossed yellow and pink flowers, hoping the pedals would land on the tail feathers of the towering rooster, and then symbolically they too would be center stage in the festival of The Rooster Palace. By having had the good luck of tossing what touched King Rooster, maybe their fortunes would change.

Up front, Sadhu Ricki stood straight and searched across the crammed Square for The Fat Man. Using his piercing eyes, Sadhu man saw him sitting on his Kashmir throne made of silver birch next to his mammoth prized cage of twisted vines, curled branches and bamboo - with the door propped wide open, waiting for King Rooster. Beyond the cage, a head taller, stood Nandalla with his powerful arms crossed over his hairy brown chest.

Chaleea was wondering how and when The Fat Man would pay us the other 1000 rupees. The Fat Man was dressed in a long dark brown robe, looking like a monk or an executioner. A gouge and two sharp knifes for cutting and shaping the bamboo and vines, hung from his belt. As our procession was halfway across the Square, the sound of flutes and drums began, and those in the crowd with enough space to move, waved their hands above their heads while twirling their bodies.

The dancing, surging crowd pushed in closer, unstoppable and relentless like a rising tide, and Annapurna began to fear for herself. Hands of smiling, eager Indian men, both Hindu and Moslem, reached out to her, their eyes wide at seeing so much of a woman's skin, her shoulders, her neck, the beginnings of the curves and cleavage of her breasts. She hesitated, lost her regal composure, and raised one arm to pull the top of her sari higher. With that gesture the men went wild and the women grew nasty, yelling curses at her.

Sadhu Ricki sensed what was happening behind him, but could do nothing. He knew if he broke ranks their arrowhead shape would be destroyed and the crowd would engulf all of them. I was concentrating on keeping the throng from closing in and panicking King Rooster.

From The Fat Man's throne, Nandalla was watching like a hawk above a valley. He was driven by Annapurna's beauty and daring and their provocative history together. He knew the crowds were growing dangerously unpredictable. The men closest to Annapurna were pushed against her by the masses behind struggling to get a glimpse of this Western nymph. Annapurna stared straight ahead and tried to keep moving.

Finally she shrieked, "Stop it. Stop it." The men up front tried to obey, but they were getting squeezed and flattened by the waves of humanity behind them.

Nandalla moved. He didn't call out any warnings. With long strides he shoved through the crowd, knocking children and women left and right like puny, unworthy wrestling opponents. He didn't care. He hardly noticed the contact. A few fortunate ones saw him coming and somehow got out of his way.

Annapurna was being swallowed by the giddy masses while Sadhu Ricki was engulfed but calm. He just let the crowd carry him whichever way they wanted. Was this disaster? He didn't know. At one point both his feet were off the ground, as the surging men pressed around him and through friction held him up off the ground.

Nandalla nodded in recognition of Sadhu Ricki before he charged through the rabble to scoop up Annapurna from the sandy, earthen Square as she was about to be trampled. He tossed her over his broad shoulder, where she hung limply. Thinking clearly, like a Gurkha general in the midst of battle, he now yelled to Chaleea to follow him and bring King Rooster to The Fat Man's throne. One shoulder down, Nandalla led like a battering ram. Our procession tucked in behind him, as he forced his way to the smooth circular stones beneath the throne and

King Rooster's waiting cage. We could see Annapurna floating above the crowd on Nandalla's shoulder like a damsel carried to the altar to be sacrificed in a pre-Aryan ritual to the god Kali.

King Rooster's composure snapped on the final push to the cage, and anyone that brushed him got a brutal clawed kick or in one case a vicious peck that opened a fallen woman's bottom left cheek. Chaleea and I fought with the ropes tugging the rooster forward, choking him when we both pulled hard in opposite directions.

The raised stone Square where The Fat Man reigned was still clear of the masses, kept that way by his guards and servants. The Fat Man watched the debacle with sinister appreciation, and quietly tucked away the remaining 1000 rupees, the fee he would charge them for saving their lives.

With too many bodies too close to him, King Rooster was fighting off panic, though still able to kick and slash in a controlled fashion, sensing that now was not the time for desperate ferocity. One man though, fell underfoot and fell victim to the full weight of the rooster, his chest and lungs punctured by King Rooster's claws.

Even from afar Nandalla was recognized by the dispossessed of the streets. He was one of their leaders, their Nehru. As he carried the creamy white Annapurna over his broad shoulders, her dress waving valiantly, a cluster of his followers started to yell, Nan-Dal-A, Nan-Dal-A. Soon like rolling thunder, the thousands in the Square took up the chant, Nandalla! Nandalla! When he strode up on the primitive stage, he gently placed her on a large stone used for crushing grain, while a servant slid a straw cushion under her head for a pillow.

"Get her some water," The Fat Man commanded. Nandalla then postured, and much like after his most decisive wins in wrestling, after a takedown and pin from the neutral position, with the opponent lying prostrate and wounded, he exalted, held both arms high, looked in all directions, and responded to the crowd by thrusting his arms triumphantly to the rhythmic beat of Nan-Dal-A, Nan-Dal-A.

XXII

The Final Stage

Though Sadhu Ricki was physically tired, he maintained his poise and with delicate deliberateness sat down next to The Fat Man. Keeping in mind his religious stature, albeit self-appointed, Sadhu Ricki was determined to be the serenity at the center of a storm. The Fat Man munched on dusty blue grapes while watching King Rooster through puffy eyes. He spat out the seeds on the minions below. Finally Chaleea and I struggled up the stone steps with our frayed ropes and our monster bird in tow.

Using long bamboo poles, The Fat Man's servants guided and prodded the prehistoric King Rooster towards his cage. With his beak, King Rooster snapped off the end of a bamboo pole a servant poked too close to his eye. The nervous servant stepped backwards, and to the uproarious delight of the crowd, fell off the stone stage. The moment of entering the cage was the only time King Rooster showed any hesitation, not knowing whether to resist or submit. Ultimately the cage was safer than the crowd, and King Rooster made a show of entering of his own free will.

King Rooster stamped his claws in the cage. From his menacing beak hung his black hood torn to shreds. Chaleea and I were near collapse. We looked around for assurance that our task was complete and it was safe to let go of our guide ropes. The vine and bamboo door had yet to be shut.

For the first time The Fat Man stood. He ceremoniously unfastened the longer knife hanging by his waist, and with no outward show of fear, reached in the cage up to the neck of the beast. The crowd hushed, not sure of what was going to happen.

While staring hypnotically into King Rooster's eyes, he skillfully slid the knife under King Rooster's leather collar, with the glistening blade facing outwards, and yanked back, splitting the collar the ropes were tied to it. Chaleea and I pulled the remnants of our ropes out from the cage, and two handlers quickly closed the door. They kept their eyes on the rooster and his beak and tied the door shut. The crowd responded with a growing cry of King Roos-ster, King Roos-ster, King Roos-ster - which smothered the remains of their chant for Nandalla.

In a rare show of his crooked yellow teeth, Nandalla grinned from ear to ear, basking in the scene. The Fat Man sat, pleased with himself. Annapurna rubbed the cool stone with her fingers, conscious but bruised. Chaleea and I wearily stayed by her side. Chaleea took his shirt off to cover Annapurna's bare shoulders, and made sure her sari was smoothed out, covering her legs down to her ankles.

As the noise from the crowd subsided, those of us on the stage heard a hissing sound, like the return of the great winds after the eye of a typhoon had passed. The hissing was King Rooster inhaling . . . in preparation. King Rooster cocked his head and let go the loudest crowing ever heard in Calcutta. "Cock a doodle doooo. Cock a doodle doooo!" trumpeted the grand bird. The crowd was stunned and then responded with wild cheers and wild dancing. This was a bird for all times. King Roos-ster! King Roos-ster!

I needed water and was suffering from the resurfacing pain of my ribs. Chaleea's youthful energy had revived, and after a whispering plea from me, he was about to dart away to find some water. But before he went to leap off the stage, Nandalla reached out with a long arm and grabbed him by his billowy pants, nodded knowingly to The Fat Man and his servants, and told Chaleea to ask them for water. Chaleea was silent, then crossed his arms over his own small pounding chest, and shook his head no. He would have nothing to do with The Fat Man.

Nandalla knew that if they used The Fat Man's local power and position, they would have quick access to pure and cool water. Nandalla released his grip and told Chaleea to sit for a moment. He motioned to one of The Fat Man's servants, and in English asked for a large cup of water for me, the Sahib.

Since the request came from Nandalla, the response was "Certainly." With a snappy little bow the servant turned to another servant waiting behind the blowing silk curtains leading to the labyrinth of paths and rooms of The Fat Man's tent-like domain, and repeated the request in Hindi to bring some water for me, the Sahib. Nandalla had successfully circumvented The Fat Man, and gotten his water without insulting the admirable boyish pride of Chaleea. Restraining myself, I at first sipped, and then gulped down the cup of water, with the servant standing over me.

"Another one, please, is that possible?" I asked.

"Yes, of course, we have plenty of water," he chuckled. He snapped his fingers. His gesture was relayed through a chain of servants until another large yellowish ceramic cup of water appeared from behind the silk curtains.

I held the organic looking vessel in two hands, admiring it and its contents, and took another long refreshing drink, and then passed the heavy cup to Annapurna, who sipped silently, and finally to Chaleea who begrudgingly drank. Sadhu Ricki did not drink. He sat cross-legged, his back upright, his eyes closed, meditating.

The crowd grew less raucous, taking time to gab among themselves, call out to friends, giggle and in general enjoy one of the more notable and unpredictable of the many festivals of Calcutta.

A servant brought out a large black linen sheet which he hung on one side of the Rooster's cage, and then another servant appeared with another black linen cloth until each side was covered and darkened. Between the bamboo bars of the cage, a servant with thick leather gloves, slid a tall thin canister of water for King Rooster, along with an odd-shaped bowl of grain. Everyone was refueling and resting.

In the background the mountainous pyramid of all the lesser roosters, possibly sensing their opportunity to be the focus of the festival, started to crow and sway, and beat their wings against their cages; such that the entire seven story pyramid looked like it might come apart, with cages flying and falling everywhere. The roosters knew something was afoot. Never before had so many thousands of humans gathered about their pyramid. Even the feeble, scrawny roosters at the center of the pyramid, barely able to see any light, covered with droppings from the others, occasional trickles of life-sustaining water filtering through, stumbled and raised up in their coffin-like cages, to throw out weakened crows to add to the cacophony of the festival of the Rooster Palace.

XXIII

The Furious Festival

The pyramid rumbled and swayed, while the tottering yet still revered royalty of India, the Babus, made their way through the Square. Their procession consisted of two 1948 blue Rolls-Royces, and three carriages followed by rickshaw wallahs pulling the young plump princesses, all of whom had come to watch and bid on the roosters. The presence of King Rooster had drawn out the old guard as well, tucked in the back seats of the Rolls and the Carriages - leathery skinned old men of wisdom who had never done a day of physical labor except in their younger years when making love to their concubines. They were beyond that now, and clung desperately to their station in life, much like the city itself, which knew it had seen better days.

A festival like this turned the clock back. A true attraction, a beast from the country, could draw the myriad distinct yet interwoven societies of India together. A captured man-eating Royal Bengali Tiger of the Sunderbans might have been the equivalent attraction of King Rooster in the colonial days. But the feared tigers were rarely seen anymore, and hunting them was banned and punishable by a public whipping.

King Rooster was a superior replacement, a fine aberration of nature, which Calcutta, a city that thrived on excesses, embraced. In every conversation the chatter in the crowd was about King Rooster.

"Do you believe me now? He's huge, isn't he?" said one man near me with a silver turban.

"My friend, he's a dinosaur," his companion answered, clapping his hands above his head, because he couldn't clap them elsewhere; everyone was so squished together.

Nandalla stood over Annapurna and put a comforting hand on her shoulder. She looked up at him and smiled weakly. She was a aware that from him, a gentle, consoling gesture was rare.

I watched their brief exchange and when a pang of jealousy lingered in my gut, I grew annoyed with myself. What right have I to be jealous, I thought. I don't own her. In my mind I was swept back to the bliss of our night at the edge of the jungle, and it occurred to me that she was really the one making the sweet unspoken decisions of love.

With a furrowed brow and growing desire, I raised my head to look again at Annapurna, who was slowly reviving. Nandalla had released her hand from his and stood tall surveying the crowd. Like a general overseeing his camped army, his political self rose once again to the forefront.

I felt doomed and tired, dizzy with aching ribs, and slid towards the one other risk-taking American. She reached her hand out to mine as I moved closer. Touching hands was heavenly. I was awakened and delighted by the notion that she wanted me closer. I pictured her always brimming with confidence, picking and attracting men, the way wild flowers attract bees.

But Annapurna too was having her doubts about her life, and was losing her way in Native Town. She was trying to grasp on to some muddled picture of her future. But instead she saw nothing. She reluctantly concluded that Nandalla was a lingering and now passing storm, a typhoon of swirling hostilities that was part of her adventure.

The two of us sat huddled side by side while Nandalla and The Fat Man argued in terse phrases, each careful not to overtly threaten the security of the other, but each wanting to gain something from this grand opening ceremony of theirs. Perhaps Nandalla wanted to turn the festival into another political rally. They were dueling with words rather than swords, knowing that when darkness fell each had the power of physical reprisals; Nandalla through his secret cell of Naxalites and The Fat Man through control of most of his servants. I saw that Nandalla was not afraid of anyone even Ali Kahn, The Fat Man. The only time I saw Nandalla show some caution was when the soldiers appeared, and then he simply disappeared.

Nandalla despised the indolent wealth of the decadent Maharaja's, though he risked alienating the masses, who still respected the Maharaja's historic role in Indian society. He had secretly placed his cell of Naxalite followers throughout the crowd, waiting on his orders to strike at any symbol of colonial British dominance of India.

The Fat Man, on the other hand, was calculating the best way to make the largest profit. He was debating whether or not to stage cockfights, or haul King Rooster to the top of the pyramid and then auction him off to the highest bidder. His problem was he didn't know what gamecock to put against the King. Though King Rooster hadn't been bred for battle, The Fat Man was positive King Rooster's size alone would assure victory.

With The Fat Man and Nandalla sparring, Sadhu Ricki sensed an opening, an opportunity, and for the first time rose silently from the stones. The crowd nearest him quieted. His orange rob still commanded a certain respect as a genuine religious man among the rabble. Sadhu Ricki was revived and centered after his twenty minutes of meditation.

Next to him Chaleea stood straight with a serious look on his face, amazed that he was here in the center of this grand gathering, strong with flames of anger in his eyes when he glared at The Fat Man.

The peculiar forces of this Rooster festival of Cal were all accounted for. Annapurna and I, two adventurous Westerners, were attempting to meld into the Bengali society of Calcutta, while the two power brokers of the riffraff of the city, Nandalla, the political anarchist, and The Fat Man, the decadent entrepreneur, were competing. Lastly Sadhu Ricki, representing revered religious street-traditions of India, was protecting and teaching the naive yet wise-beyond-his-age street urchin, Chaleea.

Annapurna and I were sitting back to back, supporting and warming each other. If one moved beyond a sway the other would fall. Even in this evening heat, I had become chilled from my fever brought on by broken ribs and an eye-popping squeeze from Nandalla. I was comforted by the closeness of Annapurna, and it brought me back to our touching everywhere our night together in the jungle.

I silently drifted back to my first feelings of love for a girl. I was dreaming of home and a lost innocence and a lost first love. I reached up to my face and with the back of my hand, wiped the smallest of tears from my eyes. Time to return to the present. Forcing a smile I thought here I am back to back, having been belly to belly, with a young American woman wiser and tougher than I.

In a way, I knew it was my greatest strength, the ability to be consumed by the present, and I was working on that right now, like a good present-day, going-to-have-some-fun, American. I was reviving. I waved for one of the servants to bring more water. The servant dutifully returned with a yellow cup. I sipped some and then slid the cup behind me on the stone floor to Annapurna.

"Have some" I whispered. She did, and slid the glass back. But instead of reaching for the cup, I surprised myself and reached beyond for her hand. I pressed my hand over hers, and turned my head to her cheek. I whispered, "Together?"

Annapurna stayed quiet, but she turned slightly to look at me. She held my hand, thankful for the touch, glad that I cared for her, feeling vulnerable herself. Rather than answering she held onto my hand turning it over in hers, rubbing my one callous with her finger. "Your hand is like the cushioned paw of a baby tiger. I like the feel of your hand."

He answer was better than a simple yes. Annapurna needed to like hands that caressed her. She knew that these hands would touch her again if she wanted. She was inspecting them, lovingly, for my hands had touched and penetrated her.

Sounding far away, she told me she had decided she was an American at heart. Lazily scanning the crowd, she said aloud to herself, "It has been a wonderful experience." She looked upwards at Nandalla who looked at her with a feeling of abstract disdain. Drained of emotion, Annapurna thought simply, I am who I am. What she didn't realize was that Nandalla was transforming himself. He was gearing up for a long awaited wrestling match; he was steeling himself for a deed for the cause - for the Naxalite formula of anarchy and then Communism.

Night was falling. Matches were struck. Thousands of candles ringed the Square. The Fat Man gathered his servants and handlers around and decreed that before the auction and the crowning of The Rooster Palace, he must entertain the people with a cockfight.

Turning to his handlers and placers he said, "Prepare the pit here," pointing to where Annapurna and I sat back to back. "Climb for two nine-pounders bred to fight to the end," he commanded.

The placers dashed off, arguing about which gamecocks to bring back. They huddled near the base of the pyramid and put on thick leather gloves and strapped strips of leather around their ankles. As they climbed the cages roosters would be pecking at their hands and ankles.

The climbers' hearts were beating fast, like the drums of the tribal villages some of them had come from. The pyramid was ringed with fiery, illuminating torches. This was time to show their skill and daring. From the stone stage, in the flickering darkness, Sadhu Ricki began to play a high pitched, haunting tune on his flute. The birds of the pyramid and the people of the Square cocked their heads. Two placers began to climb up the bamboo corners of the cages, headed for near the top and the healthiest birds. They squinted, holding their torches in one hand grabbing the cages in the other, searching for the roosters with the longest spurs, the sharp bony spines on their ankles which were their fighting weapons.

Two of the most experienced placers, Singha and his partner climbed skyward. "Singha" one called to the other in a British accent, "Where are those pugnacious two we took in yesterday? The ones from Madras."

"Watch out, or you will fall!" the other warned. Then they both turned to look out over the crowd. It was like a restless army bedded down for the night, and now these two handlers were the attraction. All eyes were raised to them, and the hushed noise of the crowd was like a distant train, comforting and alarming at the same time.

Singha felt proud, and turned to climb higher. He reached too far with his right hand and his grip on the corner bamboo wasn't solid. A rooster immediately pecked away at it. Singha slipped. He instinctively flattened out against the cages, and was forced to drop his torch and grab a vine with his other hand. The torch ricocheted down off the cages like an errant comet, and the crowd gasped, leaning forward as one and then pulling back when the torch scattered its flames on impact, quickly lighting a small fire. Just as quickly, the other handlers danced around on the matted hay stamping out the fire. The crowd clapped as if the two climbers were a high-wire, circus act.

Singha was panting but inspired. "Climb next to me. I need the light of your torch." Together they climbed higher, resting maybe ten feet below the summit, knowing the cages at the top were the least stable and the most likely to topple. "He will do. This is one of the birds from yesterday."

Singha grabbed the torch from his partner and thrust it inside the cage at the rooster, who made a ruckus and backed up into a corner.

Singha saw that the rooster's fiery red comb had been trimmed, cut back; a sign that he had been trained for fighting. "We have one," he yelled down.

Out of the darkness below a group of handlers tossed up a hemp rope, which the other climber caught and relayed to Singha. He tied the rope onto the corner of the cage by the one knot they both knew wouldn't slip, an Indian version of the climber's bowline with two half hitches, and then yanked the cage outward while they held onto the other cage, praying the top of the pyramid didn't collapse. Two cages above toppled into the opening and a third teetered outward, but the pyramid held.

The cage with the pugnacious gamecock sporting the trimmed comb, tumbled downward as they let out sections of slack in the rope. Once at the base, servants opened the cage, and a designated handler for the cockfight looked over his bird, firmly but gently grabbing him out of the cage. He began to massage its body in preparation for the cock-fight.

Up on top, the two climbers winked at each other. One down and one to go they thought. Singha and his acrobatic partner dangled out into the airy darkness with their flickering torch, putting on a show for the crowd below. They leaned back into the smelly tangle of cages, like the impenetrable under growth of the jungle, and searched for the tell-tale longer spurs of the natural fighter. In the teetering cage they found just such a bird, perhaps another bird from the province of Madras.

"Send it down," Singha said.

"But we don't have a rope," his partner replied.

Eyeing the caged rooster, the prideful handlers spread apart about two yards, and together they jerked the teetering cage from the rest. Singha kicked out with his right foot where a rooster had bitten through the leather and blood was trickling down between his toes. Singha knew he could not lower the cage and hold the torch at the same time. Deciding to add to the aura of the spectacle, Singha tossed the torch straight out into the night air, arching well out into the crowd, like a flaming arrow, causing a great commotion but no injuries when it landed. Tier by tier, their outstretched arms aching, Singha and his partner began lowering the cage in the darkness. The two sweaty, sinewy Indian workers fell into a speechless, awkward rhythm lifting the cage out and down over each terraced outcropping of cages. They were at home now, their eyes adjusting to the blackness, feeling for firmness with hands and feet the way rock climbers do. Slowly, they descended, their confidence up.

But blood covered the bottom of Singha's foot from his cut ankle, and half way down he slipped again. To save himself he had to let go of the cage. Gallantly, his partner tried to hang on, swinging the cage and its rooster beneath him like a monkey with a prize. But he couldn't hold, and yelled down "Cage!"

The handlers below knew not to look up and with their heads down scattered. It wasn't the first cage to fall from The Rooster Palace. The cage smashed into the stones, pieces of vine, rope and bamboo exploding in all directions as the rooster sprung upward, momentarily free. One of the handlers quickly swooped up the rooster and put a gloved hand over its head to calm him. To protect himself, the handler clutched tightly at the bird's spurred heals.

Now both gamecocks were brought over to be hosed down in water. The roosters liked the cleansing shower; strutted about afterwards, flapping their wings, pleased at the attention and the open space, but wondering what was next?

Like everybody else, Annapurna and I had been gazing skyward, watching the search for cockfighting rivals. In the spirit of the festival, we pushed against each other back to back and rose up without using our hands, rather proud of our nifty stunt which was witnessed by the young Indian men up front, who giggled and smiled, all eyes on Annapurna. She made sure her shawl covered her bare shoulders and stood dutifully next to me.

Two servants shinnied up wooden, electric poles to install two floodlights, and everybody clapped when they were turned on. Other servants descended on the area where we had been sitting and unfurled the largest woven carpet I had ever seen. Around the edges they placed heavy flat field stones side by side. The design in the center of the carpet looked like a blossoming red rose surrounded by pink jasmine and had a luminous quality.

While I was marveling at the glowing design, Annapurna covered her mouth with her hand and said to me. "Do you see the red at the edges? Those are bloodstains."

One man politely warned us, "You're going to be in the way."

From farther back someone shouted, "Get down, get down."

Annapurna and I moved off into the shadows, unsure of where to go. We hesitated, then I plunged down into the crowd, wincing, squeezing myself into the front lines, repeating, "I'm sorry, I'm sorry." I nudged the Indian men away creating a space for us and turned and held my arms up, motioning for Annapurna to jump off the stone platform. She was fearful of reentering the masses, afraid again of the dark brown gleaming eyes of the men.

But there was no choice. The rug for the cockfighting pit was in place, the handlers or pitters were in their corners, and the crowd was eager and restless. She let herself fall into my shaky arms.

In our weakened state, the two of us packed together was unnerving yet comforting. The Bengalis in dear old Cal took for granted the state of being pressed together with strangers; they had no choice. Lines and crowds and lack of privacy were a way of life. I often wondered where and when couples found the space and time to kiss, to make out, to make love.

XXIV

The Cock Fight

The Fat Man rose and one of his servants handed him a mega-phone. Even with the amplification, The Fat Man realized most of the spectators in the Square beyond the front rows could not hear him, so he exaggerated his gestures as he spoke. Like watching a pantomime, the crowd was able to read him.

Two handlers carefully untethered one of the blindfolded fighters, and held the rooster up above their heads. Torches all around illumi-nated the bird as The Fat Man bellowed, "See, my countrymen no gaffs have been added." pointing at the bird's long natural spurs. "No metal spurs. These birds are strong natural fighters." The handlers put down the one rooster and picked up the other, pointing again to the long natural spurs, a sign of a true fighting cock. These spurs were the bony sharp spines on the legs the gamecock used in fighting, much like Mu-hammed Ali used his jab, drawing blood with repeated hits. "These are big roosters. Nine pound gamecocks," blustered The Fat Man.

Two large Indian pitters, one with a red cape, the other with yellow cape, each removed the black hood from their fighter, and tied the same color kerchief as their cape around their rooster's hackle. Briefly, the crowd forgot about their monster, King Rooster, at the darkened back edge of the stage, tense, in a shrouded black cage big enough for The Fat Man himself.

"I don't want to see this," said Annapurna, crossing her arms.

"Let's just wait a minute. I've never seen a cockfight before." I slid my arm around her waist. "We're trapped here anyway."

The entourages stepped back and crouched near the far corner of the stage. The two pitters, the two fighting cocks, and The Fat Man stayed center stage. The Fat Man held a brass copper gong in one hand and a padded mallet in the other. He circled the stage, and began a rhythmic beating, slowly and then faster.

Heads of strangers inches from ours struggled to get a better view of the birds, and off in shadows at the base of The Rooster Palace, daring youngsters climbed the first tier of cages to get a view of the contest. Everybody jabbered, smiled, and shouted, shoving their rupees back and forth. The betting enhanced the excitement. Fearful of pickpockets, I instinctively padded my passport and money hanging around my neck.

The gamecocks writhed in the gloved hands of the pitters, who held them a foot apart face to face. The roosters were bobbing and thrusting their heads, lifting their hocks to free their kicking shanks with their bony spurs. When the birds were bursting with fear and aggression and the crowd was pumped up and riveted to the stage, and all bets on the yellow rooster or the red rooster had been placed, The Fat Man ceased his drumming and the cocks were unleashed.

They whirled around each other colliding in a tumultuous ball of flying feet and feathers, both birds screaming and hissing. They kicked and clawed fast and hard and neither gave ground. At first bits, and then chunks of skin and feathers hit those in the front rows.

Even though fighting to the death was forbidden by the government, this was a night to defy the government. There was no time limit and a pitter could not withdraw a badly injured cock, as was usually the case. The fight would last until one was killed.

The wheat-colored rug surrounding the flowered center was now covered with drops of blood. The red rooster rose up and pecked away at the trimmed comb of the other, trying to crack the skull and smash the brain. The worried pitter for the yellow bird, peered into the flickering shadows for The Fat Man. His bird was getting the worst of it, and he wanted to pull him out while he was still alive.

Instinctively the yellow bird fought to get out from underneath the deadly pecking of his red rival. Somehow the frantic yellow bird escaped upright. Anticipating the red rooster's instant charge to finish yellow off, yellow spun around and leg-whipped high, aiming for the head of red. Yellow's spur caught the dilated eye of red, taking its sight away with that one swipe.

The crowd roared its approval. Yellow had come back with a fighting vengeance and a well placed roundhouse kick which had equalized what had started to be a one-sided match. The red cock seemed bewildered and off balance, his eye ball dangling from his eye socket. The yellow cock was bleeding and severely dazed from his own head wound.

"I'm leaving," said Annapurna firmly. But leaving wasn't that easy. She could barely turn, and when she did her face was inches away from the faces of gawking strangers.

"Jack," she said, with a do-something tone of voice. Now that the cockfight was in progress, no one was looking at her. Instead they were trying to get a look at the killer roosters. The Fat Man had stepped from the shadows into the pit to act as referee. The wounded birds were circling.

For protection, I kept one arm bent firmly beside my rib cage, clasped Annapurna's shaking hand, turned sideways, put one shoulder down and drove through the crowd. People yelled at us, but only because we were in their way and they couldn't see. In some cases, lighter boys were sitting atop the shoulders of bigger boys, many of them having never seen a cockfight.

The farther back we pushed the less crowded it became. Soon we came upon the normalcy of street vendors selling peanuts, and women with their scrawny deformed babies, begging for rupees. We passed them by, thankful that in the darkness we were not easily distinguishable.

Almost running Annapurna led me blindly onward. A hoarse groan went up from the crowd. I turned around, and above the heads of the crowd, in the center of the two floodlights, The Fat Man held the red rooster above him, dripping blood from a now empty eye socket, looking like the pitless half of an avocado, but still alive and the winner.

Annapurna cast not a glance. She was headed back to her ruined apartment at the edge of the Square, hundreds of yards from the stone stage. Some waifs from the street were up there, sitting on the slanted floor, legs dangling where a wall had been, smoking Beedes cupped in their hands, inhaling through the crack between their thumb and forefinger.

Annapurna leaned up against the cool pink plaster wall in the courtyard below and looked up at the cluster of street urchins casually rummaging through the remains of her apartment. She wasn't angry at them, but she felt violated. Then she thought of all the locals, the Bengali's who year after year had to recover from tragedies. How did they do it? Maybe that was part of the reason they were so fatalistic and accepting of their own misery.

I was stirred from inside by the frenzy of the cockfight. I put my hand on Annapurna's neck, and gently brought her head towards mine. She saw the quiet determination in my steely blue eyes and guessed what I was up to. Right away I knew she was thinking now is not the time. She let me kiss her, and lingered out of fatigue, not out of any quiescent passion.

"Please, not now," she whispered to me. "Let's go up," motioning to her demolished apartment. "We can watch from there, where we're no longer center stage." Or so she thought.

A lull on the stone stage set in after the cockfight. The loser was put in an empty burlap sack which once contained grain. A group of Untouchables waited around back. The yellow handler tossed the bag to them with its dead, brutalized rooster in it. After a brief tug of war between two clothed skeletons, one ran off with it. Within hours, every bit of that once glorious gamecock would be cooked and eaten, probably serving a family of eight living in a field on the Maidan.

I squinted through the gray darkness and wondered what was next. I could still make out Sadhu Ricki and Chaleea side by side, on the edge of the stones, observing. I wondered about Chaleea, and how he would react once again to being right there with The Fat Man.

The Fat Man stood with his arms outstretched while his handlers swept the carpeted stone pit clear of blood and feathers and bits of flesh. Two men bent over the red rooster and smeared some sort of salve in the eye socket, tilting their heads and shrugging their shoulders when asked if the bird would survive.

XXV

Nandalla Strikes the Maharaja

Behind the bulk of the crushing crowd, over near the street hawkers, the chauffeur of the old right-hand drive Rolls tapped on his horn. It was a distinct tinny sound from the British era, and many in the crowd stopped talking to listen. The chauffeur kept honking at the command of his Maharaja in the cracked, leather back seat.

This particular Raja enhanced his wealth long ago with gold enshrouded in legend. Reptilian-like army ants can be found in remote parts of West Bengal, and it is believed that underneath the large ant hill mounds, lies gold. The Raja's servants dug up much of his gold from beneath the ant hills, and, in the process, the ferocious army ants, some a foot long, would sting and bite the servants.

The wrinkled, wealthy Raja in the back of the Rolls wore some of that gold for the festival. His chauffeur carried a pistol, licensed by the army whom his master supported with periodic cocktail parties for the commanders at his garden mansion on the banks of the Hooghly River.

Wearing a white turban and a large gold nugget pin in the knot, the Maharaja of Cooch Behar leaned forward and commanded his chauffeur to tell The Fat Man to begin the auction. The chauffeur dutifully nodded his head, opened the wood-paneled door, gracefully got out as he had a thousand times before, and locked the Rolls behind him. Radiating regal presence, he strode towards the stage to deliver his master's message.

The Fat Man was well aware of what the wealthy aristocratic clients in the audience wanted. They wanted to bid on King Rooster and display their wealth and presence to the masses. Besides that, they wanted an event which would make for grand stories in the parlour rooms.

While the chauffeur was on his mission, four lieutenants of the Indian Army who had kept well back from the main throng, circled slowly around the Rolls, inspecting it.

The Maharaja rolled down the window and in a raspy voice called the tallest over. Inexplicably, the tall soldier found himself bowing slightly to the old aristocrat. As a boy that's what he was taught - to defer to royalty. The old Raja handed him four, hundred-rupee notes and said, "If this crowd gets unruly, I want your protection." The Raja slipped the rolled bills into the soldier's hand without fanfare or hesitation.

When asking a favor, when you wanted a specific result, money was expected. The soldier clicked his heels together, bowed his head slightly, and said "Right, Sir."

One of the other soldiers was buying a bag of cashews and salted peanuts from a vendor, a puchkawalla who had dragged his display cloth and hibachi near the Rolls, the luxury car being a natural attraction for people to mill about. The vendor was listening and observing. He noticed the exchange of money between the Maharaja and the soldier. The Raja was physically weak and the seller of nuts was his sworn enemy, a Naxalite and part of Nandalla's cell.

"Your peanuts, sir." He handed the soldier a bag. The soldier absently flipped him some coins, and walked straight to the tall one. The two soldiers discussed something, while cracking open the peanuts. The soldier who had paid didn't share the cashews, his favorite snack.

The vendor couldn't hear, but he didn't see the tall soldier give any of the Maharaja's money to the other soldier.

The vendor was clever at observing the smallest details, without appearing to be watching. He fancied himself a spy. Maybe there was a little extra something here for him, he thought, something even Nandalla need not know about. He slid the package Nandalla had delivered to him from the left side of the red ground cloth to the right.

The chauffeur returned to the Rolls. The Fat Man was about to announce the auction, but he wanted the anticipation to build. It was a beautiful warm, moonlit evening in Calcutta. The crowd deserved more. First the cages from the top, and then King Rooster.

Again the handlers climbed The Rooster Palace, this time roped together holding wooden gaffs in gloved hands. They climbed to the pinnacle and secured the top cages to their snagging device. After a series of yanks, the top cages came tumbling down like tumbleweeds. The helter-skelter act was actually more orchestrated than it looked, and the cages did not splinter on impact. The cages swung suspended a few feet above the hard-packed, tamped ground by the long ropes the handlers had used for safety on the way up.

A handler plucked the first rooster out of its cage and carried it over to The Fat Man. After seeing the giant King Rooster arrive and after watching the nine pounders fight, this rooster appeared small. But he was perfect. His points on the base of his head were undamaged, his blade was a bright orange, his hackle dark blue, his saddle and tail feathers a golden yellow. The coloring was highly unusual and therefore prized, not as a fighter, but as a showman.

"A distinguished bird, for a distinguished buyer," bellowed out The Fat Man, glistening with his own perspiration, which he wiped off every few minutes with a white towel.

The Fat Man was looking far to the back of the crowd at the bevy of wealthy aristocrats that the four soldiers still hung about. But no one

207

raised a hand or relayed a number. Up front, a farmer raised a wad of rupees, and yelled "A hundred rupees."

But The Fat Man laughed an exaggerated laugh. "One hundred rupees? Just look at his beauty!" And as if on cue, the rooster strutted forward and thrust out his colorful breast, while he trumpeted a melodious cock-a-doodle-do. Hundreds of boys scattered in the crowd, cupped their hands and echoed the same back. The bidding rose. One of the young princesses in a golden colored sari, the same color of the saddle of the rooster, whispered something in the ear of her prince languishing against the Rolls, chatting with the revered Raja in the back seat through a crack in the car door window.

The prince casually raised both hands and with his fingers doubled the price of the current bid. One of The Fat Man handler's situated about a hundred yards closer in the crowd eagerly relayed the bid to the stage. Finally thought The Fat Man. "Eight hundred rupees. We have a bid here for eight hundred rupees. Going once, going twice. . . . Sold!"

The relay man ran to the stage reached up and was handed the colorful, proud, and perfectly proportioned rooster. Holding him respectfully and talking to him, humming almost, the relay man dodged through the crowd back to the young prince near the Rolls. All eyes followed. Everyone wanted to know who in Calcutta had such money. Breathing hard, smiling broadly, for he should get a handsome tip, since he had both relayed the bid and delivered the bird; the relay man bowed slightly and presented the rooster to his princely buyer. The prince pushed his lower lip out, and nudged the relay man towards his wife in the golden sari. Her servant accepted the rooster, and now the relay man trotted the few paces back to the prince for the money. The Bali Crown Prince Sin Sin Dower of the Marwaris looked around serenely and showed his handsome light brown face to the crowd. He passed the roll of money to the runner, who quickly counted it and backed up bowing, knowing the excess above the bid was his cut.

Though still accepted as having a place in Bengali society, the wealthy were walking a dangerous line here, parading their money and position among the abject poor of Calcutta. The young prince outwardly had enjoyed the moment, but inwardly he was now disturbed. He had gotten a better look at the crowd, and did not like what he saw. Every walk of society was here, including, he suspected, communist revolutionaries.

The Fat Man assessed the crowd and wondered if the time was right to present King Rooster. He felt pressured and uncertain. Through his clenched teeth, he snapped at his servants, "Bring me another one. I want something unusual."

The handlers scurried around, but could find nothing unusual about the available roosters other than their coloring, which was too much like the rooster they had just sold. The crowd was getting restless. The Fat Man decided he couldn't wait.

"And now, good people of Calcutta. From the southern province of Tamil Nadu, long breeders of the largest roosters, we have the rare privilege of offering for bid, the largest rooster I have ever seen, a true giant, the largest in the continent of India and probably the world, sent from the Gods, a true giant, a true king, King Rooooooster!!!"

From the back three handlers worked feverishly at untying the knotted vines, realizing that now was the time, the coronation of the festival. Like peeling back a patch of jungle concealing a rare beast, they bent back the resisting cage door, and King Rooster emerged, dragging vines attached to the leather collar around his neck, stomping directly towards The Fat Man, who was busy with duties as master of ceremonies and had momentarily forgotten how imposing a beast King Rooster was. When he turned and saw King Rooster, he hollered at the handlers, "Grab his vines!"

Once the giant rooster was reigned in, The Fat Man felt safer and back in control. His servants lit more torches around the stone stage which shown upwards on King Rooster highlighting his features giving him a ghostly, prehistoric look. The crowd hushed. Those in the front rows gasped, putting their hands to their mouths.

The only persons not mesmerized by this moment were Nandalla, Sadhu Ricki, and Chaleea. Each of them was concentrating on his own mission. Nandalla was infiltrating the crowd, making his way back towards the vendor and the cluster of wealthy aristocratic bidders, while staying hidden from the soldiers. Chaleea was fixated on The Fat Man, and Sadhu Ricki contemplated whether or not he should put a stop to Chaleea's mood of revenge. Sadhu was sworn to uphold a peaceful world, but then again, he understood and respected Chaleea's rage.

In the distance across the Square, from the heightened ruins of Annapurna's demolished flat, she and I, unsure and needful of each other, looked through the smoky darkness and witnessed the gaudy action while feeling other emotions.

Sitting side by side we were growing closer in this foreign land, wondering if we had found something lasting. Annapurna put her arm around me. We drifted from watching King Rooster on the stone stage in the distance to watching the Rolls-Royce down below and closer to us.

"Annapurna," I hissed, pointing to the chauffeur, the tall turbaned Sikh, opening the rear door of the Rolls. The commanding Sikh carried his Gurkha dagger at his waist and an embossed sword hung across his chest. He thrust a stiff arm inside, and the old prince grabbed on to it with all his shaking strength, prying himself off the worn red seats up and out into the sweet smelling air of the festival of the Rooster Palace. Those natives standing close to the Rolls moved back, as if propelled into their place of respectful distance by decades of caste and tradition.

The Raja was dark brown, gnarled and bent over. He kept holding the tall Sikh's arm for support while he walked around in jerky movements, in small circles, like a toy soldier whose batteries were running down. Apparently the Raja was trying to loosen his knee joints.

"Better master?" asked the Sikh chauffeur to his Raja.

"Over there, on the car, next to my son." The Sikh placed his lord in a bent position, leaning next to his son and wife, the prince and princess of Marwaris, who now owned the perfectly proportioned, radiantly colorful rooster, which sat in the front passenger seat of the Rolls, looking quite pleased with its new bell-shaped cage.

Not far away, the peanut vendor, spread some fresh chestnuts over his small portable hibachi of coals, waiting for his leader, Nandalla, to give him a signal. The vendor kneeled statue-still and stared at the coals to give him strength for his deed. He was calling forth the necessary political trance. Soon his eyes burned like the coals with notions of a daring deed and a new India.

A thunderous crowing turned everybody's attention back to the stage. The handlers used all their weight to pull the vines tighter to hold back King Rooster, who had been edging closer to The Fat Man.

"Let the bidding begin. Who wants him? How much for this once-in-a-century King Rooster. In all my years I've never seen one so large. He's mammoth. A dinosaur from another time. A Rooster fit for a king! A Rooster fit for a king! Who wants him? How much? How much? A thousand rupees? A thousand rupees?"

The crowd rumbled and swayed as it came to life again with excited chatter. Who had a thousand rupees to spend? Only the Bali clan or some international merchant or a Maharaja.

Leaning against the Rolls, the prince turned sardonically to his Dad, "Well father?" he queried, "What's your pleasure?"

The Raja held up his hand and in a raspy voice said simply, "Wait. Let us see who else bids."

Meanwhile partially blocked from view by a cocoa tree, Nandalla was close to the cluster of Indian aristocrats and in the fading moonlight would decide when to strike. He dared not get too close to his Naxalite vendor for fear the nearby soldiers might recognize him. During the moment of peak crowd commotion, Nandalla would give his vendor a signal to act.

Several in the group were patting Nandalla's back, taking liberties in the excitement of the festival, happy to have said they touched their revolutionary leader. They were proud that Nandalla was not afraid, and that he had the will to fight to change the dusty, hapless ways of the decadent Indian government. Nandalla surveyed the scene in widening circles out from the Rolls, until he happened to spot Annapurna above rows of boys dangling their feet from her ruined apartment.

As sometimes happen in large crowds with searching people, for no apparent reason Annapurna turned her head just slightly and found him with her eyes. Her expression remained as it was, neither smiling nor frowning. She would never forget him; his dangerous ways and her early yearning for his exotic foreignness. From afar, they couldn't turn away, both remembering the past, knowing it was slipping away. She fought off any bitterness and felt a maturing acceptance of reality. She had the spontaneous urge to take away her arm from around my waist and blow him a kiss, but then she thought that would be going backwards.

Nandalla, who was steeling himself for what was to come, felt himself falling into the quicksand of his violent jealously and fought against that wasted energy. She closed her eyes, blessed him, and opened them again to look directly at him, with two cultures and the gulf of a teeming Square of Native Town between them. Nandalla bowed his head slightly to her. He knew he had meant something to her, and she had been the only foreigner he had slept with that he didn't grow to despise. He whispered good-bye and turned his back. Engulfed by the crowd, he looked for the shadows where he would be unseen by all but the vendor.

As was my nature, I tried to remain tolerant and neutral to the passionate exchange of looks, full of knowing, between Nandalla and Annapurna. After all, I kept repeating, she's entitled to a history apart from me. I didn't need to know everything about someone I loved.

A loud roar of exclamation and approval rose from the crowd. Up front on the stone stage, King Rooster had flapped his wings and knocked down The Fat Man in the process. His handlers were helping him up. The Fat Man behaved like nothing happened, and scanned the audience for a bidder. Finally a shill in the crowd, one of his own, yelled out "500 rupees."

The Fat Man put on a look of repugnant disgust, and repeated the bid through his megaphone. "We have an opening bid of 500 rupees, 500 rupees. I will not let this one-of a-kind-rooster go for 500 rupees."

"750!" yelled another of The Fat Man's plants from the opposite side of the crowd. The Fat Man glanced to the far back of the Square, where the rich congregated.

An arm rose. A white sleeve of the finest silk, embossed with 24 gold thread, revealed a hand covered with gold rings, which shimmered in the fading light, floating above the crowd signaling a bid. The Fat Man saw the prince's mouth move, but he could not make out the words. He looked to his relayer, who had shinnied up one of the electric poles, pushing some boys off in the process. The relayer yelled down to the stage, full of excitement, "4000 rupees!"

This was more like it thought The Fat Man, and with gut-felt satisfaction, he called out the Raja's bid, "4000 rupees! 4000 rupees!" He encouraged the crowd for an opposing bid, but as he expected, found none. Addressing the crowd, he announced, "The most honored Maharaja of Cooch Behar has bid the sum of 4000 rupees. Do we have a counter offer? Is there another bid?" The crowd was attentive, as thousands of heads swiveled to gawk at their Raja or to look for another wealthy bidder.

"This is a final bid. Going once. Going twice." And here The Fat Man paused, relishing his control of the crowd, and turning to look eyeball to eyeball at King Rooster, who had made him this nice profit, "Going Three times and sold to the Honorable Maharaja of Cooch Behar for the sum of 4000 rupees!"

The relay man and several of The Fat Man's servants pushed their way through the crowd to the winning bidder, who was now exhausted leaning against his dark blue Rolls. His son Prince Sin Sin Dower was undoing a 24 carat gold nugget bracelet from the father's leathery left arm. "Are you sure father?" he asked, questioning the wisdom of his father giving up his gold bracelet. But the father insisted.

Nandalla eyed the scene from his partially hidden corner on the edge of the Square. He stood with both arms back above his head grabbing a water drain pipe. It was a physically distinct position. In the distance the street vendor moved slightly this way or that to keep the line of sight open between Nandalla and himself. The vendor reminded himself to breathe. The relayer and the handlers were about to push through in front of him, and Nandalla saw that and knew his vision would be cut off. He brought both his arms down seconds before they passed and pointed his fingers directly at the vendor. That was the signal. The vendor drew the dagger from its sheath and trembled trance-like unbelieving that he was gripping a fabled Hyderabad dagger. When the relayer and his gaggle had passed, only the vendor's cloth and the white coals of his hibachi remained. The small, wiry vendor had slipped in between two handlers behind the relayer. The vendor's right hand was at his waist under a fold of his loose shirt clutching his bejeweled dagger. With his left hand, he pulled up his red kerchief, used to filter smoke from cooking, over his mouth and nose. Only his eyes were visible. And they gleamed of an evil deed.

The young prince had handed the gold-nugget bracelet back to his father. The Raja tried to unbend and stand erect. But there was no use. He hefted the weight of the gold in his hand, and looked up at the towering rooster in the distance. A most visible symbol, he thought; I will be remembered. The relayer and his entourage approached.

The relayer bowed slightly. The aging prince took no notice, as was his right, and held out the gold bracelet. The relayer cupped his two hands underneath, and the old man his hand shaking, dropped the bracelet into his trusting hands. Native Town peasants mobbed the scene. The relayer clutched the bracelet desperately, immediately secreting it away to a place next to his body. Everyone was watching the aged Raja and the young prince and the glittering gold bracelet.

At the instant the relayer pocketed the bracelet, the vendor struck. Yelling a Naxalite slogan, he leaped from behind the relayer, gripping the dagger in his fist high above his head, and plunged the tip into the Raja's neck. The Raja flashed a look of bewilderment and then the screaming started. The shocked young prince reached out after the assassin who had been knocked to the ground while blood the color of burgundy poured out of his father's neck. The aged Raja reached up with both hands to grab his own neck and crumpled against his son while the crowd stampeded. The young prince tried to kick the dagger away from the downed assassin, but the Sikh chauffeur yelled, "No! We must get out." The assassin vendor crawled and scraped his way to underneath the car, amazed to find himself still alive. The chauffeur picked up his dying master and carried him the few feet back into the Rolls. The prince rushed to escape to the safety of the Rolls. He remembered his wife and reached back and grabbed her, throwing her down in the back of the rolls. The Sikh had already started the engine, and the prince, his hands bloody and slippery with his father's blood, couldn't close the door. Strangers were trying to get in, or were being pushed in by a frenzied crowd. The prince rocked back, and with his foot repeatedly kicked a peasant woman in the face, until he slammed the door shut on her hand. The prince was panicked. Would they all be killed? Where was the military?

Then they heard shots. The chauffeur started to drive away. Another man's hand was caught in the chauffeur's door and he and the peasant women were dragged hollering to stop. The driver had no clear driving path, and he knew only one way back to Chowringhee wide enough for the car and that was straight ahead. So he plowed onward, hitting people left and right, glancing into the back seat to see his glassy-eyed master clutching his neck.

Everybody was fleeing. Two military men, caught off guard, at first fired above the crowd, but then decided they had to protect their aristocrats, and so shot at anyone who looked like they were running towards the car.

The vendor assassin who had squirmed underneath the car had escaped being run over by inches. His kerchief was covered with red blotches of blood and dirt. He tore it off, and along with his white cloth turban, threw them down on the hard packed dirt of the Square. Everybody was running. India was not a country used to violence. The assassin sneaked back to his display cloth on the hard-packed dirt of the Square and righted his overturned habachi. In a daze he preoccupied himself with picking up the chestnuts which were strewn about. He looked over to the now deserted spot where Nandalla had given him the sign to proceed to assassinate an aged prince who had plundered the riches of their Indian society, and who was, he reminded himself in litany fashion, a glaring example of the financial inequities greed brings to a democratic society.

Even Nandalla hadn't anticipated the chaos that would follow. No one could know that the frantic chauffeur would mistake the shooting by the two army soldiers while he was driving to escape, for Naxalites shooting at the Rolls-Royce. When the chauffeur saw the natives near the car being shot, he figured the shots were aimed at himself and the prince. So he drove like a madman, thumping over bodies. Between the military shooting and the driver bowling over the panicked natives, lay a path of writhing peasants who had come to the Square to see King Rooster.

2

At the same time the assassin-vendor had squeezed unseen into the pact behind the relayer, the tall soldier patted the bribe in his uniform pocket and realized for the first time the Raja was outside the Rolls, visible and vulnerable to all. The four soldiers always patrolled in a group for protection, and he alerted the others that the masses were crowding around the Rolls and they should make their way there. They had been heading towards the stone stage, using their feared stature to push their way to the front, when the tall soldier commanded they turn around. As he did so he noticed another tall man across the Square above the heads of the masses make a pronounced gesture towards the increased activity around the Maharaja. Immediately the soldier commanded his men to brandish their weapons and release their safeties. Even from two hundred yards across a festive crowd, he recognized Nandalla.

He dared not take his eye off him. "Ready men. It's him, the Naxalite Nandalla. Watch yourself."

They veered towards the post where Nandalla had given the signal and away from excitement around the Raja and the Rolls. The tall soldier moving through the crowd, knocking people aside, still had a bead on Nandalla, who did not yet know he had been spotted.

Then an explosion of shrieks, and a recoiling of the crowd packed near the Rolls froze the four soldiers.

"Oh, my God," muttered one of the soldiers, fearing the worst.

"Shoot Nandalla," barked out the tall soldier aware now of what Nandalla's decisive gesture was all about. Intent on stalking and killing the revolutionary, the tall soldier commanded two of his men to go to the Raja and protect him at all costs, using lethal force if necessary.

The tall soldier was even more determined now, because between his gritted teeth he knew he had not been vigilant. Whatever had happened to the Raja, the soldier privately blamed himself. If he could capture or kill Nandalla all would not be for naught.

Nandalla, meantime, was walking at a brisk pace in the torchlit darkness, angling away from the assassination scene back towards the stone stage. In forty more feet he and the soldiers would cross paths.

"Move," yelled the two soldiers at the rabble, as Nandalla stepped unknowingly into their sights. The tall soldier stood erect, and squeezed the trigger, but as he shot, an old woman, an untouchable in rags whom the soldier had pushed aside, kicked him in the groin. For her audacity the other soldier cracked her in the head with the butt of his rifle, and she collapsed holding her bloody skull. Nandalla, closer now, saw the soldier aim and hadn't flinched. After the errant shot, he raced towards the soldiers yelling obscenities, urging the crowd to turn against their oppressors, the soldiers. The two soldiers stood poised to fire again and Nandalla dove aside into the crowds who drew around him. The soldiers fired anyway, and a man covering Nandalla was hit in the back.

Nandalla felt a sting in his muscular calf. He reached down with his fingers and touched his wound, brought his hand to his face and licked the blood. Intoning a Hindu prayer, he rose up, threw off the peasant who sacrificed his life and rushed the soldiers. As he charged, the panicked crowd running from the stabbing of the Raja crashed through them like a breaking wave and knocked the soldiers off balance. Nandalla was stronger and more agile. Fifteen feet from the soldiers, his dagger drawn, he flew through the air, and slammed into both of them with his shoulders. Without a second's hesitation, Nandalla stabbed one soldier in the heart and left the dagger sticking out from his chest. While peasants wrestled the soldiers' guns away, he whirled to face the tall soldier.

Nandalla instinctively attacked the tall soldier with one enormous blow after enough, surprised that the soldier wasn't giving him a ferocious battle. What the dazed soldier was trying to do was reach for his own pistol strapped around his chest. Otherwise the soldier knew he had no chance. Nandalla spun around behind him and clasped him in a bear hug.

By now the military was on its way in force, and Nandalla should have run. A small unit of military police was marching across the Square searching for the two who had radioed for their help, disregarding for now the moaning bodies strewn about who had been shot or hit like cricket balls by the terrorized chauffeur. Then they got a whiff of the tall soldier's struggle near the center of the square and broke into a disciplined trot.

With the soldiers marching forward on the run, the protective masses had fled, leaving the soldiers and Nandalla naked in the Square. Nandalla was in a rare state of suicidal rapture, cackling at the success of his campaign, convinced by the surrounding chaos that a decadent Maharaja was undoubtedly dead. The soldier had finally managed to get a hand on his revolver inside his uniform, but Nandalla's bear hug pinned his arms. Nandalla saw the advancing soldiers and knew he was trapped. He switched his grip to a deathly choke hold around the neck of the soldier who was struggling furiously. As the tall soldier crumpled unconscious from Nandalla's strangle hold, Nandalla held him upright and grabbed the soldier's pistol. He felt a thump, thump hit the soldier's body. The marching soldiers were kneeling and firing. Nandalla yanked the dagger out of the other soldier's chest. He heard a row of pops, and experienced a searing hotness which forced him back to one knee. Using the tall soldier as a shield, and biting on the dagger with his teeth, he faced the two dozen soldiers running forward firing in rows. Carefully he aimed the pistol at the commander of each line of soldiers, killing with each shot. The sack that he was holding, that was once a human being, was pounded with fire. From the side of the square those loyal to Nandalla wailed in anguish. One boy rushed out to try to pull Nandalla to safety yelling, "Long live Nandalla! Long live the Naxalites!" The boy was shot dead by a soldier taking careful aim. Nandalla aimed his last pistol shot at that soldier hitting him in the center of the forehead. The attacking unit of soldiers was that close. Nandalla threw the bullet-riddled body of the tall soldier aside and stood. He was instantly hit with a fusillade of bullets. His last act was to take his beloved dagger from his teeth, hold the point of the blade to his chest, and fall forward.

XXVI

Fallen Idols

Up above the Square in her destroyed apartment, much like her destroyed life in India, another idol was falling. Annapurna had been watching Nandalla prior to the assassination, and clearly saw his arm movement signaling the time was right. She had witnessed a murder, and she didn't like it. Having never before attached herself to someone who was dedicated to a violent cause, she found herself disillusioned. She now fully understood that Nandalla had given the command to kill the aged Maharaja.

Annapurna and I both stood breathless, trembling in the smoky darkness, breathing hard from witnessing the raw danger. She was silent and consumed by what she had witnessed of Nandalla's work. A modern day guerrilla warrior, she thought. But that glorified what he did. He had ordered another man killed. She turned away and stared downward. "Jack, we have to leave here," she said shaking.

"Yep, this is too much. Let's think this out. What's the easiest way out of the Square?"

"Jack, I mean, yes we have to leave here. But, Jack, it is time for me and maybe you to leave India. I have had enough. It is time to go back to America." Annapurna was speaking from her gut, and she touched thoughts that were welling up in my mind.

Noise from behind us startled me. A cluster of boys were tossing bricks into the Square, hitting some of the fleeing men. That peculiar brand of Indian non-violent, disorganized, order was disappearing, and chaos was taking its place.

"Let us go" commanded Annapurna to me. Carefully we descended the rickety ladder down into the turbulence of the Square. I looked up, no bricks. The brick-throwing orphans were pointing to The Fat Man's stage. It looked like a mob was trying to rush the stage. Maybe to steal the gold bracelet The Fat Man's spirited away from the dying Maharaja.

Annapurna grabbed me by the sleeve as I took my foot off the last rung. We dodged through bewildered groups of people, and ended up leaning against the same white pillar in the same shaded corner where Nandalla directed the assassination operation. We were the only ones standing still, while everybody else was racing about in insane motion, like the worker ants of an invaded anthill, losing its gold.

XXVII

The Rooster's Revenge

The Fat Man's festival was in shambles. But there was Ali Kahn, The Fat Man, standing still clutching the golden bracelet the shaken relayer had brought back as payment for King Rooster. Only two other living things weren't dashing around. One was King Rooster, back in his cage still tethered and encircled by The Fat Man's handlers, awaiting their employer's next command. The other was Sadhu Ricki sitting motionless in his orange robe to the right of the cage.

Sadhu Ricki opened his eyes from a sonorous chanting. He immediately turned to see if Chaleea was near him, but Chaleea was absent, having jumped down and off the stage during the melee. "Namesti," he said dutifully, preoccupied with the loss of Chaleea, his charge.

But Chaleea wasn't as far away as Sadhu Ricki had imagined. He was sneaking around behind the stone Square crawling to the back edge of King Rooster's cage, trying to methodically rip out and shred the vines wrapped around the bamboo poles which secured the side of the cage to its frame. He had brought a handful of grain with him which he tossed to King Rooster so the bird would know he was his old friend, the one who had helped rescue him from the cyclone.

With his own dagger, which Nandalla had given him, he sawed and sawed at the vine. Finally in the dark he cut through one end. Using both arms he unwrapped the vine from the bamboo pole, until it reached the corner and he had about a ten foot length. Then he set to work on the other end. Seeing that he was up to something daring, a cluster of young beggars and such had gathered behind him.

Chaleea knew he was admired by the street urchins as one who was resourceful, and they would protect him by remaining silent. His skinny forearms ached, and he motioned to one of the boys in the gang to come over and help him.

Chaleea had a scheme. He slipped in under where he had loosened the vine, and stood looking up at King Rooster. Chaleea leaned his head against the towering rooster's bright orange breast, the feathers tickling his ears. But neither Chaleea nor the rooster flinched. King Rooster recognized Chaleea by his smell, and knew him as a friend. Chaleea started to speak quietly standing there in the cage.

"Listen, glorious one. I'm getting you out of here. We're making a break, you and I, and were going to leave The Fat Man naked and wounded. Naked and wounded my friend."

The street urchin had tired quickly of sawing through the vine with Chaleea's dagger, and another ragged soul took over. Soon the vine was cut. Chaleea held a two-inch thick, yard-long piece of pliable vine in his hands. Inside the cage behind the black shrouds surrounding it, Chaleea looped the vine up over King Rooster's head and around his neck. King Rooster bent down to receive the tether as if he were receiving a medal on a ribbon. Chaleea stood holding both ends of the vine, one in each hand, like the reins of a horse.

But one of the handlers glimpsed the gathering gang, and peered into the cage. "A boy is in the cage! A boy is in the cage! " he yelled. The handler was most concerned about the boy's safety, expecting him to be knocked unconscious with one swift kick.

Dispensing with whispering, Chaleea called to the gang of boys. "Tear down the curtains!" Before the handlers could push the boys off the stone stage, the boys had yanked down the black curtains enshrouding King Rooster's cage. King Rooster flapped his wings and the cage jerked about, further loosening the one side where Chaleea had cut out the vine.

Chaleea swung himself up and around behind King Rooster, and pinching in on his feathers with his knees and sandaled feet, climbed up on his back, choking up on the vine around his neck, and rode him like a elephant. Emboldened by the day's events, and being a boy, Chaleea was feeling for the first time a man's smoldering anger turning to rage.

"Charge," he yelled," Charge!" The street urchins backed up screaming with delight at Chaleea's audacity. They didn't know Chaleea was burning with thoughts of avenging The Fat Man.

"Look!" pointed the handlers. Hundreds of worried-looking persons now milling in the Square, stopped and stared in the direction of King Rooster and The Fat Man.

"Grab that boy!" commanded The Fat Man.

"Now charge, King, charge!" begged Chaleea. And King Rooster head-butted the loosened side of the stage, until the whole side was twirling by a corner, and King Rooster with Chaleea on his back, plowed it down.

Sadhu Ricki watched motionless sitting in lotus position on the stage.

"Yahaaaa! Yahhhhaaaaaa!" screamed Chaleea, riding atop of the world's largest rooster. The handlers dove off the stone stage. The Fat Man remained frozen in place, gawking in disbelief.

Like riding a horse on the polo field of the Maidan, Chaleea tried to turn the agitated King Rooster with his reins. Chaleea had a special target before they escaped the Square. A few feet before King Rooster was going to fly off the stage, they skidded to a stop, almost sending

Chaleea catapulting over King Rooster's head. Then King Rooster whirled around, and staring at the solitary, robed figure of The Fat Man at the other end of stone stage, let go with a mighty cock a doodle dooo! All eyes were riveted on King Rooster. Holding tight to the vine, Chaleea burrowed deep into King Rooster's feathers, squeezing with his knees, the points of the feathers sticking through his roped sandals helping to keep him on.

"Yes King! Yes King!" shouted Chaleea with surprising ferocity into King Rooster's ears. King Rooster charged forward straight at The Fat Man who now registered that he was about to be run over by a giant rooster.

"Noooooooo!" The Fat Man wailed in a strange voice. He looked for cover but there was none. King Rooster was closing fast, his wings spread. There was no escape. King Rooster rammed into The Fat Man full force flattening him like a diesel engine running over a rickshaw.

"Now keep going, keep going," pleaded Chaleea having accomplished his mission. King Rooster stretched his wings farther and soared off the stage. The crowd below hugged the ground. King Rooster flew a good hundred yards before he and Chaleea landed on the run heading through the gates of the Square and out into Native Town.

2

Before and after the collision Sadhu Ricki worked at staying calm, chanting faster than usual. At the instant of impact, a golden bracelet flew across the stage landing at Sadhu Ricki's crossed feet. Without hesitation, and even before it slid to a complete halt, Sadhu Ricki scooped up the bracelet in his right hand, gently tossing the precious payment from hand to hand as he continued his chant until the commotion stopped. After the Fat Man was trampled to death, Sadhu Ricki held the golden nugget bracelet in his hand and one by one yanked the nuggets apart wondering about wealth and luck as he did so. In the torch-lit darkness, the tattered group of homeless street urchins gathered around the stage, gaping in disbelief. One by one the holy Sadhu Ricki called them over to his temporary throne and distributed a nugget and a kiss to each boy, until a circle of skinny boys sat around gleefully patting him on the back.

Meanwhile, the Fat Man lay motionless on his back. A servant slithered up on the stage crawling towards him on his hands and knees with one eye looking about fearful the rooster and his rider might roar back like a bad dream.

3

Annapurna and I were speechless. I said, "We should go see him, Sadhu Ricki. He's still on the stage." Annapurna followed, numb from witnessing Nandalla's true nature, his primary mission.

He picked out Annapurna and I slowly and sadly walking towards him, growing closer to each other and more distant from Calcutta step by step.

"Namesti." We smiled weakly and bowed together, in prayerful fashion.

We needed a plan. I put my arm around Annapurna. She and I had witnessed too much in one day too far from home. We looked at Sadhu Ricki, who said simply. "Go my children, it is time to go home."

Annapurna and I strolled off into the night, knowing we had some decisions to make. Aimlessly we headed back towards Sadhu Ricki's tent avoiding the soldiers, ambulances and wailing souls caroming about. Annapurna was emotionally torn apart by the death of Nandalla, desperately wishing she had never denounced him, sobbing, proclaiming her love for him as we walked along the alleys of Native Town, arm in arm, half expecting to see Chaleea fly by on King Rooster and offer us a ride back to the tent. I reached over and wiped a rare tear off Annapurna's cheek.

"You're one tough woman. You know that Annapurna."

"Yes, but why me? Why does it always have to be me.?"

I wasn't sure what she meant by that, and to this day I'm not sure.

XXVIII

Epilogue

That time of my life and that day and night at the Rooster Palace lasts forever in my mind. Sadhu Ricki kept the single largest nugget for himself, as he said was his right, and from that day forth he was revered in Native Town as the holiest of holies.

Chaleea showed up at Sadhu Ricki's tent strutting a new found confidence and a burgeoning reputation. He had tried to return King Rooster to the family of the murdered Raja Cooch Bahar, but they wanted no part of King Rooster. Instead Chaleea arranged for the return of King Rooster to the Rooster Palace, and in exchange came into possession of the fabled, blood-stained dagger of Hyderabad, and the right to carry forth the mantle of the martyred Nandalla. Now Chaleea had much to consider, as well as being wanted by the soldiers for questioning about the death of The Fat Man.

A few weeks later at the spot where Nandalla died, his followers planted a sapling banyan in the middle of the packed earth, a place where ordinarily no tree would grow. But the downtrodden of Native Town watered the tree daily and today it stands as a spreading monument to Nandalla and his doomed Naxalites - the only shade tree in the Square. Each year at the anniversary of his death, the homeless and dispossessed of all castes camp out by the hundreds under the banyan tree and tell tales all night of the marvelous struggle Nandalla put forth to try and change Calcutta. The greatest story told is how he held off a regiment of soldiers single-handedly, killing six, one for each bullet in the revolver, and in the end like a true martyr, took his own life.

For two days, Annapurna and I stayed at Sadhu Ricki's tent where we slept, mourned and made love. Annapurna and I were confused about how we felt towards each other. Christmas was approaching, so I did as I planned, gave Sadhu Ricki my army surplus sleeping bag as thanks, and, alone, took a train north to Nepal. Before I left we held each other and cried. She headed to the airport to catch a flight en route to London and then back to JFK and Albuquerque.

A month later, I flew back to the States, to the Adirondacks, all traveled out. I wrote her a couple of times to an address she had given me, and even called, but we never connected, and never saw or spoke to each other again. Sometimes I feel sad, thinking what might have been, that we never should have parted in Calcutta, and I say to myself, "Why me? Why does it always have to be me?"